ONE GOOD
AND DEADLY
DEED

Where there is mystery, it is generally
suspected there must also be evil.

LORD BYRON

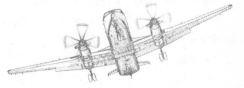

CHAPTER 1

The fact that none of the body parts was covered told me no one from Dr. Konstantina Smyth's office had arrived at the hangar yet.

Doc Konnie was adamant about not contaminating a victim's remains. The fastest way to get on her bad side was to throw a plastic sheet or a tarp or a couple of towels over a corpse. Or over body parts.

And it wasn't only our outspoken Greek-born medical examiner who was dyspeptic on the subject.

It was the law.

I memorized the statute word for word. This way, I could spell it out in no uncertain terms when people at a crime scene got careless, not keeping their hands off the deceased. Or, for that matter, off the dead person's possessions. I'd point out that anyone who — quote, unquote —

willfully touches, removes, or disturbs the body,
clothing, or any article upon or near the body . . .
shall be guilty of a misdemeanor of the first degree.

So in West Texas's Abbot County, at a crime scene involving loss of life, even we law enforcement types waited for the ME's white van to show up before touching the body. Until then, we looked for clues elsewhere. Or else we stood around and waited.

When I entered the hangar, that's what a half-dozen people were doing: standing a few steps inside the door. Gossiping, kibitzing, pointing.

Waiting.

All of them were dressed like I was — in protective gear. But they were acting like they'd just gotten out of church. Clustered in a group, they were enjoying a social moment before heading to the parking lot.

Or maybe I was thinking that because I'd stepped out of a church building a few minutes ago myself. A church building where I'd been the preacher.

I was quite certain there were other sheriffs in America who preached. Just about anyone can run for sheriff. That includes country preachers, many of them self-taught in theology. Some of them preached every Sunday morning.

But I wasn't one of those. This was the first sermon I'd preached since becoming sheriff nearly seventeen years ago.

I had a copy of the church program jammed in my inside coat pocket. The cover offered the bare details of the morning's activities.

Today's sermon by
Sheriff Luther Stephens McWhorter,
B.A., M.A., Doctor of Divinity

"Sworn in, eyes up"
How heaven and your local sheriff view
wearing a badge and carrying a gun . . .

But no one in this group was going to ask about any of that. They were too busy taking extreme care where they rested their eyes. I didn't blame them. I'd never seen a crime scene like it.

Pools of crimson and body parts of all sizes littered the hangar floor.

In all directions.

But it was the plane that dominated the view.

I knew what kind it was. The twin-engine Beechcraft King Air 350i was an iconic plane from a lineup of aircraft with a distinguished pedigree. I knew all this because I'd always found the King Air 350i more princess than king.

Even at a moment like this, it looked like a resplendent metal sculpture as much as an aircraft. Walk around it, and the very nature of what you were looking at seemed to change before your eyes. This was a consequence of the craft's exquisite, complicated design. I found the sight of one mesmerizing.

"You ever see anything like this?"

A woman's voice came from behind me. One I knew well. It belonged to one of my deputies. A detective actually.

Detective Rashada Moody.

Detective Moody was my department's only woman deputy. Only African-American deputy. Only left-handed deputy. Only deputy who'd been a beauty queen contestant. And the only one of us to have a four-year college degree in criminal justice. "Deputy Only," we jokingly called her. But at the moment, there was no humor in Deputy Only's voice. And I knew she wasn't talking about the airplane.

"No," I said after a moment.

"Somebody didn't want these poor fellows viewable at their funerals," she said casually before reverting into the professional I'd always admired. "I was the first officer here . . . if you'd like to know what I've noticed."

Her tentativeness was more than a courtesy. It hadn't been that long since I'd been the first one to roll up on another horrendous crime scene, a sickening scene near a remote, abandoned house thirty miles west of town.

The smell of rotting corpses and the sight of buzzards devouring them had made me ill. After several episodes of acute gastronomic distress, I'd managed to withdraw a short distance and summon help. Detective Moody was one of those who had responded. Now, here we both were again.

But before she could propose a place to start, I issued a directive to the others. "People, why don't we vacate the hangar until the ME can get this sorted."

Detective Moody turned to join the departures, but I caught her wrist. It felt warm. She seemed embarrassed, likely for not immediately recalling that I had seen this much ugly and more not long ago — and had been physically devastated by it. How could she ever forget the sight and smell of me and my vomit-drenched clothes and car.

I released her wrist and squeezed her shoulder reassuringly. "If we're careful, you and I can walk through this."

She nodded and pointed to the plane's starboard engine — the right wing from the point-of-view of the pilot looking forward. "I think the poor guy hit by those propellers was shoved into them from the side."

I looked from the propellers to the body parts and then back to her. "You're going to have to show me why."

"It isn't pretty."

"Ugly is all I'm expecting to see today."

□□□

Detective Moody headed for the largest body part visible on this side of the plane, staying a half-dozen feet away from it. That was close enough.

Her point was undeniable. The upper part of the body had

been hacked in two, beginning with its head and proceeding just below its waist.

I thought of pig carcasses I'd seen in slaughterhouses. Cleaved neatly in halves. Only pigs weren't butchered with their clothes on. This individual had been. And the propellers had cut through them like a seamstress's clippers.

To say the human remains we were looking at had been chopped into symmetrical parts was not quite accurate. One side of the face had most of his nose. But if the propellers had struck another inch to the right, the nose too might have been sliced into matching parts.

The sight was so divorced from my sense of the normal that my judgment felt unplugged. Sounded like it too. "Wonder if the blades sliced his belly button in two."

Detective Moody gasped.

I wished for a hole I could crawl in. But she understood. "Like I said, it isn't pretty."

The body had no legs. They'd both been hacked off at an angle at similar locations below the knees.

My mind tried to picture how this could have happened. But it wasn't having much success. The geometry wasn't working out.

I'd once investigated another accident involving a young woman who'd failed to notice that a plane's propellers were still spinning. Jousting with heavy slabs of knife-edged metal spinning at hundreds of revolutions per minute hadn't been a good idea. Thinking about it, I could still picture the blood droplets on the hanger ceiling — ample testimony to the extreme forces involved. That plane too had been a Beechcraft King Air.

And I recalled one other thing.

Most airplane propellers on conventional twin-engine craft spin clockwise, as viewed — again — by the pilot looking forward.

This time, the body of the victim I could see had been nearly sundered by the four powerful aluminum propellers spun by the engine on the right wing. But beyond that, my mind's re-creation of the scene wasn't meshing with the evidence.

The remains of a victim struck hard enough to have been split in two at the waist should have been thrown back toward and under the plane's left side. But if this had been the case, where did all the carnage on the plane's right side come from? It desecrated the hangar floor almost all the way to the white-paneled wall.

And why were there large pools of blood near the plane but not in significant amounts close to where the victim's main body parts were lying?

And how had the perpetrator or perpetrators of this hideous *mise-en-scène* managed to corral the blood used to disfigure the hangar wall?

The graffiti-like object was what mathematicians call an inequation symbol — an equal sign with a slash through it. Lengthwise, it probably ran for six feet and was almost four feet tall. A bloody sock had served as a paintbrush. It and a blood-smeared container — about the size of a large coffee can — had been discarded beneath the graffiti mark at the foot of the wall.

I had no idea what the strange symbol meant, only that it seemed oddly appropriate under the circumstances. Things certainly weren't adding up.

Otherwise, there wasn't a lot of blood visible on this side of the plane. Not on the hangar floor. Not on the plane itself. Not pooled around the several body parts.

I noted as much to Detective Moody, asking her if she thought it was possible for the heavy blades to strike with such force that they'd seal off the body's circulatory system. Right down to the capillaries, so that there'd be minimal bleeding.

She said she didn't know. But she did have a good idea where the blood for painting the symbol on the wall had come from.

We walked around the King Air's sleek conical nose. I took one glance, and an all-too-familiar feeling speared my innards: instant, gut-wrenching nausea.

This time, I fought it down. But I knew I was looking at something that would creep into my mind again and again in the days and nights ahead.

The other victim had been decapitated. His head was lying on the floor halfway to the hangar's other wall. Otherwise, his body was almost miraculously unmarked. It lay on its stomach, arms stretched outward. As if in a deep slumber.

We agreed we were leaping to conclusions, but neither Detective Moody nor I had the slightest doubt that this was where the killer or killers had procured the blood used to paint on the opposite wall of the hangar.

"Could you stay and oversee the sheriff's department activities at the crime scene?" I asked my detective.

"Of course, Sheriff." She nodded. "Oh, and there's one other thing you need to know: a college student who did odd jobs around the airport has gone missing. We're not sure what happened. No one has seen him. But we need to find him."

"Agreed. And I need to start thinking about how to describe all this to the media," I said. I didn't tell her my next thought: that the hangar looked like the Colosseum after Christians had been fed to the lions. As my mind did another run through of the bare facts, I tacked on a silent codicil: "To be continued." I was still clueless about what — and who — was behind all of this.

Then clues seemed to start becoming as available as Saturday night pizza delivery. Only, as I'd been reminded repeatedly in my law enforcement career, having clues wasn't the same as having answers.

CHAPTER 2

M y new chief deputy, Charles "Chuck" Del Emma, had given me a ride from the church to the hangar. When I'd asked if he could stick around until I could assess the lay of the land, he'd agreed. He was still in his car, talking on his smartphone, when I exited the hanger.

When I approached his car, he waved me inside and immediately motored off. No conversation was needed. He knew I needed to be taken back to the office so I could pick up my personal SUV. Drive home. Change my clothes. And switch over to my patrol cruiser. As befitting the speaker of the hour, I'd come to the church building in a suit and tie. This wasn't my usual workaday attire. That was khaki pants, denim vest, button-down-collar white Oxford shirt, low-heeled black roper boots and, if I was headed out of doors, the white-with-black-band cowboy-style hat that I loved.

Whatever the occasion, I also wore my custom-made, light brown leather eye patch. I'd lost the sight in my right eye at age seven in a foolish mishap involving toy swords.

I'd hired Del Emma after an employment campaign lasting only three weeks. No question about it — I'd been in a hurry.

His application had jumped to the top of the pile when

I saw what he'd been doing the past five years: heading the Miami-South Florida Crime Task Force. That was pretty tall cotton for a guy applying for a second-echelon law enforcement job in Boondocks, West Texas. I hadn't expected to attract someone so qualified. His application made more sense when he told me his aging parents lived in Flagler and that he'd grown up on a ranch not that far away.

Picture Vincent van Gogh. Then ask your sensibilities to transplant everything visible above the Dutch painter's shirt collar onto Del Emma's torso. And be prepared for a remarkable sight.

All his features were either reddish-gold or orangy-pumpkin in color. This included his carefully barbered hair, bushy eyebrows, corn-silk eyelashes, red-rimmed ear lobes, richly colored chest hairs, and anywhere else his flame-tinged skin was visible — a myriad of freckles dappling a sea of red flesh. Other than living more than a century apart, the main departure between the two gents might have been their eyes. In his numerous self-portraits, the enigmatic Dutch artist had changed his eye color as often as he changed his clothes. My new chief deputy's eye color stayed constant: a buoyant blue, floating in a sea of white.

At the church building, Del Emma and I had been delayed because a churchgoer asked for my autograph. Without giving much thought to the consequences, I'd reached for her worship program and scribbled "God bless, Sheriff Luke." Other parishioners noticed. Soon, a dozen people were lined up, clutching something for me to sign.

I gave them all autographs. And I hoped word of it never got back to any of my future re-election opponents. Politicking at a church service didn't look — or sound — good.

Del Emma had watched all this with amusement. But after we'd gotten into his vehicle, he never mentioned the autographing. The bizarre crime scene at the airport wasn't foremost on his mind either. He wanted to talk about something else. Or maybe, kindly, he wanted to distract me.

"Heard you studied to be a minister."

"Long time ago."

"Went to Yale Divinity School."

"Guilty as charged."

The sunglasses-coddled skin around his eyes tightened. "So this morning's sermon wasn't your first, uh . . . rodeo."

I laughed. "Paid my way preaching through both undergraduate and graduate school."

"After all that, you became a sheriff instead."

"Yep, started in the summer of '02."

"So you were pretty young."

"Twenty-six," I told him.

"Worn the star for several terms, then?"

"Four."

"That's impressive."

"Some folks think it's getting a little monotonous."

I didn't mention the reason I'd gotten a divinity degree from an Ivy League school was because I'd been planning a career as a gospel preacher. That's what most folks in my part of West Texas called the local minister. Then 9/11 struck.

My loss was devastatingly personal. My fiancée of four months had been sightseeing at the top of the first tower when the airliner struck.

After the memorial service for Mary Austin, with encouragement from home, I'd returned to Yale and finished my degree. Right around that time, my father abruptly retired for health reasons, and at age twenty-six, I ended up appointed by Abbot County's commissioners to replace him. I became the third generation of my family to serve our community as its top law officer.

My driver's thirst for information still wasn't satisfied. This insatiable curiosity would likely make him invaluable as a chief deputy.

He wanted to know what sermon title I'd used this morning. I reached for the church program inside my coat, handed it over to him, and watched as he took his eyes off the road long enough to read what was printed on the cover.

He whistled. "Mind if I take a guess at your text?"

Curious about how much more interesting this could get, I told him to go for it.

"Romans, chapter thirteen, verse four. For he is God's minister to you for good. But if you do evil, be afraid; for he does not bear the sword in vain; for he is God's minister, an avenger to execute wrath on him who practices evil."

I smiled to let him know I was impressed. "That's the New King James version of the scriptures. I prefer the New American Standard version."

"We always used the King James version in our Sunday School classes."

"You taught Sunday School?"

"Back in the day, yes." He handed the church program back to me. "How'd you apply that passage in the Book of Romans?"

"Well, I supplied some things I think the writer could have said but didn't."

"Specifically?"

"Won't bore you with a list. But ways law officers can protect against evil without, as the scripture says, executing wrath."

He said he wished he'd heard my sermon. I thanked him but said I hoped I'd never feel a need to deliver it again.

It wasn't necessary to remind him he was sitting here because of the horrors committed by his predecessor.

Not long ago, my former chief deputy had slipped into madness and murdered twelve people. He'd apparently come to see himself as an avenger executing wrath against evil-doers. One of our department's own snipers had fatally shot Chief Deputy Sawyers Tanner. If he hadn't, I might not be sitting here.

For reasons I'd never understand, my long-time employee had looked like he was about to fire a bullet into my back. Or the back of my fiancée, FBI special agent Angie Steele, who had been walking beside me. Or both of us. This was after he'd already tried to poison me. Another courthouse employee had gone to the emergency department in danger of her life because she'd drunk iced tea Tanner had mixed up for me.

I didn't mince words with my new second-in-command. Told him the behavior of the late Sawyers Tanner had been the worst imaginable application of Romans 13:4. In my sermon, I'd argued that if law officers insisted on seeing themselves as avengers bringing wrath on evildoers, there were far better ways to go about it.

But I didn't go into those for my new chief deputy. I didn't want to reprise my sermon. Not on this occasion. And not to this audience.

Del Emma's phone rescued us before our conversation got any more awkward.

He listened a moment, then signed off. "The missing airport employee has been found alive but badly hurt. He was beaten unconscious, dragged into a janitorial closet, and hidden under a tarp."

We met paramedics for the Flagler Fire Department running with lights and sirens as we were exiting the airport. Probably transporting the injured young man to Flagler General Hospital.

I gave my new chief deputy a quick glance. "Hopefully, here endeth the lesson."

He had an instant comeback. "Don't count on it. I'm sensing here beginneth the chase."

CHAPTER 3

At the house, I did more than merely change into my work duds. I donned my duty belt. Pinned on my badge. Slipped my gun into my holster. And did it all with more than my usual dispatch. I didn't have that long to get prepared for the news conference Detective Moody had been telling reporters about. It was scheduled to get underway at five o'clock on the courthouse steps.

That meant I was going to need to disrupt the Sunday routine of my long-time office assistant, Helen Grainger.

If I could find her.

Helen was a good Baptist. If asked, she'd work on Sundays, but I knew not to ask her to do it often. And I didn't.

Nobody else seemed to be at work either. The courthouse was as deserted. It was likely to be empty all week except in the middle of the night. As I approached, our office suite looked dark and empty through its outer glass walls.

A bit lonely, in fact.

I located the door key amid the others on my split-coil key ring and inserted it into our scarred door lock. I'd done that so many times I could do it with my mind a thousand miles away.

The security deadbolt lock in the door to our office suite was like all the other locks in the courthouse. Outdated, well-used and often a tad rattly. But ours had always worked.

I expected it too this time.

Only, it didn't.

The lock wouldn't admit the key past its first couple of grooves. Pushing harder didn't make any difference. To the lock.

But it did to the door. It opened a few inches. It was already unlocked. No doubt by the person I could now see sitting there at her desk. I wasn't going to have to ask Helen to join me. She was already there. She must have just arrived and hadn't had time to turn on the lights.

This was when I noticed she wasn't by herself. One of her visitors' chairs was occupied by a square-jawed young man.

He wore his dark hair in a short, spiky devil-may-care style. His finely etched roseate lips had a hint of permanent pout to them. There were beguiling shadows around his eyes and a carefully tailored look to his thick eyebrows.

He could have been a model.

But he wasn't.

He was a cop.

From Mexico.

That was clear from the patch on the left shoulder of his trim-fitting black uniform. It featured Mexico's three-colored flag — green, white, and red.

Three white stars tracked prominently between white bars at the end of both the wide, dark epaulets on his shoulders. He was a high-ranking cop.

I didn't have a clue as to why he was sitting in a visitor's chair in our departmental offices with his briefcase in his lap.

He'd not made an appointment. At least, not one that I knew anything about. An even bigger mystery was why Helen had been there to let him in. Then I saw the weekend's mail piled on her desk. She'd been to the post office to pick it up and was dropping it off.

She sent one eyebrow and a shoulder upward in a gesture that said, "I know as much about this as you do." Then she slid my visitor's business card toward me on the protective glass covering her desk.

I transferred the file folder I was carrying to the other hand. Used my thumb and a fingernail to flip up the card so I could grasp it. And looked to see who'd come calling.

The card had us gringos in mind.

It was in English.

It introduced me to Antonio Aguirre Obregón, Assistant Chief of the Investigations Division, Mexican Federal Police, Guadalajara, Jalisco, Mexico.

I extended a hand. "Sheriff Luke McWhorter, Chief. You're a long way from home."

When he answered, his English was like that on his card — flawless. "Call me Antonio, please. Nice to get out of the office occasionally."

"How far is it from Guadalajara to Flagler?"

"As the crow flies, about 1,650 kilometers. A thousand miles."

"You must have something on your mind. Why don't you come on into my office?"

I invited him to take one of the three chairs parked around my makeshift conference table. I pulled out one of the others and joined him.

He reached into his briefcase. Found the file folder he wanted. Extracted it. Rummaged through its contents. Removed a four by six color photo. Handed it to me. And made a request. "I'm hoping you can tell me how to go about finding these gentlemen."

There were two men in the picture. I didn't recognize either one. But the same couldn't be said for the object behind them.

Seeing it again so soon sent competing sensations careening through my nervous system, one of paralyzing confusion and a stiff reaction to an overload of adrenaline.

I couldn't afford to surrender to either set of emotions. In the end, rationality won out.

I looked at the photo again, double-checked to make sure this was the same Beechcraft King Air 350i I'd left behind in the blood-soaked hangar only minutes earlier, and saw there wasn't any doubt.

The wide, royal-blue stripe on its belly swept backward from the nose and undergird most of the plane before finally disappearing near its tail. And the same *N* number — the government registration number — was reversed in white near the tail.

I realized the stranger in the natty Mexican federal police chief's uniform sitting across from me was a victim of the worst kind of timing. He couldn't have picked a more inauspicious moment to arrive at the Abbot County Sheriff's Department asking about the persons visible in that photograph.

Or there was the other possibility.

That he was somehow involved in one of the most horrific slayings in modern American crime annals. Or at least Texas's crime annals. For certain, in Abbot County's crime history. Perhaps he was even the perpetrator of our double murders. Or one of the perpetrators.

Either way, he had some explaining to do. And I didn't intend for my office manager and me to be the only ones around when he did it.

I rose from my chair, took three quick steps to my desk, reached under the narrow overlip and pushed my panic button.

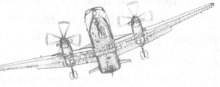

CHAPTER 4

The buttons had been installed by my predecessor, "Sheriff John" McWhorter. My father.

There was one under my desk and one under Helen's. I'd only pushed mine once before — when five members of an upset family had started fighting in my office.

Pushing it would cause a red alarm light on the wall in our ready room down the hall to start flickering on and off. I didn't know how many deputies were there at the moment, but I knew I wouldn't have to wait long to find out.

The first officer through the door was Detective Matthew Salazar. Young Salazar was the department's clothes horse. You never saw him wearing anything that didn't look new and starched and freshly pressed.

He had his gun drawn.

Detective Tobias Coltrane was next. The look on his lean, well-razored face was as fierce as his body was tone. He'd honed both during an earlier career as a military policeman.

Now, I had two officers in the room with drawn guns.

Deputy Carter Ratchhammer was the last to arrive. With his short, chubby physique, he didn't move as fast as the others. As always, his curly gray locks were bouncing around his forehead. He too had drawn his gun.

I ordered Assistant Chief Antonio Aguirre Obregón of the Mexican Federal Police to stand and extend his arms.

He did so, and I told my deputies we needed to frisk the guy.

Detective Salazar holstered his gun and did the honors. It wasn't much of a haul. He found a packet of gum. A set of car keys. A wallet. And a neatly folded handkerchief with the logo of one of Mexico's famous beers imprinted in gold ink in the center.

I told the Mexican policeman he could lower his arms. Retrieve his possessions. And return to his seat.

From the dumbfounded look on his face, he was ready to return to Mexico.

I asked Detective Salazar to stay — he spoke Spanish, and because of his frequent trips to Mexico to see family, he was familiar with the culture.

I asked the others to see if Helen would join them for a cup of coffee. During the whole ordeal with the Mexican police officer, to the extent that I'd noticed anything on the other side of the glass wall, the only thing I'd seen move were her eyes.

CHAPTER 5

I suggested that the Mexican cop and Detective Salazar join me around the small, circular table I'd found at a garage sale. I called it my conference table. We each took a chair.

My suspicions about Assistant Chief Obregón had ebbed to the point where I felt casual might be helpful, especially after the rough handling he'd gotten.

The Mexican police officer clearly felt he'd earned the return of his dignity. And perhaps an apology. Certainly, an explanation.

But we weren't close to that point. Not yet. To my thinking, we'd made progress on only one front. I'd established he wasn't likely to pull a firearm out of his shirt and shoot me in my own office.

"Between eight-thirty and, say, eleven o'clock this morning, you were where?"

He sent an exasperated, Groucho Marx–like look to the ceiling before letting his eyes fall on me. "Until about nine, in my bed at your South Breeze Motel."

"And then—"

"And then breakfast at a place across the street. Eden Junction Bar and Grill, I think it was called."

"And then?"

"Drove around town a bit. Sightseeing, you could say."

"You brought a gun with you?"

"My service revolver, yes. It's in my luggage."

"And your luggage is where?"

"The *cajuela* of my rental car."

Detective Salazar chuckled. "The trunk."

For the first time since he'd laid the photograph in front of me, I saw a hint of a smile on my Mexican visitor's face.

I still wasn't ready for pleasantries. "We'd like to take a look at it, please."

Assistant Chief Obregón reached in his pocket, extracted his keys, selected one, let it dangle between a thumb and a finger, and handed them to me. "Only one suitcase."

I reached for the key chain and handed it to my deputy. "When we're finished here, make sure the gun hasn't been fired recently. Then give Chief Obregón his keys back. And his gun."

When we'd made the move to my conference table, I'd brought along the photo and placed it on the table. I was staring at it.

So were the others.

Our visitor was the first to take his eyes off it. He looked up at me. The flesh around his eyes tightened in a slight squint. He was still waiting for an explanation.

I considered it. Then decided he was going to have to earn it. "You took this photograph?"

He raised both his hands a short distance off the tabletop. Flicked them both outward twice in an opposing sweeping motion. Then brought them to rest again on the tabletop. "De ninguna manera, José."

No way, José.

The Mexican police official knew he had to tell me why he'd shown me the photograph. I'd let him figure out where to start.

He tapped the photo. "We found this on the film in a camera we confiscated."

I gave him a slight head nod. But kept my thoughts to myself.

"At Miguel Hidalgo y Costilla Airport, in Guadalajara." He tapped the photo again. This time, his finger was landing on the airplane in the picture. "This plane, it has been seen frequently in the past year and a half. Flying in and out of our international airport. Sometimes with strange passengers. And, sometimes, strange cargoes."

This time, I was the one tapping the photo. "Do you think these two characters were smuggling drugs?"

"Maybe. A few times. Or computer chips. Or Rolex watches."

"But—"

"But they didn't act like normal smugglers. Too — how you say it? — nonchalant. Too visible. They didn't try to hide anything."

"So why didn't you just ask them what they were up to?"

"We did. I did so myself. Again, very strange."

"How so?"

"One time they even showed me what they were transporting. It was some medical vials. In a chest with ice that smokes. Dry ice."

"Could most of these have been simple business trips, then? Or even pleasure trips?"

"With no luggage? Leave the airport in a taxi? Return in a couple of hours and fly off again? All the way back to Texas?"

"Doesn't sound much like smugglers."

"We didn't think so either."

"So what did you expect to find in Flagler?"

He raised his palms from the tabletop, flipped them over, and left them suspended in the air. "Answers. Answers that I've been missing in Guadalajara."

"Surely, you've had suspicions."

"Those, yes. But more curiosity — and concern."

"Because?"

"Because of what our agents saw not long after this photo was taken."

"More test-tubes packed in dry ice?"

"No, not that."

This was when Assistant Chief Obregón told me about a scene at Miguel Hidalgo y Costilla Airport that sounded like it was ripped out of an old James Bond movie.

The Beechcraft King Air from Flagler had been positioned on the runway for takeoff when a heavy, Hummer-looking vehicle burst through a chain-link gate. The chunky truck was headed for the plane.

"The pilot saw it coming. Goosed his throttle. Picked up speed enough so that it kept ahead of its pursuers," he said.

But the other thing the pilot had done could have been the saving grace of the plane and its occupants. He'd kept fish-tailing the plane's tail. He could only do this so long, but it was long enough. He'd prevented the person who had been firing the automatic pistol from the front passenger window of the pursuing vehicle from having a clear shot.

The lull in the conversation was on me. There had been a lot of dots in this new turn in the conversation. It took me a few moments to decide which ones to try to connect first. "Did your agents see what the Hummer's occupants looked like?"

"Only that they didn't look Mexican."

"Did your agents chase them?"

"Only a little ways. My guys were in the terminal, watching through the windows. By the time they got to their cars, the attackers had crashed through another wire gate at the other end of the airport and disappeared."

"Did you check to see where the plane was going?"

"Of course. Flagler, Texas. At least, that's what the flight plan said."

"So that's why you came to Flagler?"

"Yes. I was hoping you'd know something about these two gents in the photo. Maybe help me ask them some more questions."

"So you don't know anything about what happened at our airport this morning?"

The puzzled look on his face answered that question for me.

I tapped the face of one of the pilots in the photo, then the other. "Hopefully, we'll get some answers from what's left of these gentlemen. But I think most of the talking is going to have to be done by someone else. And by the hangar. And the plane."

CHAPTER 6

My detective left with Assistant Chief Obregón to check the gun in his car. After that, I suggested they get some lunch. Talk some more. See how we could assist each other. It was possible he had more information than he'd already given, but I didn't think so, and for now I needed to work my case. It wasn't an easy one.

I walked to the door to our office suite and watched them leave. I stepped out into the hallway. Stopped. Looked both ways. Listened. Heard nothing. Saw nothing.

The only creature stirring anywhere within earshot — or the reach of my single peeper — was me. It was another of those times when the courthouse was quiet as a tomb.

Re-entering our offices, I locked the door to our office suite behind me. Returned to my chair. Picked up a ballpoint pen and began to doodle on my blotter pad. Did that for a couple of minutes. Laid the pen aside and leaned back in my chair.

For the first time since I'd stood in front of my electric range that morning and fried myself a couple of eggs for breakfast, my mind was my own. I had a chance to reflect on the day's fast-moving events.

The first thought out of the chute couldn't have been more

encompassing. *The Abbot County today's sun had risen on was not going to be the Abbot County it bid ado to at day's end.*

Far from it.

Was that making too much of the mind-boggling developments at the airport? Not to mention, the Mexican cop's materialization in my office with a story straight out of *The X-Files*? Possibly. But I was dealing with another kind of feeling. I'd felt it before. I was descending deeper and deeper into the clutches of one of my hunches.

I had these experiences from time to time. These awakenings. Moments when the universe chose to dispel some of my ignorance about a new one of its entanglements in a very personal way. No more than a half-dozen people on the entire planet knew about my brain reorderings. I say "brain reorderings" because, over the years, I'd become aware that this was what they were — my mind's scab-ripping capability.

That's what it felt like emotionally when I had one of these episodes. Like a scab had been ripped off the realities I lived amidst, and things weren't going to grow back. Not the way they'd been.

What awaited underneath, at least for me, was a new ordering to the world. One to be pondered and probed. Sorted and lived through. And adjusted to as the only sheriff the county had had in the past sixteen-plus years.

The reason I didn't talk more about this was doing so usually produced blank stares. A few times, I'd tried to articulate to my classmates how it felt. But even some of the country's top religious-studies students ridiculed my instincts for problem-finding and problem-solving.

One of them had joked my problem was that I was a one-eyed visionary.

This graceless comment sent me to the Yale library. I wanted to know everything I could find out about the psychological consequences of monocular vision.

I learned a great deal from my research. People with only one eye often suffer a loss of self-esteem, and there can be a lot of anxiety, mostly from a fear of losing vision in the remaining eye, but because I'd been so young when I'd had my accident, I'd seemed to have sailed right past — or maybe it was through — those kinds of concerns.

Physically, I'd long since realized the center of my field of vision wasn't the same as other people's. This meant I not only had to watch where I was going, especially when driving, but I also had to watch where others were going and anticipate possible consequences they paid no heed to. Indeed, possibilities they were literally unaware of.

I'd also learned what "motion parallax" meant. This was a fancy term for constant head movement. It's what cats do just before they jump. And it was why I moved my head from side to side more than most people. It is more than merely making up for the fact that my field of vision is smaller than people with both eyes. It helps my one-eyed brain judge distances. That is, tell how far apart things really are.

In the end, I'd concluded that being one-eyed had helped me develop my unusual hunch-making abilities. And sitting here at my desk, leaning back in my chair, I knew one of those hunches had arrived. I again went through today's signature events in my mind.

The hideous, improbable murders of the two men in the hangar — presumably, the plane's pilots.

The enigmatic, unexpected arrival of the Mexican policeman at my office.

And the growing evidence that both events might be connected to a much larger narrative with multinational fingerprints all over it.

This was beginning to feel like what had happened with the Roswell UFO fragment not that long ago. Once again, Flagler seemed to be on the verge of larger-than-life developments that extended far beyond our city limits and county boundaries. And reached deep into its civic, political, and private underbelly.

The "deep into our underbelly" part was at the core of my hunch. Whatever was happening, and about to happen, was in substantial part home-grown. Cooked up by local folks. Mostly, in Abbot County, by Abbot County, for Abbot County. For whatever reasons.

I wanted to talk at length with my chief deputy and the others I had sifting through these events. ASAP.

But the only one who seemed to be at a point where they could break away was Chief Deputy Del Emma.

Since neither of us had eaten since breakfast, I radioed him and suggested we meet at a hole-in-the-wall Korean restaurant I liked not far from the courthouse.

□□□

I ate at Kang's Healthy 'n Happy Korean Food often enough to know that owner Fred Kang wouldn't object if we ordered something to eat, then sat around and jawed for a spell. The only issue for my chief deputy and me would be how well we coped with the odor of the fermenting kimchi.

Kang refused to tell me how many weeks — or months — he fermented the cabbage, garlic, red chili pepper flakes and whatever else he put in his version of Korea's national dish. The odors from it were the reason you left his place eager for a shower, shampoo, and change of clothes. But, more importantly, the taste of it was one of the reasons you kept coming back.

The odor wasn't what brought me to an abrupt halt. The large, hairy hand with the stubby, nail-chewed fingers did that. The one that slammed into my chest like a pump engine piston.

The individual the hand belonged to was a couple of inches shorter than me but much broader. He was built like a bridge pedestal. Or a tank. He wanted me to stop. So I obliged.

Stared a moment at his closely cropped salt-and-pepper hair. Observed how it retreated backwards from a sharp widow's peak. And waited for him to give this awkward encounter a sense of direction.

He lost no time in doing so. "Sheriff, we have a situation here."

I kept my gaze focused on his bulbous nose, as broad and beefy as the rest of him. "Clearly, we do."

He reached in the pocket of his full-length, khaki-colored raincoat and extracted a slim, dark bi-fold wallet. Flipped it open so that I could see his plastic ID card. The biggest letters on it by far — and the only ones I paid much attention to — were the royal-blue ones reading *FBI*.

My chest was still stinging, so I wasn't inclined to be any more helpful than I'd already been. "Very nice, but we were next in line. We get the next table."

For the first time, I noticed the reason why my accoster was doing everything with one hand. He was carrying a brief-case. *Attached to it, actually.*

The irony wasn't lost on me. The second stranger with a briefcase I'd encountered today was looming large in my line of sight. The hardened security chain hung in double loops from his fist. It was long enough that he could open his case without removing the cuff from his wrist.

I was still feeling pissy about his rudeness. I gestured at the briefcase getup. "Didn't know the FBI's weekend delivery service extended to West Texas."

My impudence was so unexpected it sailed right past him at first. Then, my insult soaked through his thick skull. His eyeballs seemed to retreat a few seconds so he could reexperience the moment. When they'd done so, they returned to me. "We have an agent based here, you know."

I looked for signs in his face that he was being facetious. Didn't see any. Glanced around the room before adding to his knowledge about that particular special agent. "Yes, I intend to marry her."

The blank look returned to his face. "Special Agent Steele?"

"One and the same."

His lips pursed a slight bit. "Then you'll be interested in knowing why I've just ordered her to D.C."

Now, I was the one with the omelet look. Flat. Surprised. Concerned. Confused. And, for the second time since my chief deputy and I had walked into Fred Kang's restaurant, steamed. Infuriated, in fact.

I'd paid no attention to his name or title the first time he'd showed me his credentials. I asked to see them again. This time, I noted I was having a conversation with Patrick E. Knoke, Special Agent in Charge of the North Texas District of the FBI.

I decided exasperation was the best adult flavor of the moment. Wasn't sure I could have kept it out of my voice, anyway. "Well, Special Agent Knoke, not only are you interrupting my chief deputy's and my lunch, you have also apparently destroyed my dinner plans. Special Agent Steele and I had planned to celebrate the three-month anniversary of our engagement tonight."

The oafish fellow at my elbow didn't so much as nod to show that he'd heard me. He was too busy inviting himself to join us for lunch.

"Hope they've got good kimchi."

I gave him no indication that we intended to follow him to a table.

He turned around. Held up the briefcase, chain and all. Gave his head a come-hither jerk. "Need you to see this."

CHAPTER 7

Déjà vu is the term for what I was feeling. I'd been here before. About an hour earlier, in fact. Sitting at my desk, waiting for a total stranger to dig photographs out of his briefcase. And here we were again.

I focused a less-than-friendly glare on the special agent. "How'd you know where to find me?"

"You have a dispatcher, you know," he said with the air of a teacher speaking to a school child.

I did. One who wasn't likely to bother me at lunch unless it was an emergency. Apparently an FBI agent demanding to know where I was an emergency.

It wasn't quite *déjà vu*. This was a more-than-second-time-around feeling. More than *déjà vu*.

Déjà vu feels like you've gone down a similar road. This road felt almost exactly the same: Stranger digs through his four by six color photos. Stranger glances at them for a moment. Stranger picks four. Stranger looks more closely at them. Stranger taps one of the photos and pushes it closer to you. Onlooker leans over for a better view, although that wasn't necessary.

I'd already recognized the Beechcraft King Air 350i. If there had been any confusion, the N number on the side of the plane would have banished it. The white government registration I was becoming so accustomed to beamed at me, reversed out of the solid royal-blue belly stripe. Only this time, the two pilots weren't posing jauntily in front of it. One of them wasn't in view at all.

Somebody I didn't recognize was helping the visible pilot hoist a shallow, elongated box into the King Air. My guess was that the other pilot was inside the plane, steering the box from the other end. I might have called it a crate, except crates tend to be wooden. Or a case, except cases tend to be molded plastic. Whatever this was looked like metal. Probably aluminum, because it couldn't have been too heavy or the pilots couldn't have lifted it or the plane couldn't have carried it.

Chief Deputy Del Emma peered at the photos, then at me.

I let a quick finger drift to my lips. His double eye blink told me he understood.

The FBI special agent didn't notice. He was returning the photos he hadn't chosen to share to his briefcase. Snapping it shut. Laying it on the bench on his side of the booth. And rearranging the chain so that he could use both hands to reposition his paper napkin on his lap.

With his free hand, he reached over and moved my drinking glass without asking permission. He pushed the four photographs closer to me, one at a time, adjusted them so they made a straighter line, and tapped the one at the end. "The last photo was taken in Istanbul. That's where we lost track of the plane."

I didn't want the end of the story first. "And the first picture?"

Once again, I was ignored. He was waving for a waitress. "I always order the bulgogi."

CHAPTER 8

For the sake of expediency, we made it three orders of bulgogi. The platefuls of thin beef strips didn't take long to arrive.

Once we'd all had a chance to take a few bites, I tried again. "Where was the first photo taken?"

This time, Knoke answered. But he sounded like a baby rooster with the croup.

Ah rooh da.

I tried it. Three times. The first time, I emphasized the first syllable. The next, the second. Then the third. I was beginning to sound like a junior high cheerleader. One with the croup. I could barely resist coming out with, *Sis boom bah! Ah rooh da!*

Only two other people were dining in Kang's Healthy 'n Happy Korean Food at this hour. Both turned to look at us. The noise Special Agent Knoke's fork made when it hit his plate prompted a second look from the pair.

Knoke extracted a ballpoint pen and a small notebook from his breast pocket. Shoved his silverware aside. Wrote something, turned the notebook around, and thrust it at me. The diacritical marks made it look like he had written *Ağrı Dağı*. He provided instructions. "Don't pronounce the *g*'s and go easy with the *i*'s."

Really?

"And it means what?"

That got us over the goal line. "It means Mount Ararat. Or, literally, the Mountain of Pain."

"But obviously, this photo wasn't taken on a nearly 17,000-foot-high mountain."

I was about to miss the extra point, so I smiled at him to suggest I was joking.

He began spearing bulgogi strips again. "The photo was taken at Ağrı. That's a good-sized city 750 miles east of Istanbul. In Turkey. One of those end-of-the-world places. Has the closest airport to Mount Ararat, for what it's worth."

"And why was anyone taking photos at all?"

"That box, crate, container — whatever it is. We've got some concerns about what was in it."

"Who's concerned?"

"Everyone from the bureau to the CIA to the International Atomic Energy Agency to The Organization for the Prohibition of Chemical Weapons to Homeland Security's Securing the Cities operation to the Centers for Disease Control and Prevention. To name a few folks."

I looked at the photos again. The two I'd paid most attention to were closeups of one of the pilots walking around the plane. Doing pre-flight-check kinds of things. Or so I was assuming.

The box was visible only in the other two photos. I tapped the box in one of them. "What do they think that is?"

The special agent cleared his throat. Toyed with his bulgogi. Speared a slice. Considered moving it to his mouth. Then thought better of the idea. "Well, that's one of the questions."

"And what are possible answers?"

He started playing with his food again. "Okay."

I raised both eyebrows. Said nothing. Lifted my fork and actually took a bite. Chewed. Swallowed. Furrowed my forehead. Still said nothing.

The special agent sent his bulgogi strips through another plate dance. Then repeated himself. "Okay."

If we were ever going to get beyond okay, he was going to need help, so I set out to help him. "Let me guess. Weapons of mass destruction." I started to name every kind of WMD I could think of. "Dirty bombs? Sarin aerosols? Blood agents? Psychotomimetic agents? Biological toxins? Infectious agents?" I added one I'd only read about a few days ago. "Nuclear gun bombs? One of those nasties would fit in that box, wouldn't it?"

He looked uncomfortable, and it wasn't the bulgogi. "I suppose."

I rerouted my inquiry. "You're sitting here disrupting my late Sunday lunch with this tale straight out of *The Arabian Nights*. So I'm going to assume that the bureau thinks this box ended up in Flagler. Right?"

More non-confirming silence.

Then he seemed to decide that he should tell the poor local sheriff the whole story. But he never got the chance. I took the lead in our discussion and never surrendered it.

CHAPTER 9

I started reeling off my suspicions.

Actually, they were more along the lines of wild guesses. But they were the only explanations I could think of that made any sense. Something about the photos made them look a bit dated. Maybe it was the lighting in them, I wasn't sure. But I qualified my time assessment. "This whole question about the box could have been resolved in Turkey months ago, don't you think? Maybe a year or more ago."

To my surprise, he accepted the adjustment. "Yes."

"But somebody kept screwing up with the photos."

"Big-time."

"The Turkish intelligence guys didn't realize the possible implications of their photos for some time."

"Correct."

"Then our embassy guys in Turkey lollygagged in passing the photos on to the CIA."

He nodded. "Right again."

"The CIA didn't see anything they immediately recognized, and the photos bounced around their analysts for months."

"Yes."

"They eventually gave them to the FBI, and the bureau's counterterrorism whiz kids in D.C. sat on them for several days before forwarding them to Dallas."

He nodded.

"You guys didn't get around to checking with air traffic controllers about the airplane until this morning."

"True."

"By the time anyone realized the plane had started and ended its transcontinental journey in Flagler, the trail for the box had grown colder than a North Pole porta-potty."

"Yes."

"You could have immediately called us, but somebody in D.C. decided that this was potentially too big and too dangerous to involve a country sheriff's department. Not until you got your own boots on the ground."

Special Agent Knoke nodded.

His bulgogi was growing cold from neglect, but I wasn't finished with him. "You decided you'd do it yourself this morning. Because you'd sent your resident special agent in Flagler to D.C. for some asinine reason."

For the first time, Knoke looked sheepish. "'Fraid so. We wanted her to be briefed by our terrorism agents. But I'm here now. You can do two things for me."

I reached for the deadest of my deadpan faces. "I always knock myself out to assist FBI special agents who disrupt my visits to my favorite Korean food restaurant. Especially when they say please."

I couldn't decide whether he was hard of hearing. Or ignorant of the usual manners generally honored in a two-party conversation. Or simply two shades denser than stupid.

I was still debating the issue when he shared the thing he'd had on his mind from the start. "You can tell me what the targets might be in Abbot County."

Once again, no "please." Not even a request. It was an order.

Although I wasn't sure why, I decided to play this straight. Possibly, I was curious about seeing where it might lead. Especially if my county and its occupants were actually in danger.

I held up my left hand and spread my fingers. Each time I named a potential target, I reached over with the other hand and pushed down a finger.

"Let's start with Burford DeBlanc Air Force Base. I don't know a lot about what goes on at the big base. But if terrorists could wreak substantial havoc on a major U.S. military installation, they're going to be guaranteed serious damage and big ink, don't you think?"

He continued to stare at me. Then he wrote something down in his pocket notebook. After that, he nodded. Just the opposite of what most normal persons would do.

Next, I included our three universities. He listened, he wrote, he nodded — and this time, added a new fillip. He spoke. "Neat."

I paused, thinking about what to suggest next. I decided on the Wide Skies Wind Farm. This facility sprawled about twenty miles west and a little north of Flagler — its giant windmills and their generators made the site one of the world's largest onshore producers of electricity, all created by our relentless winds.

Listen, write, nod, speak. "Amazing."

After that, I threw in the new research park southeast of Flagler. The sophistication, sensitivity, and size of the contracts it announced and the secrecy of those it didn't announce but I heard about anyway was a constant surprise to me.

Then, the railyard.

And, almost for comic relief, I added our museum/amusement park, *7 Days: The Experience*, to the list.

Knoke flipped his notebook shut. "Outstanding! Now we can go buttonhole these clowns and get on top of all this once and for all."

This was the moment I delved deep into my college French. I needed a new term for *déjà vu*. Not a new one, but a term suitable for describing a second *déjà vu* episode coming on the heels of the first.

The term that sailed into my head was *redux déjà vu*. The *vu* this time involved telling another sudden visitor to Flagler he was several hours too late.

I informed our visiting FBI special agent we'd have to resolve the mystery of the box without the pilots' help. When I'd finished telling him why, I knew he'd leave the rest of his bulgogi untouched.

He did.

CHAPTER 10

Where press conferences were concerned, I am a firm subscriber to what I called the Ludwig Wittgenstein Method of Crisis Management.

That's how I view any encounter with the media. As a potential crisis. One unguarded slip of the tongue, and the fat could be in the fire — and the headlines — for days. Your headlines. Your fire. Your fat.

Thus when it came to news conferences, I'd developed a three-step strategy.

Step 1. If possible, don't have a news conference.

Step 2. If you have to have one, say as little as possible.

Step 3. If you don't have to say anything at all, make sure you don't.

Step 3 was where Wittgenstein came in. The Austrian-British philosopher had offered a clever piece of advice: "Whereof one cannot speak, thereof one must be silent."

Where Clyde Hazelton was involved, this wasn't always easy. Hazelton was managing editor of our local daily, the *Tribune-Standard*. I liked him — fair, curious, a good writer. He'd attend press conferences only if he thought they had big-story potential.

Hazelton was sitting in the second row of the spectators' benches when I walked to the front of the county commissioners' hearing room. Helen had transferred the briefing from the courthouse steps because of uncertainties in the weather. The season for afternoon and early evening thunderstorms was here, and the weather bureau had issued a storm watch.

I reported the bare facts of the two pilots' deaths as I knew them. About five sentences' worth. I didn't even have their names.

Said we'd be issuing further statements as our investigation proceeded. And moved immediately to the question period.

Hazelton was ready. And he wasn't the only one smelling a big story.

Reporters from Flagler's three network-affiliated TV stations were in attendance. CNN would pick up a feed from one of those. Reporters or producers from five of our radio stations had set up mike stands. I'd glanced at the slip of paper Helen had handed me when I entered the chamber and noticed we also had stringers for the *Dallas Morning News* and the *Fort Worth Star-Telegram* present. Four student journalists from the newspapers at the three local colleges were in attendance.

I always let Hazelton go first. He always went through the same routine. He always stood, stretched his neck to the left, drew his head back slowly, then dipped it as if to realign his neck vertebra. He'd take off his eyeglasses with the oversized, spotted-leopard earpieces, hold them in his left hand, let one of the temple pieces fall on the web between his thumb and his forefinger. And then read his question from the Gregg-ruled stenographer's notebook he always kept a death grip on at media events.

His questions always had at least three clauses. They could have as many as five. I was accustomed to asking for a repeat of the first two or three clauses when I got ready to answer because by then, I'd forgotten what they were.

On this occasion, no repeats would be necessary. I wasn't going to answer any of his clauses. I'd had no idea he had known anything about any of this.

To most of the people in the room, I probably looked like I was stalling. Working on concocting lies.

But that wasn't true.

I wasn't even thinking of some novel way to invoke Ludwig Wittgenstein's crisis management rule.

In my mind, I was eliminating suspects. Decided it had to have been Special Agent Patrick Knoke. He must have phoned Hazelton immediately after leaving Fred Kang's.

How else would Hazelton have known to ask how much danger Abbot County was in from the missing box; did I think the two pilots had been killed because they refused to reveal the box's location; was a reward being offered for information leading to the discovery of the box; and did I suspect that the airplane used by the two dead pilots had been used to smuggle other cargoes of concern into and out of Flagler?

Three semi-colons. Four clauses.

Vintage Clyde.

The media firestorm I'd known to expect was about to begin. But I'd not fanned the flames. Nor would I attempt to extinguish any of them until I had answers to those questions myself.

I thought Ludwig Wittgenstein would have lent his seal of approval to my reply. "At this time, I can't add anything to my brief comments earlier. We'll reveal additional information as our investigation permits."

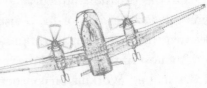

CHAPTER 11

Angie's call came after eight, our time. She'd texted earlier she would call once her briefing was over at the FBI's headquarters in D.C.

I asked where she was calling from.

She said she was in a hotel down the street from the bureau. In a king-sized bed with groovy ribbed white sheets and four fluffy feather pillows supporting her tired back.

I asked if she was naked.

She giggled. "What a dirty mind you have, Sheriff McWhorter! No, I have on my pajama top."

"I wish I was there."

"I'd like that. I'd discard my top too."

"Special Agent Steele, what a dirty mind! But you know I'd help you do that."

"I can't believe I'm having this conversation with somebody who preached a sermon a few hours ago."

"A lot has happened since then."

"So Mad Dog Knoke tells me."

"You call your boss Mad Dog?"

"Not to his face."

"What do you call him to his face?"

"I try not to call his face."

We could go on like this for hours. If anyone ever heard us, they'd have agreed with a criticism I sometimes heard behind my back. That I'd robbed the cradle in selecting a wife-to-be. Special Agent Steele was eight years younger than me. She'd stilled a loneliness that had been wrapped around my heart for more than a decade-and-a-half — ever since 9/11.

One of the reasons I'd fallen in love with Angie was that I'd never met anyone who better understood my inner imp. Or seemed to enjoy engaging with it more.

Listening to her now on the phone, I pictured her sitting in her bed, her long blond hair freed of its ponytail clip and cascading down her shoulders. She was probably in full pajamas and might still be wearing her robe. Sitting there, legs tucked under her, playing Solitaire on her iPad.

But she also had excellent instincts for understanding when enough was enough. "Sorry we missed dinner."

I matched the softening in her voice. "Me too. We'll reschedule."

"But happy anniversary, anyway."

"Happy anniversary to you. To us. And to many more."

I asked what this sudden trip was about and sensed another shift in her tone. It meant I was no longer talking to my gorgeous fiancée, who would tell me anything. Now, I was talking to an FBI special agent, who knew things she couldn't tell me. Things she wouldn't tell me. And things she might tell me after she'd thought a little about it.

In the three years since we'd met, I'd developed a good sense of which was which and when was when. In no case did I push back unduly, nor did she. Both of us knew it had to be that way if we were to stay together and still keep the jobs we had.

"Well, what Mad Dog Knoke told you had some truth to it."

"So you flew up for a briefing on terrorism?"

"That's what I thought I was coming for."

"It turned out to be something else?"

"It did after what happened in Flagler this morning."

"What can you tell me about what happened this morning?"

"We're having another meeting at 935 Pennsylvania Avenue NW tomorrow to decide about that."

"So that box — it's in Flagler, isn't it? And it has national security implications."

"What box?"

It wasn't a question to be answered but a signal. It meant that Angie and I had lost no time in running up against the "things she couldn't tell me" barrier.

I sensed the bureau was playing games with both of us. For that matter, with the whole situation in Flagler, whatever it was. And already, two of our local citizens had been butchered because of it.

Angie knew this.

So if I proceeded with care, she might be able to help me decide where our investigation into the two pilots' deaths should take aim next.

I decided to start with the personal and work outward. "Are you going to be in any danger when you come home?"

"No more than usual."

"Will you be doing anything differently?"

"May have extra company for a while."

"So the bureau is staffing up your office because of this?"

"I'll know tomorrow."

"Will these be counterterrorist agents?"

"Could be. But remember the bureau already has a Joint Terrorism Task Force team. Our local JTTF unit can pull all kinds of expertise from other Texas sources at a moment's notice."

"I know — I'm a member of it."

"That's right."

"But is this bigger than routine JTTF business?"

"I think the next few days could prove very interesting."

"What's the first thing I should do tomorrow?"

"Talk to anyone who can tell you where that Beechcraft King Air has gone in the past fourteen months."

"First thing tomorrow?"

"I would. Otherwise, you may bump into obstacles trying to get that information."

"Who's going to place the obstacles?"

"Wouldn't know much about that."

So we'd again reached the "things she wouldn't tell me" limit. That left the "things she might tell me after she'd thought a little about it" category. "The earthworm category," I often called it, because it sometimes required questions that wiggled all over the landscape.

"When did the local sheriff's favorite FBI special agent first realize there was excrement in all this that might hit the fan?"

"The first putrid smells began drifting out of the bureau's Dallas office about two weeks ago."

"Feces-based or just farts?"

"Flatulence at first. Mad Dog Knoke is famous for breaking bureaucratic wind."

"When did the odors become alarming?"

"About two days ago."

"Any of it emanating from D.C.?"

"Enough that I booked an early morning flight to DFW International with only a quick text to someone I love dearly."

That was another signal. When we suddenly injected something very personal into office talk, it meant a wrap needed to be put on the conversation.

"I love you too."

"Sleep well."

CHAPTER 12

I slept well myself.

The next day, my first meeting was in the farthest corner of our situation room. It was exactly that — a corner. No doors. No windows. And, as a rule, no disruptive foot traffic moving through it.

"Conference Room Corner" was the closest thing our department had to a good meeting space outside of the small interrogations rooms, and those weren't particularly welcoming.

In our conference room, one of the walls was writable. The other wall supported a good-sized cork board. A streamer across the top minced no words. "Be courteous! Leave the board clean!" Notes about a case could only be pinned there while a discussion was underway. When it was over, they came down. Or else.

The last time I could remember using the corner was during what one of the national tabloids had ended up calling "The Case of the Ninety Naked Toesies." This was because the corpses of the nine physicists Chief Deputy Tanner had poisoned were found at the abandoned house west of town without their shoes and socks.

There had been four of us at that Conference Room Corner meeting: myself, my CSI section leader, the medical examiner's field supervisor, and one of Abbot County's game wardens.

This time, I was again expecting there would be four of us. I'd asked Helen to notify Chief Deputy Chuck Del Emma, Detective Matt Salazar, and Detective Rashada Moody of a meeting at 1 p.m.

It was a little after that when I entered our situation room. My head was down because my mind was elsewhere, so I wasn't prepared for the sight that greeted me as I took my first glance of the Conference Room Corner. The corner space was much larger than it normally was. This was because several desks had been shoved to the side. Otherwise, there wouldn't have been room for all the office chairs that were present.

The two rows of chairs reached in a ragged bow from wall to wall. Each row had a narrow aisle-like opening near the middle. And all the chairs were occupied.

I froze in place. Then realized it was useless to try to hide the double take on my face.

This reaction had been expected. The laughter confirmed that. But now that they'd sprung their surprise on their boss, none of my employees showed any signs of leaving. I felt like a schoolteacher facing an unruly class. My mind weighed the implications of this spectacle. I didn't know how much most of my deputies and staff knew about the crime scene at the hangar.

I trusted the three people I'd asked to be at the meeting enough to know they hadn't been spreading alarmist gossip.

Still and all, my people in the department were only human. And more attracted to a good mystery than most. Here were nearly two dozen of them waiting to be titillated by the details of our latest whodunit. It appeared that crime in Abbot County had become its own entertainment, even for the people who investigated it. Most of them were people I'd hired. People I depended on. People the Abbot County citizens who paid all our salaries depended on. My thoughts sampled several possibilities. But they all returned to the same conclusion. *Your call, hotshot. You're the boss.*

On this occasion, the Ludwig Wittgenstein Method of Crisis Management wasn't going to work. I'd have to fall back on the Luther Stephens McWhorter Method of Crisis Management.

I was going to own the moment.

I made my way to the aisle between the rows of chairs. Stepped rapidly toward the writable wall. Laid my rose-colored accordion file folder containing my papers on a small table. Reached for the armless chair sitting close by. Turned it around. Scooted it closer to my onlookers. Straddled it. And once I'd gotten comfortable in it, I swept my eyes from one side of the group to the other without cracking a smile. "Here's the way we're going to play this."

The snickers in the room faded.

"I need a show of hands. How many of you will need to leave in the next thirty minutes?"

Seven people among the twenty or so in the room raised their hands. I asked these to be courteous and leave now so as not to disturb proceedings later. I didn't speak again until they had departed, rolling their chairs with them.

"Next question — and be honest — how many of you think you may need to rush from the room when you see a photo of a decapitated head? And, be forewarned, his eyes are open."

All six of my non-deputized staff people departed.

The folks still in their chairs got another stern look from their jefe-in-chief. "How many of you remember chewing Beechcraft King Air bubble gum as a kid?"

Five more hands went up. Their owners were informed their expertise was not quite what we were looking for. And they, and their chairs, departed.

I asked the four remaining deputies if they could clear their schedules and be available for special assignment at least 80 percent of the time for the next week. Maybe longer, if it took longer.

Three of them could. I thanked the other one for knowing his limitations and wished him a good week.

At this point, I asked the remaining six persons to bring their chairs forward and make a new partial circle. Then I pulled an armless chair to the front of the room and turned it around so that it faced the others.

When I'd met in Conference Room Corner to speak with my investigators about the buzzard-mutilated bodies of the nine physicists, I'd closed the meeting by going to the writable wall. Picking up a marker. And scribbling a single word in capital letters. Then I'd added an exclamation point. And underlined the whole shebang.

That's how I started this meeting. I went straight to the writable wall. Extracted a marker from the service tray. And, before anyone said a word, myself included, I wrote the same word on the wall and gave it the same treatment as before.

Almost.

The one difference was a big one. Instead of adding an exclamation point after the word, I added a question mark.

PROFESSIONALS?

Then I reminded the people sitting in front of me that Detective Moody had been charged with sorting out the crime scene.

I found a chair for myself, joined the circle, reached toward Deputy Only and pantomimed holding out a performer's mike to her. "What in Jehoshaphat's name do you think happened in that hangar?"

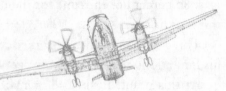

CHAPTER 13

But my employee didn't go along with the script I had in mind. "No offense, boss. But I think Chief Deputy Del Emma should go first."

I shot Detective Moody a curious look. Aimed another curious look at my new second-in-command. And used my open palm to indicate that the empty chair was his to occupy.

He might have blushed at his sudden advance into the spotlight. I couldn't tell. With all those red colorations, the doctor who'd delivered him had probably thought he was blushing when he came into the world.

The previous night, I'd sent him a brief text as soon as I'd hung up from talking with Angie. I'd passed along her concern that important information about the pilots' recent flight destinations could be in jeopardy. And shared her suggestion that we check ASAP with anyone who might keep track of pilot flight filings.

I had no reason to suspect Del Emma hadn't acted on my request. But he was quick to volunteer he had crucial information from a different source. He said it was the college student with the grievous head injury. He'd stopped by Flagler General Hospital to check on the student a couple of hours ago.

The kid had awakened from his coma. Was responding

to questions. And, remarkably, was providing clear, detailed answers to some of them.

Del Emma licked his thumb and flipped through several pages in his shirt-pocket-sized notebook until he found the one he wanted. "His name is Stockstill. Pogue Stockstill. P-O-G-U-E. Stockstill as in, well . . . still as a stock. He's a freshman at the University of the Hills. Majoring in analytical history techniques, whatever that is. And he's one more pissed dude, his massive headache notwithstanding."

He'd told Del Emma about arriving for work at his usual time on weekends — around nine o'clock. And realizing almost immediately things around the hangar weren't exactly kosher.

His first surprise had been finding the hangar's sliding doors still closed. He'd known the Beechcraft King Air's owners had been planning a departure at about 9:15. He wondered if they'd already left. Then saw that they hadn't. At least, their plane hadn't. When he'd walked onto the floor of the hangar through the pedestrian entrance, the plane was still sitting there. Unattended. Not a soul in sight, at least that he could see.

Del Emma said this was the college student's second surprise. He knew the owners of Orville 'n Wilbur Charter Services were punctilious ex-military helicopter pilots. Before every flight, they'd fuss over their plane like it was about to run in the Kentucky Derby. They never spent less than half an hour on these elaborate preflight checks.

My chief deputy said the young student was right about the pilots' backgrounds. Both Quitaque ("Kway") Haynes and Akron ("Ike") Breezer had been flying Apache attack helicopters for the U.S. Army in Iraq when the war ended in 2011. A year later they'd run into each other in Dallas.

It had happened at a weekend shindig at a glitzy fixed-based operation staffed by a Texas cosmetic queen for her customers and sales reps. Both pilots had been dragged there by the women they were dating. Their female companions soon moved on, but once they'd met, the two pilots found a bond developing between them.

At first, they'd talked of founding a helicopter service for helping ranchers round up cattle. But one of the other people they'd run into at the Dallas FBO was an executive at the Kansas company that made Beechcraft planes. One thing led to another, and the pair ended up going in deep hock for the 350i.

They'd decided to base their new charter service in Flagler because the Beechcraft guy had said there was a lot of money in the county.

Getting back to the college student's account, Del Emma said the youngster's third surprise had come after he'd been in the hangar's small office for about fifteen minutes. He'd gotten caught up reading an article in an aviation magazine and barely looked up when he thought he'd heard a small noise near the hangar doors. When he'd heard nothing more, he decided he was imagining things and returned to his reading.

Not long after, he'd heard a mechanical sound. It started as a low drone then increased to a buzz and then a hiss — like a hive of irritated bees. He knew it was the sound a turboprop engine makes when it first begins to turn over.

He also knew it was a universal no-no around airport hangars to start a plane's engine or engines indoors. The issue was more than bad manners. It was dangerous. And not only because of the deadly propellers. The wind blasts could turn anything not screwed down into a life-threatening projectile.

Then the kid heard the plane's other engine coming to life and realized what he still hadn't heard: the sound of the hangar's big roll-back doors being opened.

Del Emma took a moment to stretch his neck muscles before continuing. "The kid opens the office door leading to the hangar floor. Sees two figures standing there in black ski masks and blue buddy suits. Disposable coveralls, gloves, booties — the works. One of them even had a fanny pack strapped to his hiney. And both had respirator cups tied over their masks."

Del Emma couldn't help noticing our startled looks. "I know. Kid said it scared the bejesus out of him. Not to mention, he said the pair also looked like they'd just been splattered head to toe with blood."

And that's where my chief deputy stopped. We knew this was because this was where the college student had stopped. Anything else that happened in the hangar, we were going to have to reconstruct from other sources or our own observations. At least, for now. But we had something none of us had expected. An eyewitness. Not to the actual slayings, of course. But tantalizingly close.

Detective Salazar broke the silence. "But why didn't they kill him too?"

Del Emma flicked his notebook closed. Stared at the cover. And offered no response.

At first, I thought he was collecting his thoughts. Then I realized he was stage-managing the moment. *My latest hire had a flair for the dramatic in his storytelling.*

"Well, they almost did kill him. But the kid himself has a theory about why they didn't finish the job." He paused again. Looked toward the other side of the room. I didn't know if the others were picking up on this, but my new chief deputy was treating this like a stage, not a sheriff's office. What a ham!

"He thinks it might be because he's Jewish."

Another pause. More glancing at our faces.

"His dad moved the family here from New York when the kid was in grade school. The dad is a professor at the University of the Hills.

"He was wearing his chai medallion. C-h-a-i. You pronounce it *khy*, with a guttural sound. Like the 'ch' in Johann Sebastian Bach. Some people, even Jews, think it means 'living' or 'alive.' But it doesn't. It just means you don't want to dangle your

Jewishness in people's faces like you would if you were wearing, say, a Star of David."

Del Emma rubbed the chest hairs visible where his shirt was unbuttoned. If he'd been wearing a chai on a necklace, it would have appeared there. "Half the adult males in South Florida wear one."

His next comment was apropos of nothing that had or not happened in the hangar office. It was more likely prompted by his realization of how pompous his explanation had sounded.

"Elvis Presley wore one . . ."

CHAPTER 14

After Del Emma's offhand comment about Elvis, I wanted more than ever to hear from Detective Moody. She'd stayed at the hangar deep into the night with our CSI team and the medical examiner's people. And she'd been inside the plane.

But she was still making notes in her black faux leather padfolio. When she looked up, I invited her to take the chair.

She did so — with a beauty queen's grace and poise, an ever-present reminder that she'd been a finalist for Miss Abbot County a few years back.

Her first action was to send an emphatic hand chop in my direction. "Correct me if I'm wrong, Sheriff. But the plane's pull-down stairs . . . When you and I first walked into the hangar yesterday, did you realize they'd been lowered?"

I had to think about it. "Not until we walked around the nose of the plane. The stairs are on the other side."

That earned me my deputy's nod of approval. "I think that's the reason the college kid didn't see or hear anybody when he first arrived. Our two victims and the killers were on board the plane. If the kid had been looking for them, he might have seen them through the plane's windows. But he wasn't."

Detective Moody was using her pen to beat out a kind of rat-a-tat-tat noise on her notepad. She had a vacant look, as if she still wasn't sure what was bugging her. Then the sun peaked through the clouds. "What if the killers hadn't arrived with murder in mind? What if they'd worn the protective gear for some other reason?"

I had a suspicion what had prompted her question. "You saw something inside the plane, didn't you?"

That got a "maybe yes, maybe no" shrug. "We'll get to that. But you all help me out on this buddy suit thing. Why else would these guys have shown up in full protective gear?"

I got out of my chair and hurried to the writable wall. Grabbed a marker. And started writing as fast as I could. Because the suggestions were flying.

Avoid being recognized if anyone saw them.

Avoid direct contact with anything dangerous.

Keep away from germs.

You can't stand the sight of the person you came with.

You don't want the other person to see how scared you are.

Because the buddy suit colors go with your eyes.

To discover how comfortable the suits are.

To discover how uncomfortable the suits are.

Because you've always wanted to look like a storm-trooper.

To compete for most original costume.

Because you're a neat freak.

Because it's a bad flu season.

You plan to rob a bank next.

You'd always wanted to do this.

It might scare someone into spilling the beans.

Detective Moody waved at us to stop. "This group ought to be writing TV scripts." She put her padfolio on her chair seat, walked to the wall, and swept a hand down the list. "None of the rest of these makes as much sense as the first one."

We all looked again to see what was at the top of the list. She read it for us. "Avoid being recognized if anyone saw them."

She put both arms behind her and leaned against the wall. "Until Deputy Chief Del Emma told us what the college student saw, I'd thought all this was probably a botched interrogation. The pilots knew something their captors wanted to know. They'd been trussed up and stood in front of the propellers. To that point, any threat to push them in had been a bluff. Then someone stumbled. Or panicked. And the fat was in the fire. Or the flesh in the propeller. Whatever. So they shoved both victims to their deaths."

She reached toward me for the marker. "But look at number one again." She went up on tiptoes to circle the entry about not leaving evidence. "After thinking about it, I don't think the pilots' deaths were a miscalculation. Or a botched effort to interrogate them. I think their killers arrived planning to do exactly what they did. Dressed for the occasion too."

I don't remember who actually put the thought into words because it arrived in all our heads about the same time. *The pilots' hideous deaths were a message for someone else.*

I do remember who'd asked the obvious follow-up question. "Make a statement to whom?"

I'd been the one to ask it.

I still had my eyes on what I'd written on the writable wall when Detective Moody put my deputy chief's tendency for the dramatic to shame. "Don't have a clue. But it could have been whoever hired the pilots for their next flight. One look inside, and it was easy to see the Beechcraft had been outfitted to transport an infant. One that hasn't been here very long. It was carrying a tiny bassinet."

CHAPTER 15

I was still processing Detective Moody's bombshell reference to the Beechcraft plane and a baby when my cell phone rang.

It was Helen. She said Dr. Adele Lovejoy had called, wanting to know if she could come see me. Helen said her voice had sounded strained. Like she was under a lot of pressure.

The dean answered on the first ring. And she did sound stressed. Not because she sounded hurried. She always sounded hurried despite the fact that she was one of the most control-oriented people I knew. Her tendency to try to rush you was one of the ways she tried to control you.

This time, she sounded like she was almost frantic with worry. She said she realized she didn't have an appointment, but she was wondering if she could crash my schedule.

I told her my office suite was a beehive today, and we'd have more privacy in hers. When she agreed, I told her I'd be on my way as soon as I took care of a few things.

Thirty minutes later, I was walking into Dr. Lovejoy's office. Only to be reminded again how much of a neat freak she was.

Her gleaming mahogany desktop screamed that fact. It was always as clean as a furniture showroom sample. Not so much as a blotter pad was permitted to call it home. So I'd have noticed the large book anyway.

But then, books with a glossy, full-color photograph of Mount Ararat on their cover don't tend to go ignored. Especially if they've been positioned just-so in the middle of a large, burnished, empty desktop.

Had Special Agent Knoke been in touch with her too? Or had she'd heard something on the news I'd missed? Or was she just better informed than I was?

Spotting the book left my mind feeling like it was trying to scramble eggs without a spatula. And Dr. Lovejoy herself wasn't helping.

Even as middle age approached, she cut a figure — and had one — worthy of a thirty-and-older dating service promo. "Athletic and toned" were words that came to mind. Fortunately, she hadn't noticed my eyes' involuntary once-over. Or maybe she was just used to it. Maybe she reveled in it.

She pushed the book in my direction and got things on track with her usual curtness. "You're probably wondering if anyone on our faculty is responsible for this."

I picked the book up. Observed that it was a softback book, not a hardcover. Glanced at the back cover. Saw it was published by Wanderer's Planet Press. It was about more than Mount Ararat, but that was the majestic, snow-capped 16,800-foot volcano on the cover. I checked to see if the book was inscribed to anyone. It wasn't.

I laid it back on Dr. Lovejoy's desk. Carefully. If that desk ever suffered a scratch, I didn't want to be the one to put it there. "So, you know something about our murdered pilots' travels?"

"Not really. But I know something about my faculty's travels. It's Dr. Bender I'm worried about."

I pointed toward the book. "Has he been to Mount Ararat recently?"

She actually rose from her chair and straightened her designer skirt before answering. I swallowed and let my mind travel for an instant. *Back in my student days, the Bible professors had all been men, and if they'd so much as bothered to straighten a tie, it would have been like Moses descending Mount Sinai with the Ten Commandments.* I tried again: "So one of your faculty members has been to Ağrı recently."

"Dr. Bender says he has. Associate professor. He's one of our experts on ancient Middle Eastern religious cultures and history."

"Older guy?"

"Oh, no. Barely thirty."

"Ambitious?"

"Very."

"Intense?"

She looked as if the question had surprised her. But her answer came quickly. "Tightly wound."

"Risk-taker?"

"Like most millennials, he thinks he is . . . well, indestructible most of the time, I suppose. He reminds me of Dostoevsky's quote."

Divinity students don't get much exposure to Russian novelists. But I thought I knew which famous quote she was referring to. "'Only one thing matters, one thing: to be able to dare.'"

"Yes, that one."

"Dr. Bender gone a lot?"

"More and more. And the places he says he's been going seemed to make sense. After all, his area of expertise is ancient Middle Eastern religions. Lately, he says he's been making trips all over the eastern Mediterranean countries."

"Any idea what he's been doing?"

"He says research and excavating. But he's never written research papers about his finding or activities. I find that odd. At one point, I had a dark thought that he might be dealing in black market antiquities. But that's a shady, buccaneer sort of world. Dr. Bender, for all his excesses, doesn't really seem the type."

"And you're worried about him?"

Now it was clear what her agitation was about. I could see it in her face just before she said the words: "I think he may be missing."

"You last saw him when?"

"Last Thursday. And again on Friday morning."

"Thursday's when he gave you the book?"

"No, he gave me the book the second time — on Friday."

Even on his Thursday visit, she said Bender had not seemed his normal self. She searched for the right word. Settled on "preoccupied."

Said they had engaged in small talk for a while. Trifling stuff, she called it. That was a departure for Bender. Usually, he got straight to the point. Then apropos of nothing, he'd asked a peculiar question. "He wanted to know what I thought about the story of Korah."

CHAPTER 16

Her mention of Korah didn't ring a bell for me. I suggested it sounded Hebraic.

She said it was.

Korah was a character in the Book of Numbers, chapter 16. A greedy, arrogant Israelite who angered God and Moses. And gotten himself and 250 of his friends and their families buried alive by the Almighty for his poor choices and bad behavior.

I grimaced. "Sounds like a man with a problem."

"Oh, just another human a little too full of himself."

"And Dr. Bender's interest in Korah?"

"He said something about using that text for his sermon Sunday morning."

"He preaches regularly?"

"Nearly all my faculty have preaching appointments."

"And you found something concerning about using that text for a sermon?"

"I didn't believe him."

"Didn't believe he was going to base his sermon on it?"

"I didn't believe he'd brought up the Korah story because of his sermon preparations."

"Why not?"

"Because he kept wringing his hands. Dr. Bender is an experienced public speaker. They don't normally do that while they're talking about preparing their Sunday sermon."

"Did you ask him what his sermon would be about?"

"He said betrayal . . . betrayal and its consequences. He said that's what Korah and his friends did. They betrayed God, betrayed Moses. Betrayed their families and their friends. And, in the end, betrayed themselves."

"What did you make of that?"

She took several breaths. "I remember thinking the betrayals Dr. Bender had in mind must have involved someone other than Korah, Moses, and Yahweh."

Yahweh.

I'd not heard that word in a while. It was more or less how ancient Hebrews would have pronounced the name of God. But only before 300 BCE After that, they didn't pronounce it at all. Thought it was too sacred to mention aloud.

"Got a photo of Bender?"

She reached for her smartphone. Punched in a web address. Tapped the screen as she waited. Apparently saw what she was waiting for — almost. Did a reverse pincher thing with her thumb and forefinger. Made the image bigger. And turned the screen so I could see it.

The figure in the photo was obviously on the youngish end of the professional adult spectrum. And, to my thinking, sported a look a little too fashionable for a member of a university religious faculty.

Fashionable? That word didn't seem strong enough, so I searched for another one. Rakish. That was more like it.

The dean hadn't lowered the phone yet. She was watching my every eye blink. So I did the gentlemanly thing and indicated what needed to happen next. "You need to tell me the whole story."

This was when she switched her phone off and laid it flat on her desktop. "I know."

Then Professor Lovejoy said something that anyone who knew the value she put on safeguarding her public image would have been shocked to their shoe soles to hear her say. I know I was. I viewed it as another indication of how upsetting her encounters with Dr. Bender last weekend must have been.

"But first, I've got to go pee."

CHAPTER 17

On her return from the ladies' room, Dr. Lovejoy did something else I'd never witnessed when visiting her office. Or rather, she didn't do something.

She did not retreat behind her massive desk. Instead, she stayed in front of it. Walked over to the stiff-backed chair matching the one I was sitting in. Pulled it away from the wall. Turned it to face me. Seated herself. And resumed her story.

You'd have thought her lungs remembered the exact position they'd been in when she'd left to attend to her body urgencies.

"Dr. Bender called me at home Friday morning around ten. Asked me to meet him."

My hat was still resting in my lap. Without losing eye contact with the dean, I laid it on the small accent table at my elbow. "Here at Hills-U?"

"No, he wanted to meet at Cummings." She saw my eyebrows arch. "I know, I found it strange too. And it gets stranger."

Cummings University was one of the other two church colleges in Flagler. Our three schools had different religious affiliations and were in different parts of town. This meant there was little intermingling between staffs, faculties, and students.

"He didn't want to be seen with his boss at Hills-U?"

"Not sure."

"You declined to meet with him at Cummings?"

"Oh, I met with him. Didn't press him for his reasons for meeting there."

"Meeting where? At Cummings?"

"Campus chapel."

"He had a door key?'

"Said it was always unlocked."

"Wonder how he knew."

"I have a lot of things for you to wonder about if you'll let me get to them."

I made a closing-the-zipper gesture along my lips. I'm not sure she even noticed.

She told me how she'd arrived at an otherwise-empty chapel to find Bender seated on a pew toward the front. He'd ask her to sit beside him. Wanted to know if she remembered a speech she'd given in Philadelphia several years back at a convention of religious college administrators and faculty where she'd said church colleges too often forgot God was enrolled in their institutions. That they lacked vision, daring, and courage and needed to take more advantage of their wondrous opportunities.

He said that speech had made a deep impression on him. And had been providentially timed and that not long after, he'd had an opportunity to become involved in something he described as grand, epic — something breathtakingly Biblical in size and potential.

This was when he had handed her the Mount Ararat travelogue book. He told her there was an envelope in the back. Said it contained an important clue to what his grand project had been about. If something happened to him, he said, she should open it. Otherwise, she was to leave the flap sealed and the note unread. He said the wording was obscure so that innocent people would be protected, but the right people could figure it out.

I walked over to her desk and picked the book up again. Bent the back cover away from the facing page. Inspected that space.

There was nothing there. I clasped enough pages at both ends of the book to be able to turn it upside down and shake it. Again, nothing.

I shot the dean a questioning glance.

Her response was somewhere between a sigh and a sniff. "You really didn't expect me to leave it lying around, did you?"

She went to her credenza. Got her purse. Extracted a key. Unlocked the middle drawer of her desk. Removed a plain white standard envelope. Took a sheet of white paper from it. And handed it to me.

I don't know what I'd expected, but it wasn't what I was reading.

You shall not breed together two kinds of your cattle;
you shall not sow your field with two kinds of seed,
nor wear a garment upon you of two kinds of material
mixed together.

If the dean had been expecting me to say something profound, it didn't happen. "This is supposed to be a clue to something?"

"Yes, if something happened to Dr. Bender."

"And something has?"

"Nobody has seen him since I met with him in the chapel. Not his wife. No one here at Hills-U. He missed his preaching appointment Sunday. He's missed four classes. He seems to have vanished."

My first thought was in poor taste. *At least we know he didn't hire Orville 'n Wilbur Charter Services to fly him somewhere. They're out of pilots.*

My second one wasn't any better. It was an old Sunday School joke about why Noah hadn't caught many fish. He'd only had two worms.

That was when I asked Dean Lovejoy if she knew anyone else in Flagler who had been to Mount Ararat recently. She said Craft Roberts.

I didn't need any further explanation. Half the town knew that he was the creation-story-crazed entrepreneur. The one who was building a huge museum and amusement park based on the first ten chapters of Genesis at the far northeast edge of Flagler.

After saying thanks and goodbye, I made my way to my patrol cruiser. Once seated, I texted Helen to see if she could make me an appointment with Roberts. It seemed logical he was the next person I should see.

I'd only driven a few blocks when she replied. He was available now and would be waiting for me.

CHAPTER 18

Roberts's museum/theme park abutted the right side of County Road 9 about four miles north of East Main Street. It was an instant assault on the eyes.

First came a black, freshly striped ocean of asphalt — the immense new parking lot. On the back side of the massive lot loomed an enormous gray monolith. My first thought was that it looked like a crunched-down, spread-out Hoover Dam. Splashed across its monumental facade was a huge sign with sky-blue letters in bold but minimalist type. 7 Days: The Experience.

Not far below the sign was an array of towering glass doors. I knew how many without counting them.

Seven.

I counted them anyway.

Fourteen.

Each of the seven oversized entrances was occupied by a set of larger-than-life-sized double doors. The imposing guard shack at the entrance to the parking lot would have easily dwarfed the double garage at my house. The two security guards standing outside it wore campaign-style hats with chin straps that dangled in front. The headgear caused them to look a lot like the state troopers I'd seen back east. I couldn't help noticing that their duty belts held Glock 22s, Tasers, and handcuffs. This was the kind of outlay carried by my own deputies.

One of the guards waved me to a halt and made a phone call. Then he saluted and motioned me through. "Go through the last entrance on the left, sir! And show your credentials at the door!"

Under my breath, I mumbled a few words in reply. "Always do at Fort Knox."

I got a glimpse of Craft Roberts striding toward me across the cavernous atrium floor. But only for an instant. Another figure quickly captured my attention. This one loomed before me like Gary Cooper coming down the street in *High Noon*. A twenty-foot-high Gary Cooper.

My likeness was being reflected before me from tip to toe. The only aberration was a slight shimmer toward the center where the building's airflow made the giant image flutter.

I soon realized the letters over the door on the wall behind me had been reversed. The reflection was making them read "God's most prized creation."

"It's foil, actually."

That information had come from the jaunty voice at my elbow. "It's been the rage lately in stage productions and rock concerts around the globe. Lisbon, Amsterdam, Hong Kong, Vegas."

And now, Flagler.

Roberts shouted a warning. "Watch your head!"

An airborne device buzzed past, a few feet beyond our reach. It was the size of an omelet pan, had several spinning rotors, and was moving about as fast as I could run.

A white banner the length of a beach towel trailed behind it. The black lettering on the banner read, *Then God Rested, The NOVAplex, 3 times daily.*

"Aerial drone."

The voice at my elbow again. "Ultra-lightweight. Flies at whatever altitude we set it at. Goes where we want. Never gets lost. Kids are going to love it. We call it the Littlest Air Angel. Drones are the rage in entertainment complexes everywhere, you know. Shanghai, Dubai, Mumbai, Johannesburg, Los Angeles, Houston —"

I finished his sentence for him. "And, now Flagler."

Roberts steered me to the closest of the big entrances opening off the atrium. The sign said it led to Day 1. Just inside the door, Roberts showed me a display as large as my high school chemistry lab. He said it was an atomic clock.

I couldn't begin to guess what the device cost, and Roberts wasn't saying. "We want to talk about more than just what God did and when he did it — we want to feature *how* he did it. That exquisite clock is a marvelous thing to contemplate. How God keeps time. I come in here all the time just to watch the diodes and dials and the flashing lights."

Roberts had been born into oil money, lots of it. Enough to live a wealth-lubricated existence. But his life path had been shaped by both parents.

His wildcatter-father had ignited his passions for the entrepreneur's chase. His mother was on the board of trustees at Hills-U and involved in numerous charities and other community outlets for altruism and uplift.

Their only child spent most of his time with his own "inner circle" clique, so it had been a couple of years since I'd gotten close enough to him to get an impression. What I was seeing at the museum fit well with what I remembered.

He was another of Flagler's short people — five-foot-two at best. And anyone who knew Roberts, and anyone else who had encountered him on the back roads of Abbot County knew, knew he took great pride in staying fit.

More than that — in *looking* fit.

Watching him out of the corner of my eye, I could see that he still looked like a nattily-attired, sun-bronzed, tightly coiled precision spring.

"See you're still biking."

"Oh, every afternoon at three — if I can get off. Just bought a new bike."

He shared the details. "It's a Bianchi by Gucci. Carbon-fiber flat-bar road bike. Set me back nearly 16,000 clams. Plus ten Benjamins for a Gucci helmet. Gloves ran three hundred forty, water bottle one hundred fifteen." He was beaming again. Apparently, he had no inkling how this sounded in a cathedral-sized facility devoted to humanity's most sacred and cherished focus of faith — the "I Am That I Am."

I leveled my eyes at Roberts. "So you're here to argue against evolution and science and things of that ilk."

He looked a little surprised. "Where'd you get that idea?"

"Let's start with '7 Days.' Sounds like a reference to the Genesis creation narrative to me."

His easy smile didn't quite reach his eyes. "And it is, of course. But there are a lot of different ways to talk about the first ten chapters of the Book of Genesis. You can argue that He did indeed create it all in six twenty-four-hour days and not a ticktock more. Made Adam with a belly button but no penis, and all that — yadda, yadda, yadda."

Easy laugh again. But again no smile around the eyes. "But we didn't want a 'How Science Ruins Everything' feel to our place. Come on, let me show you."

We didn't have to walk far before I understood why the facade of 7 Days: The Experience looked as big as a flattened-out Hoover Dam. It needed to be. The cavernous atrium it fronted for was not all that much smaller than the indoor stadium where the Dallas Cowboys played professional football.

Each of God's creation days got its own huge chamber filled with displays, rides, visual effect spectacles, and performing artists.

On the north side of the atrium were entrances to chambers for Day 1, Day 2, and Day 3. Then came a facade ablaze with Broadway-style billboard razzle-dazzle. This was the entrance to the NOVAplex Theater. Roberts said it seated 2000.

To the right of that, completing the picture like more folds in a giant Chinese fan, were the entrances to the chambers for Day 4, Day 5, and Day 6. All six entrances were announced by signs in the same bold, sleek, minimal typeface as the pretentious sign out front.

Day 7 was assigned to the atrium itself. It was filled with lounging areas, refreshment stands, and sit-down cafés. There, patrons of 7 Days: The Experience could join God while He rested.

Roberts didn't show me everything. I could hear construction hammers issuing from behind a set of dull-gray drapes shielding an area in Day 5. Two more of those Glock-wearing guards were never more than a few feet away from them.

They'd amble past, then circle back. Sometimes walking past separately, sometimes as a pair. They were trying to be casual about it, but it was the casualness of a mother eagle trying to make you look everywhere but at the nest housing her young ones. The mother eagle, though, would have made a much more vigilant decoy. The two guards looked bored.

I'd already decided Craft Roberts was rich enough, ambitious enough, and devious enough to be involved with Flagler's newest outbreak of mayhem and lawlessness. It really didn't matter whether he'd been to eastern Turkey recently. I wanted to ask him if he knew anything about Dr. Bender's whereabouts, but I never got the chance.

My phone buzzed.

The text was from Angie. Her plane had landed from Dallas/Fort Worth International, and she was en route to her office. She wanted to know if I could meet her there.

She had an urgent need to talk.

CHAPTER 19

My usual routine when I walked into my favorite FBI special agent's office was to close the door behind me. If I neglected to do it, she'd remind me. Our discussions had a way of turning private, and we both wanted to make sure they stayed that way.

But this time, Angie's actions were something different. Seeing me enter, she walked over to the window overlooking her reception area. Lowered the blinds. Then turned and walked straight into my arms. Laid her head on my chest. Loosed a huge sigh. And for the longest time stayed still as a sleeping infant.

I went still too. She was in some kind of spell, and I didn't want to be the one to break it.

When she finally stirred, she took me by the hand and guided me around her desk. Pushed her office chair away toward the wall as far as it would go and motioned for me to sit in it.

She positioned herself at the front of her desk. Braced herself with both arms and gave a little hop that landed her above the chair well. She started swinging her legs and directed as stern a gaze as I'd ever seen on her beautiful face straight at me. "I gave the bureau my resignation letter."

The silence that followed was subject to whatever interpretation I chose to give it. I chose neutrality. And waited for more information.

It wasn't forthcoming, so you couldn't call what was happening a conversation. Then I got it.

There *was* a conversation going on, but I wasn't involved. Not yet, anyway. It was between two FBI agents, both occupying the same brain.

One of those agents was so angry she was almost incoherent. The other was — what? Perplexed? Aggrieved? Unsure of what to do next?

This insight was rewarded with more information from FBI Special Agent No. 2.

Again, it was only a few words. And it was still obvious that Angie No. 1 was mostly addressing Angie No. 2, but I was beginning to get a sense that both Angies were becoming more aware that a third party was monitoring their internal exchange. "They tried to buy me off with the Dallas bureau chief's job."

At this point, I realized how shallow both our breathing had become because she took a breath so deep it was almost a gasp. My psyche seemed to view this as an act of permission. I took several deep breaths myself. But I still didn't speak. This had been her show from the beginning, and I couldn't begin to imagine how it was scripted to end. I thought it best to keep doing what I'd been doing since I'd entered the room. Radiate acceptance. Reassurance. Security. Love.

She said something that confirmed that I'd made the right judgment about my role. "I'm so glad that you're here."

Now I could speak.

"And I'm so glad you're home safe and sound."

CHAPTER 20

"**S**o you're no longer an FBI special agent."

"Oh, but I am."

"So they refused your resignation?"

"They did when I told them what I was about to do."

"And what did my Angie girl say she was going to do."

"Go home and tell her sheriff boyfriend everything she knew."

"And is she going to do that?"

"When she and her sheriff boyfriend can find a place that isn't bugged."

"You think the bureau has bugged its own agent?"

"I do. Or none of this would have happened."

"How about my office."

"You're bugged too."

As she told me this, Angie's voice had gradually been dropping to a whisper. That gave me an idea.

I flattened the palm of my left hand and used the thumb and index finger of my right hand to make a writing motion.

Angie understood.

She hopped off her desk. Opened the narrow drawer over the foot well. And removed a writing pad and ballpoint pen. I held up two fingers. I wanted each of us to have something to write with and something to write on. For two reasons.

First, we'd make faster progress. And second, if anyone found either one of the pads, they'd have only half our discussion. She found more writing utensils. I sidled close to her and wrote first. *Bugged for how long?*

Angie wrote on her pad. *Ur office 2 wks.*

I pointed at her.

She shrugged. She didn't know how long her office had been bugged.

Angie was a skilled lip reader, so I could have shaped my next question with my lips. But I wrote it down anyway. *Who?*

Her reply took a moment. *Probl'y counterintel.*

Watching her write, I didn't wait for her to finish before I started. *Bureau? CIA? Military?*

She pointed to CIA. Then wrote a clarification. *Just a guess. CIA's illegal.*

Not every time.

I understood. The CIA is generally supposed to keep its operations offshore. But it can sometimes get involved in domestic intelligence-gathering if it involves foreign parties. That explained my next question. *Foreign terrorist threat?*

That brought a head nod.

You knew?

She nodded again.

How long u know?

Months.

You didn't tell me?

Couldn't.

Because of Bureau politics?

No. Too !!!

Dangerous for you?

For us both.

I realized the intensity of my look carried its own message. I wanted to know more.

She wrote more. *And !!! for my moles.*

I let both arms drop so that they rested on my legs and looked at her in amazement. Got my pad and pen back in place. *Moles? Plural?*

She held up two fingers.

What I wanted to write couldn't be said in only a few words. And it had to be phrased just right or it was going to sound like an out-and-out accusation. But then, it was an accusation.

She'd been conducting elaborate surveillance in our county. No problem with an FBI special agent doing that, but she had done so without so much as a hint of her activities to the head of local law enforcement. An individual whose bed she shared, on average, once a week. Sometimes more.

I needed to know everything she could tell me. *U been bugging too?*

Angie seemed relieved to be able to answer. *Sometimes.*

Who?

Folks u know about.

Lovejoy?

Almost. But — no.

Craft Roberts?

Not yet.

So who?

The Professor.

Bender?

She blinked once. *Yes.*

I wanted to know more. *U bugged his office?*

Yes.

Got a judge's okay?

Always.

He's missing.

The judge?

Bender.

Again, my fiancée made an entry on her pad. *Wanna tell me?*

On mine, I wrote in all-capitals. *WORST WAY!* Looking at her face, I saw that we had just allowed something new into the atmosphere in her office. Maybe it was called oxygen.

She wrote something more and held it up for me to read. *Wanna go somewhere?*

I wrote a very honest answer. *Lunch.*

She gave me an exaggerated head nod. But lunch was going to have to wait.

Hungry as we were, we couldn't continue this interchange in any of our favorite Flagler restaurants. It was too easy for your conversations to be overheard.

I could think of only one place where we were almost certain to have complete privacy. I'd used it for such purposes more than once. I'd met there with an emissary sent by the president of the United States.

A tumbled-down old tin shack. It stood — barely — in a back corner of the Beware the Junkyard Dogs Company's abandoned wrecking yard at the edge of Flagler's northern city limits.

CHAPTER 21

You got to the old salvage yard by motoring to the end of one of Flagler's less picturesque streets. Removing a rusty padlock from an ancient oxidized chain. Pushing open an old gate and cowering at the screeches. Then weaving your way to the decrepit shack far in the back. To complete your journey, you had to wind your way through or around piles of junk sometimes as high as your shoulders.

"So, this is it, is it?" Angie said, teasing. "Where you bring all your serious girlfriends when you want to whisper sweet nothings in their ears?"

The rickety packing crates that the president's guy and I had sat on were still there. But the temperature was a whole other ball game. That day last summer, it had been hot enough in the shack to scald a lizard. Now, if there was a lizard anywhere in the vicinity, he was outside sunning on a rock. There was no question that it was springtime.

I scooted my crate closer to my beautiful companion and took her gloved hands in mind. "Well, yes, I bring all my serious lady friends here. When I want to be sure nobody's listening. So tell me about your moles."

She rearranged her crate. That way she could look me square in the face. "It's not what you'd expect."

I was feeling a hint of impatience in myself. Maybe a little irritation.

She'd caught me off-guard with her mention of moles. I had no idea what I was expecting. But I didn't sense this was stage-management we were involved in. Rather, I felt she was still being cautious, maybe excessively so. Still wondering how much she should tell me. How much, I gathered, it was safe to tell me.

I tried to reassure her. "Your call. Tell what you can."

She formed a tiny smile, but it was not meant to be intimate. It said thanks. And quickly faded. "The pilots who were murdered?"

Not where I'd expected her to go. But when you are confused, silence is the new loud. I did the head nod thing once. And stayed loud.

"One of my moles was a friend of the pilots. In fact, she managed the office for the charter service. She couldn't say enough about how much she admired Kway and Ike. Said she kept urging them to talk to me about joining the bureau. I didn't encourage the idea because, frankly, they didn't seem quite the type. Too rambunctious, maybe. And, oddly enough, too much 'save the world' types."

Brief conversations with Chief Deputy Del Emma and Detective Moody had already armed me with a few basic facts about the pilots.

One of the reasons they'd first struck up a friendship was they'd realized both had been named after the towns where they were born. Quitaque, Texas, for Haynes. Akron, Ohio, for Breezer.

I still saw no need to speak. Head nodding sped us along, until I realized Angie's facial features had frozen. I didn't think it had anything to do with the weather; the temperature was pleasant enough. It looked like guilt. I needed to move the conversation along before it broke down completely.

"And the other one?"

"The other one?"

"Your other mole — what does she do?"

Once again, my beloved threw me for a loop. "What do you know about genetics?"

I searched my memory. "Been a long time since Biology 101."

"Never took it myself."

"One of your moles is involved in genetics?"

"Strangely enough, yes. Again, just as a lowly office manager. But it's for that research company out on the Brownwood Highway."

"The one with the funny name?"

"You mean you wouldn't name your genetics research company Thesaurus of the Gene Corporation?"

"Don't believe so. But back to these two individuals — your moles. Is there a connection between them?"

"Well, the original connection was me. I arrested them both."

She said her apprehension of the two women had had something to do with illegally customizing BlackBerry phones to make them extra secure. The young women hadn't been the ones to tinker with the phones. Their mistake had been to keep company with an enterprising young geek who had. Then they'd passed a couple of the illegal phones along to friends.

The primary culprit in all this had gotten a suspended jail sentence. The women had gotten off with a stern warning and a private phone number for the local FBI agent. Their instructions were to be available anytime she called and to pass along anything of interest even if she didn't.

I didn't push for details because it didn't seem compassionate to push the woman I loved too fast or too far. This was her story. In a real sense, it would be her neck and job at risk if she disclosed the wrong thing at the wrong time to the wrong person.

This was hardly the first time I'd sensed the dilemma our relationship created for the FBI special agent I was betrothed to. But I'd never felt it this strongly before. A cow-country metaphor popped into my mind. *While we both rode similar kinds of horses, we didn't ride for the same outfit.* Or necessarily have the same people eying us. Or judging us. Or, for that matter, always depending on us.

I reached for my companion and pulled her close. Put my fingers under her chin. Tilted it up. Gazed into her eyes and sought to transmit how very okay I felt about her.

She kissed me lightly. Then walked to the door opening. What came next proved to me just how high the stakes were in all this.

She looked outside briefly, folded her arms across her chest and turned back toward me. "The pilots and the girls did one dumb thing after another. All too often, that meant putting the best laid plans of a lot of dangerous people at risk. Not only in Flagler. Some very unsavory people on at least three continents."

I gave my fingers a come-hither ripple, inviting her to tell me more. But I'm not sure the gesture was necessary. Or whether she'd notice it at all.

When she refocused her attention on me, she used her thumb and forefinger to mimic the shape of a pistol and pointed it at me. She sometimes did that when she wanted to emphasize a point and didn't want me to miss it. "So that's why what happened in Vegas didn't stay in Vegas."

I fanned my fingers at her again, soliciting more details. "For example?"

"The metal box."

"The one that has Special Agent Knoke's boxer shorts tied in knots?"

"That one. According to my Mole No. 1, it was supposed to be used to haul some special artifacts found near Jerusalem to Craft Roberts's Biblical museum."

"Instead, somebody stuffed it with WMDs?"

My gun-totting sweetheart sniffed. "I don't know what they stuffed it with. But I've been told recently that instead of flying from Flagler to Ben Gurion International Airport outside Tel Aviv and back with the box, the pilots flew to Istanbul, then a lot deeper into Turkey."

"You've told D.C. about this?"

"That was one of the reasons for my quick trip."

"And they listened to you?"

"Not sure. There's so much international pressure behind the WMDs-in-the-box idea that they weren't that interested in anything happening in Flagler."

"And the two women — they were involved in all that how?"

"Again, not sure yet. But for one thing, I suspect they were the reason the pilots didn't go to Israel like they were supposed to."

"They have that kind of influence?"

"No, they have that kind of big mouth."

I was beginning to get the picture, but I let my beloved FBI special agent continue uninterrupted. All it took on my part to get her there was a pair of barely raised eyebrows and a little patience.

She started to lean against the wall of the shed but quickly backed away. Too flimsy to hold her. "The girl who worked at the genetics institute let it slip to a work supervisor that a girl-friend had told her about a trip the pilots had made to Turkey."

"And so . . . what happened? The genetics people outbid the original client? And arranged to use the box themselves?"

"Apparently so."

"And all this unfolded . . . when?"

"What was the date written on the back of the photographs Special Agent Knoke was showing around Sunday? The ones of the box being loaded in the plane?"

"About fourteen months ago."

"So about then."

I suggested we have a chat with both of her CIs. Angie agreed but asked which one I thought we ought to talk with first.

After thinking about it, it seemed obvious. The one who had managed the pilots' office. If we started with the other one, what we were doing could quickly leak back to her employers. The one who'd worked for the pilots had to be traumatized enough about what had happened to keep our discussions confidential. And besides, she had no employers left to tattle to.

That's where we intended to start the next morning. And we'd have done so if we could have found her.

CHAPTER 22

Her name was Nina Kendricks. At least, this was how she was known by the staff at Flagler's modern, if smallish, new air terminal.

The lone commercial carrier using the terminal operated eight regional jet flights a day to DFW International. That meant the airline's ticket and check-in counters were not much larger than the walk-up areas in most fast food restaurants. The two-room office for Orville 'n Wilbur Charter Services sat directly across the lobby from them.

My calls to the charter service's listed phone number were going to voicemail. Ditto for the personal number for Nina Kendricks supplied by the phone company. So one of the first things I did on arriving at the office Tuesday was to ask a deputy to take a fresh look at the pilots' offices.

In his sweep through the terminal on Sunday, Chief Deputy Del Emma had found one witness who remembered seeing Kendricks moving about the offices prior to the close of business Friday, but no one he'd talked with could recall having seen her since.

The deputy reported the office was still locked, unlit, and apparently unoccupied.

He did come away with one item of possible value. An

emergency phone number. It had been posted on an index card taped at the bottom of the office's glass door. But when I called it, all it produced was another automated instruction to leave a number at the sound of the beep.

I was pondering my next move when I saw Angie approach the entrance to our offices. She was wearing one of her blue-green FBI windbreakers and a gimme cap with the agency's yellow logo. Dressed to impress?

Intimidate was more like it. Her pace reflected that too. It was her power-walk gait. This was a notch above her normal brisk-walk gait. It meant decisions had been made, actions initiated, and any intrusion or diversion was unwelcome. And unwise. The train had left the station.

So I didn't begin by informing her that her mole in the pilots' operation had disappeared from the radar. I started with something more neutral. "Looks like you're planning on a productive day."

Her response confirmed my evaluation of her mood. "Well, love and candy kisses to you too."

Then she apparently decided that comeback had been a bit too snappish. She took a couple of steps in my direction and pecked me on the cheek. "You ready to go to work?"

"You have something in mind?"

She ignored the double entendre. Told me she did have something in mind. Showed me a printed sheet signed at the bottom. It surprised me. I'd been thinking of putting in a request for exactly such an item myself, but now that wasn't going to be necessary. She'd gotten a warrant giving her permission to enter the premises of one Nina Kendricks without consent for purposes connected to a criminal investigation.

My sense of amazement was strong enough to solicit details. "How did you manage to procure this so early on 'yon wondrous morn'?"

"I work in a courthouse."

"So do I. But it usually takes me a day or so to weasel one of these out of a judge."

"You don't know how to ask. And besides, you're just a lowly sheriff."

"Ew-ow! You surely know where to aim a low blow."

"And besides, you didn't have a judge who owed you a favor."

"So you know that your mole has disappeared?"

"All I know at this point is that Socrates was right."

I knew what she meant by invoking the Greek's paradox. It was one of our private codes: *I know that all I know is that I do not know anything.*

I looked again at the search warrant she'd somehow finagled out of one of our district court judges before he'd finished his first cup of coffee. It was for the lady's apartment, not for the charter service's offices. "You're thinking Ms. Kendricks keeps secrets at home?"

Angie reached for the warrant. Refolded it again in thirds. And tucked it in one of the side pockets of her windbreaker. "We all have personal secrets. But after what happened in the airport hangar, I'm wondering if Nina Kendricks was more than she tried to make us think she was."

"You'd done some checking on her?"

"Yes. And so have some others in the bureau."

"And you did this because . . ."

"How do I put this?"

"Well, close friends usually try to tell each other the truth."

"The truth can sometimes come in a variety of flavors."

That was another of our private codes. At a minimum, it meant an official inquiry one of us was working on had taken an unexpected turn. Unless the one who had used our private signal felt it unwise to do so, it was usually followed by a few sentences of explanation.

But that wasn't happening here. Sunday afternoon, after Angie's warning, I'd had our bomb squad sweep my office for electronic listening devices. They'd found only one — in an electrical outlet. Now, I was wondering if she suspected a new bug was already operating in its place.

The atmosphere in my office was too weighty for a light-hearted remark, but I wanted to see if intimacy had any chance in this encounter, so I tried one anyway. "Perhaps I could respectfully request a caramel macchiato with whipped cream and a cherry on top."

She turned to look at me like I'd pinched her behind. "Oh, I'm not being circumspect about anything. Let's just go see if I'm right."

I reached for my own windbreaker. "Right about what?"

"About whether Nina Kendricks is a double agent."

But the instant we stepped outside, we both knew nailing down the truth on that issue was going to have to wait. I'd known it was coming. But, with everything else on my mind, I'd forgotten it.

As is usually the case in the spring, the jet stream had cooked up a low-pressure system and was hurdling its winds down the Rocky Mountains onto the Great Plains. There they would be colliding with moisture flowing in from the Gulf of Mexico. The weather service had said that meant thunderstorms. Big ones.

Already, the cars in the parking lot were rocking like cradles in Godzilla's baby nursery, so I knew the weatherman had made the correct call. And I knew it was likely to be all-hands-on-deck for the Abbot County Sheriff's Department before long.

But I hadn't expected it to start as quickly as it did. Or happen in the way it did.

CHAPTER 23

The weirdness commenced almost immediately.

Angie and I were still watching the local weather update on our office TV when my mobile radio went off. My dispatcher said the highway patrol was reporting multi-vehicle pileups on both sides of the interstate closest to the big towers at the wind farm. They were asking all available agencies to respond.

Wide Skies Wind Farm sprawled over the prairie about twenty miles northwest of Flagler. Its scores of giant windmills made it one of the world's largest wind-generated producers of electricity.

I held my mobile radio up so we both could hear the details. "HP says there's something wrong at the wind farm. Drivers are rubbernecking, and it's turned into a wrecking derby in both directions. There are injuries."

I had a choice to make. I could head for the interstate, which was fourteen miles north of Flagler, then barrel west for another fifteen miles to help at the site of the pileups. Or I could head straight for the wind farm to render what assistance I could.

This would involve going north of Flagler a short distance and taking the Sweetwater cutoff. I'd be at the southern entrance to the big generating site inside of twenty minutes. In either instance, I'd have to decide how fast to drive through the mercurial winds.

I knew that even seventy mile-an-hour wind gusts shouldn't be posing any grave danger to those big towers. Their massive blades and the electrical generators that made them such a desirable source of renewable energy were designed to protect themselves. That is, to disengage long before winds got that blustery.

So what could be wrong?

It was this uncertainty that helped me make my decision.

I had at least three deputies who should be closer to the highway crashes than I was. I told my dispatcher to make sure they responded. As I passed Helen at her desk, I told her I was going directly to the wind farm. Angie followed me into the hall, and I turned to tell her goodbye.

She brushed past me, on her phone. I heard her tell her office manager she was going to the wind farm with the sheriff.

I kept one hand on my hat, wrenched the courthouse door open and charged out into the bushwhacking winds after my headstrong companion.

I'd driven into strong, angled crosswinds on many occasions, and the drill was nearly always the same.

First, there was what I called "the 10/30/5 rule." For every ten miles an hour the wind surged above thirty miles an hour, you decreased your car speed at least five miles an hour from what you'd normally be driving.

Second, you gripped your steering wheel with both hands like you had an enraged bull by both horns and banished any thought slacking off. You get better at this with practice — you played a game with the elements called "Catch Me Unawares If You Can." It was all about guessing what the winds would do next and reacting the moment they did it.

I knew the FBI operated something called the Tactical and Emergency Vehicle Operations Center in Quantico. I assumed

Angie had taken the center's driving course, likely more than once. She confirmed that even before we reached the cutoff and headed west by northwest — almost directly into the wind. But she said there had been no instructions on how to drive in hurricanes or a Texas weather hissy fit. "It's not like they've got a wind tunnel for you to practice in, you know."

I corrected her on one point. This wasn't a Texas weather hissy fit. This was only a feisty little late spring blow.

Privately, though, I had to admit that it was pretty feisty. And more erratic than I'd been expecting.

One moment, the winds were huffing and puffing and threatening to blow the house down. An instant later, they could go all sweet-faced and tranquil, barely stirring a tumbleweed.

Because of this, my patrol cruiser advanced up the highway like the town drunk was driving. Maybe a tad less crazy than that. But I kept changing the angle of my steering wheel and that changed the angle of the car on the road. Otherwise, it was barrow ditch, here we come.

I felt Angie peering at me. Probably wondering how wise it had been to entrust her life and limbs to my faux Mario Andretti driving skills. Not to mention my single working eye.

Not so, as it turned out. She had something else on her mind. "Can you drive in this and talk at the same time?"

I found her comment amusing. When I laughed, she blushed, and one more time, I felt I was walking on emotional quicksand anytime I was around this complicated creature.

I figured a good offense was the best defense. "Okay. And I can walk and chew gum at the same time too." One of our Texas-born presidents — LBJ — had loved that riposte. But Angie ignored it. So this was not a good time for frivolity, historical or otherwise.

"I need to tell you about Special Agent Knoke," she said.

She was staring out the windshield. "In some ways, and I know this may be hard for you to believe, Knoke is one of the best problem-solvers the bureau has in the field. You know what they say about surgeons. You don't really care about their bedside manner if they are brilliant at saving your life. That's the way Knoke can be when he's on top of his game."

"You mean, an incision here, a suture there. Here a transplant, there a transplant."

"It's just when it's time for the rubber to meet the road, he has a way of cutting through the clutter. Getting needed results. Producing good outcomes."

When I thought about it later, it wasn't surprising to me that I'd chosen that moment to remember another term from one of my psychology classes:

Cognitive dissonance.

This feeling of psychological distress can show up when you realize some of your beliefs are in conflict. Only I wasn't sure the phrase was strong enough to describe what I was experiencing. *Cognitive consternation* was more like it.

Here was this FBI agent, trained to meddle in people's thoughts to try to get closer to realities they might be trying to hide. There must be some reason why she'd felt the need to mention Knoke's unique skills in this moment — motoring down the road in a thunderous West Texas rain-and-windstorm. What was her purpose? Why had she brought it up at such a chaotic instant? And what in holy thunderation was I supposed to do with the information?

I had no idea. I couldn't get more than three sentences into a conversation with Knoke without having to suppress a burning desire to plant a McWhorter fist just above his belt buckle, then slap his ruddy Irish face silly. I couldn't imagine what he'd done to command the admiration that Special Agent Steele felt for him. I'd found him to be a total donkey.

And until I understood more about where Angie was coming from, I was going to take what plane geometry calls the shortest distance between two points. A straight line. Or, in this instance, a clear progression from her logic to my logic: "If Agent Knoke is so good, why isn't he somewhere else?"

I don't know whether Angie noticed it, but the subtle shift from amiability to neutrality in my tone was there for the observing. "I mean, what's he doing in the hinterlands? Why Dallas? Why isn't he holding the fort — or a scalpel — in a D.C. or a New York City or a Los Angeles?"

"He's . . ."

She gazed at me long enough for both of us to realize that she hadn't anticipated that the conversation would go in this direction. Or at least this far. Or maybe this fast.

But here we were.

"Remember the Kennedy assassination and Oswald's murder? Dallas's worst hour. *Ever.* A Fucked Up Beyond All Recognition week beyond all FUBARs for everybody, including the bureau. I think that's when the powers-that-be at headquarters said never again. Since then, the agency has been careful to assign some of its best people to head up the Dallas office. Knoke's the latest. The guy's trained as a lawyer too, you know."

Since Angie was being so candid, I decided to stay with the flavor of the hour. "If he's so good at this, why can't he tell us what happened to our pilots?"

"He thought he was getting close to finding out. But all the hubbub in D.C. over WMDs got in his way. That, and some other things."

I felt a need for a little more clarity. "Which other things?"

"Well, for one thing, your wind farm being attacked."

She gestured at turbulence visible outside the window. Russian thistles — tumbleweeds — careening into the car. Roadside trash whipping across the windshield. Anytime we crossed through a creek bed, visibility dropping close to zero from the boiling dirt.

The howling outside the car windows was almost constant now. Angry, aggrieved, whipsawing winds.

In another mile or two, I'd normally expect the wind towers to hove into view. They'd be lined up in stately rows — in the wind farm industry, they called them corridors — of ten or so. There'd be one row of the towers after another, lined up for miles. Sitting there like a massive mechanical drill team waiting to be inspected by some fussy, demanding sergeant.

I decided to try again. "So what did these surprises keep him from finding out?"

She almost answered, but she didn't.

"To why . . . to what . . . Well, about some things a country sheriff would find it hard to have much influence over."

There she went again.

Dissing Abbot County — and me — to my face. What did she say about us when I wasn't around?

In a flash, her face colored as she realized her faux pas. For all intents, she'd suggested I was a clueless hick wearing a badge and a gun.

I took my eyes off the road for an instant and made sure she understood I expected an unequivocal answer. "What kinds of things would a country sheriff have no influence over?"

I could see that she was considering telling me less than she knew. But the thought of sidestepping seemed to fade, and her reply sounded genuine. "Knoke hasn't wavered from the idea he shared with you at the Korean restaurant. He is absolutely convinced that someone — possibly a nation/state — has put Abbot County squarely in its sights."

"Any concrete suspicions?"

"Just on the *how*."

"Something that would impact the wind farm?"

"After seeing this, we need to talk with him. He's been in frequent contact with some of our D.C. experts. They've been concerned about an attack over the internet using something like Stuxnet."

Once again, my brain was scrambling to keep its footing. "Stuxnet. That's the computer worm. The one that took down Iran's uranium processing facility."

"Yes, that one. In 2010. It didn't end Iran's nuclear-bomb-building ambitions, but it destroyed nearly a thousand of their uranium-enrichment centrifuges, and that slowed them down a little."

I answered without thinking about it. "I don't think we have anything remotely like uranium-enrichment centrifuges in Abbot County."

Angie's voice now seemed on tape delay. "Unfortunately, we do. From the looks of that roadblock up ahead, we must be getting close to them."

The ugly truth, as it so often does, almost blinded me. I realized that we had a lot of "somethings" not all that different mechanically in many ways from a centrifuge.

Only ours were giant whirligigs that sat at the top of 300-foot-high towers pushing into the sky over hundreds and hundreds of acres.

The towers were usually about 800 feet apart. Each one was attached to three 140-foot-long, aerodynamically gorgeous blades.

Each of these blade sets could turn safely at wind speeds up to fifty-five miles an hour. In doing so, each of the towers generated enough electricity to power several hundred homes.

If the ambient winds went higher than fifty-five miles an hour, the wind vanes atop each of the towers' core structures — "nacelles," to those in the know — notified the computers that controlled the giant pinwheels. And the computers feathered the blades. In effect, turned them off.

Unless something or someone interfered. Maybe the person manning the roadblock Angie had spotted just ahead could tell us more.

CHAPTER 24

The vehicle was straddling the center stripe of the roadway. I knew it wasn't one of ours. I was the only sheriff's car on the Sweetwater cutoff. Besides, we didn't drive pickups in the sheriff's department.

The emergency yellow lights of the late-model white truck were flashing. Its distinctive three-bar front grill was pointing back in the direction we were coming from. I recognized the driver.

He was Cale Billingsley, site manager for the wind farm. The logo on his kale-green gimme cap said as much. "Wide Skies Windpower." The cap matched the color of his windbreaker, which also bore the logo.

When he rolled down his window, I had to shout to be heard above the howling winds. "Where're your employees, Cale?"

Before he could answer, another of the turbines disintegrated. "The others are blocking roads closer to the interstate."

"How long has this been going on?"

"Not long. Just since the wind got up."

"Did you have any warning this could happen?"

"Only a phone call from Kansas City."

He said the folks who controlled the electric grid called to report they could no longer monitor the wind farm's substations. About two minutes later, his field engineer had radioed in that the towers had gone crazy. Said every turbine in the field was exceeding tolerance speeds. And none appeared to be disengaging — feathering — in the high winds like they should be. Something was interfering with their controls."

I debated about how much to tell him. "So Kansas City hasn't told you any more?" I could see both disbelief and fear in his eyes. This convinced me to tell him nothing at this point about Stuxnet or any of the FBI's other suspicions.

He was still clinging to his steering wheel like he'd float away if he let go. "We could see the turbines exploding before we got out of the parking lot. Absolutely nothing we could do."

I felt for the guy. "Anything we can do for you?"

"Mouth's dry. You have any spare water?"

Angie reached for the bottle of mineral water she'd been holding when we'd headed out of my office suite for the wind farm. She'd arrived at my car still holding it. She'd taken a couple of swigs since, but most of the water remained. She held up the bottle. Billingsley gave her a thumbs-up and began lowering his window more.

I handed the bottle across. "Before we head back, we're going to get a better look at the damage."

He glanced over his shoulder. "You can get a better view from the top of that rise behind me. But don't go any farther. Blades are still coming off and a lot of the turbines are throwing fire."

"You need the fire department?"

"Don't see what they could do."

"No ground structures in danger?"

"Not unless they take a direct hit from a blade."

"How about grass fires?"

"The road network is pretty extensive. I'm hoping the roads will stop them."

"And you'll stay in radio contact with your people up near the interstate?"

"We're checking in with each other every ten minutes."

As Billingsley rolled up his driver's side window, I realized that I'd seen exactly that kind of look on people's fear-etched faces once before. On the streets of Manhattan that indescribable September day in 2001. I asked again if he was okay.

His reply told me what was foremost in his mind. "Who in holy hell would do something like this?"

All I had to offer was the unvarnished truth. "I don't know, Cale. But we're going to find out."

CHAPTER 25

Before heading back to Flagler, I drove Angie and myself to the slight rise the wind farm manager had mentioned. It was only a few hundred feet beyond where he was parked. Every few seconds, we could see one of the massive, propeller-like turbine blades hurled high into the smoke-filled sky like a one-way boomerang. A deadlier scythe you couldn't imagine.

More than a few of the towers had been chopped off close to the ground by their own churning blades. Or a neighboring tower's.

My passenger and I could only gape at the sight. Words were not coming easy. In fact, for a while, they didn't come at all. They were superfluous. Inadequate.

Many of the generators atop the towers had already burned. Their nacelles — covers — were little more than blackened derelicts clinging to their moorings. Still others glowered like the ends of giant cigars. They were only now starting to flame. As they did, their oily black smoke began to contaminate the sky.

The inconceivable scene reminded me of photos I'd seen of the burning oil wells in Kuwait in the first Gulf War. The ones set ablaze by the Iraqi military.

When I finally started speaking, I tried to put things in context. As much for myself as for Angie.

I told her about that day in the spring of 2005 when the murmuring whispers of the giant vanes first started up. How a steady breeze began shortly after sunrise. And how it had stayed around all day.

"That first day, traffic was so heavy we had cars parked solid on both sides of the road for several miles. I needed six deputies to help me keep it moving. The crowd situation was almost as bad at night. Understandably. All those red-flashing aviation warning strobes were doing a slow dance on top of ghostly white columns. And the columns — the towers — seemed to reach to the horizon in three directions. It was spectacular."

I could feel the pride in my voice as I described how our isolated patch of the Lone Star State had become known as the world's second largest onshore wind farm. Only a monstrous installation in China had been bigger.

Now, it was all gone.

In little more than a finger's snap. A billion and a half dollars' worth of the county's capital machinery wrecked.

I flexed my neck and reached around to massage the back of my shoulders. "I mean, I understand that the internet is the new wild, wild west, but what happened here?"

The FBI special agent seated next to me sighed. "I meant to tell you—"

I interrupted her. "You knew this was going to happen?"

"Not exactly. But Knoke had zeroed in on the wind farm the moment you flagged it as a potential terrorist target yesterday. I'm almost certain this was why our Critical Infrastructure Desk reacted so quickly to the news that the power grid people were no longer getting telemetry from Wide Skies Wind Farm at their Abbot County substations."

But she insisted that the Feds had almost certainly gotten confirmation that something was wrong at the wind farm in the same way at the same time we had — from my dispatcher.

I reminded myself that I loved this woman. I trusted her. We could revisit our obligations to each other again later. Right now, I wanted to know everything she could tell me. "So we got Stuxnet-ed."

Her head bobbed up, then down, then sideways. She was being equivocal. "I doubt that anybody knows that for sure. Not yet. But like Billingsley said, what could anyone do? The turbines began destroying themselves before even the people closest to the scene could get out of the parking lot."

"In these seventy-mile-an-hour wind gusts."

"Yes. I can't imagine that the terrorists planned it this way. I mean, they might have known these kinds of winds were being forecast. But I think they were lucky. Some of the luckiest terrorists in history."

With little to be done here other than keep people out of the way, I turned my patrol cruiser around. I was betting Billingsley was wrong. The danger in the open range was going to be from fire, fanned by the winds.

We waved at him as we passed, and I gunned my vehicle toward Flagler.

CHAPTER 26

Compared to its agonized howls on the trip out, my engine was now leading a charmed life. Purring like a contented kitty.

The winds were still fierce, though gusts were not quite as strong as before. But they were coming from behind us now, not howling in our faces. Though I chose not to, I could probably have steered with one hand.

Angie was involved in her own thoughts. I welcomed the respite. Every time she'd waded into the conversation lately, my world had ended up being dumped out and reordered.

So what was bothering me? We were halfway to town before I figured it out.

A lake of fire was converting the landscape visible in my rearview and side mirrors into a fiery sandwich spread. As we drove past, we were seeing new outbreaks in the barrow ditches and flare-ups in fields around us. In the wind, all these fires were going to grow. And keep growing until they were extinguished or burned themselves out.

That was the red flag my subconscious mind had been flinging about: why weren't our firefighters from Flagler responding?

When I shared my puzzlement with my passenger, she pointed in the direction of downtown Flagler. "Maybe they already have their hands full."

I leaned closer to the windshield. "If that's what it looks like, you may be right."

Next, I changed my radio to the channel we used when something intense was going on within the city of Flagler itself.

My dispatcher was issuing directives and responding to requests like he was directing the Normandy Invasion. I waited for a lull in the exchanges, and when one didn't present itself, I decided not to add to his load by pulling rank.

There was another way.

I selected the frequency for the fire department. It too was a boiling kettle of urgent messaging.

In the couple of minutes or so that Angie and I listened without comment, we heard two more engines, a ladder truck, a battalion chief and a rescue unit assigned to what sounded to me like "the courthouse square fire." I knew those units were being dispatched from across town. That probably meant every other piece of fire apparatus in Flagler was already in use.

I asked Angie if she'd heard what I thought I'd heard. "He did say the courthouse square fire, didn't he?"

She turned the radio's volume control down. "That's what it sounded like to me."

So much for being circumspect. I dialed back to our main dispatch frequency and grabbed the mike on my radio. At the first opening, I planned to ask for an update on a fire downtown.

As if eavesdropping, my dispatcher joined the conversation. "Base to unit one."

I dropped the formalities. "What's burning, Saul?"

"From the smell, you'd think it was our offices. But it's across the street. The whole west side of the square is on fire."

"How bad is it?"

"I just heard the fire department upgrade it to all-hands. Nobody's on standby any longer. They'll have to hold it until mutual aid arrives."

"How'd it start?"

"Can't answer that. But I can tell you where. In the old Bartlett building by the rail yard."

I tried to make my next question sound like it came from any good sheriff gathering the facts, but there was a sudden shortage of oxygen in the car, and my voice sounded squeezed. "What's the status of the Bartlett fire?"

"Unit eleven is on scene there. She says it's going to be a total loss. It's fully engaged."

I asked the next question knowing that the answer could leave my bladder weak. But I had to ask it. "Any injuries or fatalities so far?"

My nighttime dispatcher and I enjoyed a special camaraderie that led us to be more informal than we probably should be in moments like these. But Peetson didn't know everything about me. This time, for that reason, our shared informality led me straight over an emotional cliff.

"Looks like there's one. Homeless fellow. The paramedics have just taken him to Flagler Regional, but they think he's going to be DOA. Looks like he may have started the fire trying to keep dry in the building. The deputy said he used it as a library."

In my hands, the steering wheel felt like a life buoy — why not, they were both round and made to be gripped and soft enough to be squeezed in places. So I squeezed and squeezed.

Angie reached across the seat and placed her hand on my arm. She knew how fond I was of the Count and his dog. She pressed down on my arm once more, then withdrew to a safe distance. "Luke, I'm so sorry for your loss."

If not for her timely, distinctly feminine intervention, I'm not sure where the rage I was feeling might have led. At minimum, I'd have begun pounding my steering wheel with both hands. When you are in control of a missile weighing

4,200 pounds hurdling down the road at eighty miles an hour, that's not the most intelligent thing to do.

So I kept the air clear and the conversation simple. "Thank you. As soon as I can get to it, I've got to see if I can find out what happened to Fresca."

I expected to be at the head of the line the next morning when the animal shelter opened.

I needed to figure out how much paranoia was justified by what had happened in the past seventy-two hours in our county. Who had Abbot County in their sights? And, most puzzling of all, why couldn't some of the best minds in federal law enforcement get ahead of the mayhem in time to do anything about it? And, now, had the animus, the retribution, the psychotic evil — whatever it was — taken my homeless friend's life too? And maybe that of a blameless animal we'd both loved?

Clearly, what had just happened at the wind farm was indisputable evidence that a lot more was involved than merely our piddling patch of a thousand square miles of isolated Texas prairie and our prized little string of mesquite-and-live-oak-studded hills. It had also confirmed that we were at least one of the bullseyes in the target.

CHAPTER 27

The powder-blue sweatshirt being worn by the pleasant, middle-aged counterperson at the shelter had *STAFF* emblazoned across the front. She shook her head. But said we should go back to the cages to be sure.

In the inclement overnight weather, three dogs had been picked up by animal control. As we walked past, all of them pressed their noses hard against the screen.

But she was right.

None of them looked remotely like they were part Great Dane and Boxer or Pit Bull.

I had explained that the brindle-colored cur I was seeking had deserved its own sweater reading *STAFF* as a reward for reaching out to human strays.

This had touched a serious chord in my helper, and she was loath to give up. "As you well know, our first responders in Flagler will nearly always take an injured animal to the overnight animal ER. It's closed now. But if they treated a patient without an owner during the night, they usually post a notice on their website."

In a couple of clicks, she had the site up on her computer screen. But the results were the same: no unidentified casualties had arrived at the animal ER vet practice during the night.

I thanked the lady at the pound.

Then headed for the one place where I hoped to learn if any of the first responders had seen Fresca.

Central Fire Station was in the first block west of the old Bartlett Machine Shop building. If they'd been in their quarters, its engine crew, truck company, and paramedics unit would have been first to respond when the alarm for the burning old building was struck. They might not have been, of course. There had been multiple fire calls resulting from the storm.

I was lost in my thoughts as I entered, wondering how to deal with my sense of loss if my search turned up futile. That's why the dog saw me coming before I saw him.

Fresca launched himself from at least eight feet away and crashed into my left shoulder like a blocking tight end.

I collapsed on my back. Rolled onto one side. Doubled my legs under me. Then surrendered to my sitting duck status.

That long, velvety, scoop-shoveled, amethyst-colored tongue refused to be stilled.

If licking a man half to death could bring this animal comfort and happiness, I was content for it to continue. It was bringing me pure joy. He still smelled strongly of charred wood, but I could see no visible injury. And he wasn't reacting as if parts of his body were seriously bruised or burned.

Two young paramedics, one male, one female, approached. They looked hale and competent in their blue-over-black uniforms. Both reached out and helped me to my feet.

"As you may have noticed, Fresca and I have met before."

Both laughed.

The woman spoke first. "Fresca, is it? He didn't have a collar or a tag, so we had no idea. We were thinking of calling him Rin Tin Tin — like in the old TV show. He's a bit of a hero, you know."

The man motioned for me to follow, inviting me into the

station's ready room, had me sit down in a dining hall chair, and told me the story.

"Your Fresca was seen clawing at the door of the station shortly before 911 got the first call for the old Bartlett building fire. The homeless man often stopped by the station when he was walking with his dog, but nobody was here. The crews at the station were already out on call because of the high winds."

He said when the dog got no response, it had raced back to the Bartlett structure and disappeared through the open front door.

When the building caught fire, arriving firefighters had heard a dog barking in the dense smoke. Followed the sound. And stumbled over the body of the fire victim.

The firefighters had carried him outside. Tried to revive him. Rushed him to the ED. But it was too late.

Other firefighters had administered oxygen to the dog, and the crew of the engine company had put him in the cab of their truck. When they returned to the station, he'd made the trip with them.

When I'd gotten back on my feet, Fresca had insisted on staying close enough to nuzzle my leg for reassurance. Without thinking much about it, I did something I'd done more than a few times when I'd visited the dog and his owner at the abandoned warehouse. I leaned over to massage the tiny canyons of warm fuzz inside his cantilevered ears.

This was when I realized that I'd really never noticed how dark all his paws were, starting at the point where his toes first appeared.

Two other things had escaped me: how wide the space was between his ever-observant, jet-black eyes and how much his broad, constantly twitching nose came to matching that width. My new buddy's brain must have a mass greater than mine.

I directed a question at my new companion. "You ready to hit the road?"

On hearing that, he wheeled, headed for the door, towed me behind. *Did I speak Dog, or did my new dog speak English?*

Over my shoulder, I shouted goodbye to the two paramedics. "If you don't mind, I'm going to take Fresca off your hands."

The moment I opened the car door, he hopped up on my car seat, hurdled the center console into the back seat, and took a position by the window looking as alert as . . . well, Rin Tin Tin.

I wanted to get him to a veterinarian to see if his lungs and throat and the rest of him were okay. We'd had a vet visit the department not too long ago to instruct us on how to respond to injured animals, especially fire victims. They can fool you into thinking they are uninjured. Then they can die on you suddenly when their upper airways swell. The first forty-eight hours were crucial, and we'd already lost twelve of those. I also wanted to get him microchipped. Get him his shots and a bath and his nails clipped. Get him his tags and a collar and a leash.

Somehow, I knew there was going to be no need to arrange for someone to go to my house to let the sheriff's new pet out three times a day. Fresca was going to be doing a lot of fertilizing of the courthouse lawn. I just hoped Helen didn't mind tagging along.

CHAPTER 28

The veterinarian's office had been getting ready to close when I barged through the door with my new dog. They agreed to look him over for smoke injury and other wellness issues and give him his shots. But I was going to have to give him a bath.

On the way home, I didn't stop at my neighborhood supercenter because I didn't want to leave Fresca in my vehicle unattended. But I was going to have to visit one soon. I needed things. Three doggie beds. One for Helen's office, one for my office, and one for the house. And water bowls. And food bowls. And a supply of dog food, both canned and dry. A cold-weather dog coat, size extra large. Dog chews and dog treats. And toys for doggies. *Running a jail was easier than having a pet!*

My backup was my neighborhood convenience store. That way, I could watch him through the windshield and the store windows from the moment I exited my vehicle until I returned.

I emerged from the convenience shop hoping Fresca liked lamb. They'd not had any other flavor in canned dog food. Maybe quantity would count for something. I'd gotten three cans.

For a food bowl, I found a chipped casserole dish in the garage. Fresca found lamb entirely suitable but the quantity was not entirely adequate.

He'd eaten the contents of all three of my cans. Licked his new bowl spotless. Continued to tongue it until he'd scooted it completely across my kitchen floor and had it pinned in a corner. Then he'd planted himself on his haunches beside it and commenced to give me the most plaintive look.

Since I was out of canned dog food, I scrambled eggs for both of us. Six for him and two for me. Once again, Fresca chased his bowl across the kitchen floor, licking it clean. Once again, it sounded like my house was being demolished.

I made a mental note to explore rubber food bowls. They might be harder to push. And even if they weren't, they shouldn't make as much noise when they clanged against something.

After that exertion, he'd accepted my invitation to spend toilet time in the backyard and trotted back into the house when I called, heading straight for the den. I found him plopped on the short end of my two-piece sectional sofa, his head perched on one of my plush throw pillows.

That wasn't going to work. Not just yet.

I summoned him to follow me to the bathroom. Checked to make sure the water wasn't too hot. Hoisted him with a grunt — mine, not his — into the tub. Told him to sit and began to fill it. He was more interested in drinking than bathing. I wonder how long that could go on before he lunged out of the tub and headed, dripping wet, for the back door for more toilet duty. Didn't happen, though. His bladder hung tough.

Eventually, I got him soaped and washed off. Insisted he stay in the tub while I toweled him down. And lifted him over the tub's side for the second time. Only then did he go all dog. He shook himself violently, sending water droplets in all directions, including mine.

I knew where he was headed. I grabbed two bathmats out of the linen closet and sprinted for the sofa. I tossed them over my throw pillows, and stood back while my new dog made himself at home.

I liked to stretch out on the long end of the sofa. With Angie, if she was staying over or had come for dinner. With my cellphone, or a newspaper, or the TV remote if I was alone for the evening and had no files to read.

The long end was the other end of the couch. If snuggling down on the short end of the sofa had long-term appeal to Fresca, we'd try it.

On my smartphone, I again called up the topic I'd been pursuing on the web the past two nights. I wasn't sure what had initially hooked my interest, but I was finding the activities of the Navajo code talkers during World War II fascinating. But tonight, I kept glancing over at my new companion. I wondered what Angie was going to think about sharing her space and routines with a homeless man's mutt.

I put the question to Fresca. "I say, old man. You think we may have a problem with Angie?"

Both ears stiffened, pointing straight up.

I gave him a serious look, although solemnity was not what I was feeling. Playfulness was more like it. "You do, don't you?"

This time, those ears pivoted a quarter of a turn. *Is this how dog talks to man?*

CHAPTER 29

The gory scene inside the hangar wasn't the one I couldn't get out of my thoughts. That image would keep me awake at night. And, when it wasn't keeping me from my sleep, it would give me nightmares.

It was the image from one of Special Agent Patrick Knoke's photographs I couldn't dismiss from my mind. The one where the pilots were muscling the low-slung, elongated box into the aisle of their Beechcraft King Air. And it wasn't the snapshot that intrigued me most. It was where the photo was supposedly taken.

I directed a Lone Ranger–type question at my new Tonto. "You ever been to Mount Ararat, partner?"

Fresca rubbed his nose with a paw before looking up at me. "No, but you're ready to mount up, are you?"

That humongous tail whipped back and forth. "Appreciate your adventurous spirit, old fellow."

I'd never been to Mount Ararat, either. And had no plans to go.

But I knew folks in a lot of places were obsessed with Mount Ararat. Several of them lived in Flagler.

I decided to test my new sidekick's knowledge of ancient Middle Eastern history. "You know who made Mount Ararat famous, don't you?"

Those ears did their contrapuntal quarter turn. "That's right. Old Noah. He's supposed to have parked his boat there after the Great Flood. Explorers have been looking for the craft since the eleventh century."

I remembered the reputed dimensions for Noah's Ark in the Bible. Three hundred cubits long, fifty cubits wide and thirty cubits high. That would have made it a city-block-and-a-half in length. So it hadn't been Noah's Ark in the Special Agent Knoke's box. But the box could have housed a few weathered scraps thought to have come from Noah's Ark.

As I'd listened to the pompous, bulgogi-loving FBI special agent two days ago, that had been my first thought. Maybe the box contained archaeological artifacts. And the pilots had been hired by someone to fly them from extreme eastern Turkey to West Texas. Flagler had more than one individual obsessed enough with Noah's Ark to have paid for such a flight.

But the obnoxious federal agent hadn't mentioned the most famous ship captain in the Old Testament at all. So I'd decided not to mention him either. One reason was the special agent's insistence that the box could be dangerous. His obsession with WMDs was being fed by higher-ups in the nation's — and other nations' — intelligence agencies.

Maybe it was tunnel vision, maybe it wasn't. I could be succumbing to the same malady. I put the question to my sofa companion.

"Deputy Fresca, do you think I've heard one too many Bible stories about Noah's Ark?"

The thick tail thumped twice.

I knew my new pet was responding to my emotions, not my words. With his emotions. And I soon realized it was working . . . for both of us.

I watched my new animal buddy fighting off the sandman. So far, his droopy eyelids had always managed to raise themselves one more time. This time, he began to snore softly. Before long, the zzzz's were more syncopated. More resonant. More confident.

Witnessing this little drama wasn't making me sleepy. It was letting me focus on Abbot County's latest crime wave one dot at a time. Try to link them. And realize where the gaps were. Or maybe thinking about rearranging dots wasn't the right image. It was more like shuffling cards. Or looking into a kaleidoscope.

Whatever the right metaphor, I had every reason to suspect it was happening again. Our extraordinary little city and uniquely isolated county were busy weaseling their way once more into deadly international mayhem and intrigue.

This time, the focus wasn't a piece of an alien spacecraft. The UFO that had reputedly crashed nearly seventy-five years ago in New Mexico; a fragment of it had improbably made its way to Flagler. The fragment was gone from our county after a case I'd handled only two years before. I'd seen it depart myself, stolen by a quasi-government agent and other parties in a military-styled helicopter. Present whereabouts unknown. At least, by me. It was, in all likelihood, gone forever.

This time, it looked like the cause or causes of our deadly chaos had been imported into the county by our two murdered pilots themselves. Perhaps in a narrow metal box. Or in a test-tube. Or a baby bassinet. Or other vessels, locations all currently unknown. Perhaps over a period of months, even years. Who knew?

I didn't yet.

But how else could I explain the Mexican police official's stories about strange cargo runs the pilots had made to his distant city? Or the FBI special agent's photos? Or what one of my officers had found on the plane? Or Angie's suspicion that evidence of where else the pilots had been might start disappearing from government records? Or the college student's horrific story about who else had been in that hangar yesterday morning.

More dots.

"You know, Fresca, it's only a hunch but . . ."

This time, when I mentioned his name, my sofa mate raised his eyelids once. Mostly what I saw was the whites of his eyes. They'd been pointing straight up.

In a matter of seconds, the zzzz's set in again. Softly at first, then louder. His closed eyelids began to twitch.

He was dreaming.

I decided to leave him undisturbed. His life had seen as much change in the past few hours as anyone else's. Gazing at him brought to mind one of my favorite descriptions of Flagler. I'd often said our town's most peculiar characteristic was its tendency to throw God to the dogs.

By that, I was referring to our predilection for religious dustups. It happened more often than any of us would like to admit. Holier-than-thou pin-up contests among church going people got out of hand. Hateful things were said in silly doctrinal conflicts. Bored, rich folks forgot the Ten Commandments and the Sermon on the Mount and began jockeying for power. Tempers were inflamed. Laws were sometimes violated. On rare occasions, bloodletting occurred.

Before long, the local sheriff often found himself dragged into these sectarian conflicts, where he was expected to do the kind of things sheriffs are elected to do. Separate the combatants. Restore the peace. See that serious lawbreakers are sent away for punishment.

Sitting there on my sofa, I pretended to read my paper. Looked over to check on my new pet frequently. Wondered when Angie would be texting me from D.C.

And pondered the question anew.

Were the deadly events of the past two days throwing-God-to-the-dogs stuff?

CHAPTER 30

The next morning, Angie gave me no forewarning before disrupting my schedule. But then, neither of us had assigned beats, so we didn't have to observe many "cop on the street" routines. That's to say, if things got irregular, we could usually go with the flow.

We also benefited from a long tradition in Texas law enforcement away from the bigger cities. Call it the "one riot, one ranger" syndrome. We were both pretty much our own bosses.

So when one of us turned up at the other's office with a come-hither signal, we tended to leap into the saddle. Usually, it was interesting. More times than not, it was worthwhile. This time, it was Angie doing the summoning. She stuck her head through my office door and asked if I had time for a ride.

The address she had for Nina Kendricks took us to the part of town that contained the town's country club and its eighteen-hole golf course. It was not a part of Flagler I spent much time in. I might travel through it on those rare occasions when I had a warrant for some well-to-do parents' wayward kid or maybe for the parents themselves for not showing up at a DUI or child-support hearing. But I was surprised to see that Angie was barely glancing at the street signs as she sped deeper into the network of wide streets.

The second time she whipped around a corner like she was hurrying home from the grocery store, I brought up the subject. "You spend a lot of time in this part of town?"

She peered at me over the top of her sunglasses. "My clientèle is better-heeled than yours."

"Beg your pardon?"

"You noticed the country club entrance, I'm sure?"

"It's hard not to notice that garish sign."

"I actually have a membership there."

"Your fussy bosses at the bureau allow you to put country club dues on your expense account?"

"As a matter of fact — they like to be entertained there when they're in town."

"And how do you justify the expense the rest of the time?"

"Their private dining rooms are a wonderful place to meet with my moles."

"They don't think meeting with you at the country club is a bit on the weird side?"

"No, they're like me. They enjoy the food. And the service. And the polished silver and linen napkins. And there's another benefit."

"Don't tell me — they find you an utterly charming conversationalist in such a setting?"

"Probably. But it helps me dissuade them from being disloyal. I tell them the Feds will always feed them better than the local sheriff."

"Ouch!"

"Bet you've never even been in their dining room."

"Well, I did chase someone into their parking lot once."

"Did they have a membership?"

"You don't need one to steal hubcaps."

And that's where the conversation died. Studying the face of my beautiful FBI special agent driver, I realized she wasn't nearly as composed as she wanted me to believe. I began to suspect that she wasn't driving more aggressively than she usually did out of a familiarity with this part of town. She was driving like she was tuning up for a NASCAR race because she was pissed. Royally.

And I had a fair idea she was dividing her pique more or less evenly between herself and her CI. Her mole.

That was confirmed by what happened next. She had to pull to the curb and consult the information on the search warrant. She was looking for the address again because she didn't know her way around this neighborhood well at all. She was lost.

When she located the address for Kendricks's apartment, she entered it into her GPS and noted the program's route recommendation. Then we continued.

I felt I was entitled to a better understanding of matters. "You really haven't been keeping tabs that closely on your moles, have you?"

My driver shot me a look that would have stripped paint off a battle tank. Next, she slapped both hands against her steering wheel hard enough to misalign the car's front axle. When she spoke again, she'd changed the subject. "You ever use a Halligan bar?"

The question surprised me. "You carry around a Halligan bar?"

"I've also got a battering ram."

"No wonder the rear end of your car looks like a low rider that needs its tires aired."

Yes, I'd used a Halligan bar a time or two. But I didn't carry one around. Most cops use the pipe-like devices with handles when they need to break open a door, which weighed only about thirty pounds. But throw in several more pounds for one of the forcible entry Halligan bars, and it added up to a drain on your gas mileage. I'd decided long ago it wasn't worth the effort. When I needed to force entry, which wasn't that often, I either waited on a rapid entry team or, if it wasn't the entrance to a fortress, kicked the door open myself.

"You're saying you don't have the apartment manager coming to let us in?"

"Oh, I do. But I've just realized something."

"Mind if I take a guess?"

"It's that obvious, is it?"

"Well, let's just say I have my suspicions."

This was when the FBI special agent for Abbot County and its fourteen surrounding counties confessed she didn't know what we were about to find in Nina Kendricks's apartment. And that the thing she'd just realized was that Kendricks hadn't been the only mole in their relationship. She'd been one too. Kendricks's mole.

The mystery deepened the moment the apartment owner inserted the key card and pushed the door open for us.

The apartment was totally devoid of furnishings. Or anything else. It was empty.

Not that it looked neglected. The floors were spotless. Through the open blinds, we could see that the windows sparkled too. We flicked light switches, and they all worked. So the bulbs were current. The manager volunteered an explanation. He received an extra payment from his tenant every month to have a cleaning woman keep the unit move-in ready.

He asked if we were looking to rent. When he understood we weren't, he instructed us to push the night latch on the door when we left. Then he departed.

Angie lost no time in expressing her displeasure. "Dagnabbit!"

"Dagnabbit" was one of her strongest expletives. I sensed this might be one of those times when it would do her good to progress to something stronger. She did.

"Holy plucking crabapples! She played me."

"So you don't have any other address for her?"

"None."

"And you have no idea where she could have gone?"

"None."

"Or maybe where she's traveled lately?"

My companion slowly shook her head. "I've never even checked her passport data. Just never suspected she was anything but what she said she was."

I revisited that idea. "A lowly office manager for two gadabout ex-military bush pilots with a charter service."

That brought another head nod from Angie. She was now leaning against a spotless wall in a spotless apartment that was providing no clues, spotless or otherwise. "Well, does the local sheriff have any ideas?"

He did. I needed to heed Henry David Thoreau's wisdom again. I'd only come across his saying once — in a college English class. But I'd never forgotten it. "Many men go fishing all their lives without knowing that it is not fish they are after."

Those words spoke to me every time I found myself facing a puzzle. One way or another, I usually asked myself the same question. "What is it I'm not fishing for here?"

On this occasion, as it usually did, my mind provided an answer. "The emptiness. Don't let it make you leave too soon."

I suggested we poke our heads in all the rooms. They too were empty. But the last one we entered had an anomaly. A windowpane had been broken from the outside. More than that, it had blood on it. And on the windowsill. And on the floor. A goodly amount of it.

Someone had suffered a consequential injury — a serious laceration. Blood, a lot of it, had been left behind. This meant clues had also been left behind.

Angie asked if one of my forensic people could collect a specimen. I told her I'd ask them to make it a priority.

I had one myself.

CHAPTER 31

L ess than an hour later, Angie and I drove separately to the airport. Rendezvoused at the airport security office. Asked to see Friday's security camera tapes for the airport lobby as the last flight of the day was loading. And, within moments, learned a possible reason why no one had seen Nina Kendricks since late last Friday afternoon. Or, for that matter, the elusive Dr. Bender.

In the security tape, we saw the pair standing together at the check-in counter. Then watched as they headed for the door leading to the concrete apron where our little regional airline loaded and unloaded its passengers with the help of pushable stairs. Our airport didn't process enough fliers to have a boarding ramp.

Both of the individuals we were interested in were pulling their wheeled totes behind them.

She was attired more smartly than I'd have expected of someone of her status, and there was a confidence in her demeanor.

It seemed to go well with a waist size that was narrower than you'd expect for a woman who was at least five-foot-six. She watched her diet. And probably did Jazzercise or Zumba.

Bender was also lithe. Much taller, though. About six feet, I was guessing. Maybe a little more.

His barber — or stylist — had given his light brown hair a deliberate rumpled appearance so that it always looked like he'd just gotten out of bed.

Rakish.

The temples on his designer sunglasses dipped as they swept forward to match the curvature of the lenses, and the casually bunched-up collar on his pale lime windbreaker could double as a hood if it needed to. Fashionable.

He didn't look like a man who'd been betrayed. Or planned to preach about it on Sunday. In fact, the confident swagger suggested he wasn't weighed down with heavy feelings at all. He looked like a man on a mission.

In fact, both of them telegraphed that idea. And it appeared they were traveling together.

I noticed one other thing. Or rather, noticed one other individual. He had approached the pair while they were getting their seat passes at the ticket counter.

Neither Angie nor I recognized him. But he looked like he belonged at the airport. Only not in the passenger area. With his short-sleeved blue coveralls and the industrial earmuffs dangling from his neck, he looked like a baggage handler or a workman.

However, the trio's intense discussion didn't look like it was about baggage.

CHAPTER 32

B ack in the airport's reserved parking lot, Angie followed me to my police cruiser.

I seated myself behind the wheel and reached through my lowered car window. I took her hand and closed it over mine, then planted a quick peck on the back of it. She said she'd be in touch and hurried off toward her vehicle.

The parking lot was too public a place for us to show any more affection than that. And yet, at the moment, despite all the vehicles parked there, it seemed surprisingly private. A good place, I thought, to collect my wits.

I eyed the manufacturer's logo mounted in the center of my steering wheel. Let my fingertips fiddle absent-minded-like with its ridges and indentations. Sent them off next to explore the array of control buttons to either side of the horn pad. And let my mind ruminate on where it might have two chances in hades of finding some answers about the pilots' murders.

That was when I realized what I wanted to do next. I wanted to have a heart-to-heart conversation with our one near-witness. If he felt up to it.

So I fired up my oversexed engine. Engaged the car's gears. And gunned my vehicle out of the parking lot with more gusto than the occasion justified.

As I brought the car back under control, I felt a bit sheepish. So this was what it felt like to see yourself as an avenger for the folks under your protection. This time, my sermon was short and to the point — and had an audience of one. *Remember, old son, you're not a prophet sent from God. You're just the local sheriff.*

I nodded to the deputy we'd assigned to stand watch outside the young man's hospital room door.

The patient's name was lettered on the door's small card holder. The door was ajar but not by much. I gave it a polite knock. An alert-sounding youngish male voice responded. "It's open."

Not really. It needed a push. I gave it a gentle one, took two steps through it, and wouldn't have come to a quicker halt if I'd walked in on Banquo's ghost.

The lanky kid with the bandaged head staring at me from the bed was the same person Angie and I had spotted in the airport security tape. The one participating in a heated conversation with the two departing persons of interest.

Near-witness, indeed.

His mental faculties were back — and so was his confidence. "Sheriff! I was hoping you'd drop by. Judson said you were a swell guy to know."

To hide my surprise at this down-home-styled greeting, I decided to start at neutral. "Good to see you feeling better, Mr. Stockstill."

He was having none of the formality. "No one calls me that. Call me Pogue."

"Hospitals are never fun, are they, Pogue?"

"I'll tell you what isn't fun — getting bashed in the head."

"Well, I want to talk to you about that."

"Shall we start at the top?"

He was watching my face to see if I'd caught the joke. I almost didn't. And might not have if he hadn't cracked a smile.

I smiled back. "Start at the top. Yes — that's a good place to begin talking about a head injury."

He was wearing his chai medallion again, but the hefty bandage covering most of the rear of his head would have made wearing a yarmulke difficult. If he wore one. I didn't know.

I don't think young Mr. Stockstill noticed how much seeing him when I walked into his hospital room had scrambled my thoughts.

He was too busy rearranging himself on his pillows. That and giving me instructions on where to transfer the reading materials piled in the room's solitary guest chair.

His instructions were helpful. Otherwise, given my state of mind and the room's clutter, I'd have been slow to decide where to relocate it all. Next to his bed there was a small three-drawer chest, but the top of it was unavailable. It was already home to a miscellany of items: Portable LED reading lamp. Gray gimme cap sporting Hills-U's Blue Knights' logo. White coffee mug with two-toned, all-cap purple letters proclaiming, *YOU LOOKED BETTER ONLINE.* His smartphone. And a boombox that I surmised was probably connected to the laptop by Bluetooth.

His friends, and probably his family, had been making certain he didn't feel neglected.

I followed his instructions to move the reading materials into the bottom drawer of the chest. Doing so gave me a moment to ponder where I wanted this discussion to go. Foremost was a question: *Was there anyone in Flagler this handsome kid didn't know?*

His tidy hair, short beard, mustache, and shadow of a goatee made him look a little like Zac Efron, the actor. "So you know Jude the Dude?"

The wide grin showcased his perfect teeth. "Best friends forever."

At that point, I realized I was going to enjoy this conversation more than I'd been anticipating.

Jude, the gigantic starting tackle on Flagler High's state championship football team two years ago had been instrumental in helping me puzzle through another of Flagler's mass murder cases. The one where nine physics professors had been poisoned and another victim struck down by a pickup truck at an abandoned old house in the far western part of the county.

At the time, part of the reason for Jude the Dude's involvement had been fortuitous. The brilliant kid had simply been in the right place at the right time. But more than that, he didn't miss much. He also had a propensity for noticing the right things and connecting the right dots. By the time it was over, Judson T. Mayes III and I had bonded in a way I'd not enjoyed with that many people, especially young adults. When Pogue Stockstill announced he and Judson were best friends for life, I'd almost blurted, "Me too."

Instead, I asked a question. "How is he?"

Young Stockstill closed the cover to his computer and moved it out of his lap to one side of the bed. "He's at Harvard, you know."

"I did know that."

"He wanted me to go with him, but I didn't have the scratch."

"Harvard does take a lot of scratch."

"To answer your question, he calls me about once a week."

"So the two of you keep up with each other's coursework?"

"Not really."

"What do you talk about, then?"

"A lot of the time, about mysteries in Flagler."

"And what mysteries have you and Jude the Dude been talking about lately?"

For the first time since Mr. Stockstill and I had started our easy banter, his eyes took on a guarded look. He flashed them around the room for a moment as if he were looking for a way to escape. Then he locked his eyes on mine. "How much do you know?"

Now I was the uncertain one. My first instinct was to say very little. That was the safest path for a law enforcement interviewer. But a feeling stirred in me that I instantly recognized. It was as if Judson Mayes III was in the room. And Jude the Dude was telling me to trust this guy.

"Okay, I'll bite . . . "

CHAPTER 33

In a staccato, near-nonstop recital, I laid out for young Pogue Stockstill what I knew about the pilots. Their grotesque deaths. Their office manager. Their clients. Their travels. Their cargoes. And about the few individuals who seemed like they might be involved in any of this.

The only reason I knew Stockstill was staying up with me were those penetrating eyes. They were watching my face with an intensity that seemed to invite me to leave no secret unshared. So I didn't. At least, not the ones I felt were important.

"First of all, the two pilots who were killed did more than haul people around. Often as not, as far as I can tell, they also seemed to be couriers. They delivered stuff.

"Second, they didn't always go where they said they were going. Especially on their cargo runs. And some of those destinations were a long ways from Flagler.

"Third, they tended to be careless about their companions. Or their employees. Some of them were pretty questionable. Confirmed lawbreakers, for example.

"Fourth, their deaths appear to have occurred in the middle of one of their intrigues. Something got interrupted, and it may have gotten them killed.

"Fifth, there may be others in danger. Which is, incidentally, why we have a guard outside your door. We'd like to talk with these folks rather than have them start disappearing.

"Sixth, there are issues connected to the dead pilots involving some of our local organizations. One of our colleges and a private research firm, for example.

"Seventh, there's the international angle. Several intelligence agencies think the pilots may have unloaded something perilous in Flagler. But we can't even find the box—"

To now, I'd not observed the slightest movement in my listener. Not a head nod, not a frown, not a raised eyebrow, not a shrug, not an idle adjustment or tug of the covers or so much as an involuntary twitch of a toe beneath them. So when Stockstill threw his sheet and bedspread back so vigorously they sailed onto the floor, I literally jumped to my feet.

My actions couldn't have been better choreographed.

When he demanded that I push my chair close to his bed so he could settle into it, it was already vacant. And when he brushed my arm away, I knew he didn't want my help getting into it.

"Look, Sheriff, I know where the box is."

CHAPTER 34

If he was to be believed, Stockstill knew a lot more about the box than just its whereabouts.

He had a working knowledge of its origins. Who'd manufactured it. The reason for its odd shape. The alterations it had undergone. And, its intended uses. The reason for all this was simple. He'd been around the box from the beginning.

As best he knew, the box's oblong shape wasn't because of anything it was intended to carry. It had been built like that so it could be fitted into the passenger aisle of the pilots' Beechcraft King Air 350i plane. That meant it couldn't be high, wide, or unwieldy. It had to be narrow, low-slung, and easily maneuverable.

As for the box's origins, he and the pilots had built it themselves with the help of a welder friend of Stockstill's dad, who was a machinist. As I had guessed from FBI special agent Knoke's photographs, the box had been constructed from aluminum, mainly to reduce its weight.

The same craftsman had helped the pilots modify the box. Twice.

First, they'd added hinged carrying handles, two on a side. In addition, a single handgrip had been attached at each end.

Mention of the handles seemed to brighten Stockstill's mood a bit. "The handles were the reason for the nickname. The guys started calling it The Coffin."

Then, a little over a year ago, they'd wanted metal clips installed in the interior of the box. They'd decreed these should go at the corners and be located on the box's inside walls twelve inches apart. Also, they'd been placed at similar-spaced locations on the underside of the lid. He said the clips were spring-activated and could be opened as wide as an inch.

While I was listening to this, I'd wondered more than once if Stockstill and I were involved in a gentleman's game of chicken. To see who was going to blink or squirm or depart from the general tenor of the conversation first. But another of my inner voices chimed in that a game was afoot, all right. Only, it wasn't chicken.

I realized this intense young man and I were involved in a game of tag. But we were not competing with each other. We were competing with an ever-shifting fog of events, personalities, and meanings.

I stepped toward the chair, leaned down far enough to place a hand on each of his shoulders, and framed a question that I felt went straight to the heart of the matter. "Why do you think the pilots were killed?"

He said if I'd help him back in his bed, he'd tell me.

CHAPTER 35

H is answer was equivocal. "Figuring that out isn't going to be easy."

I straightened up, folded my arms across my chest and continued to maintain my fatherly gaze. "That's why I need your help."

"You know where I'd start?"

"I'm hoping you'll tell me."

"I'd sit Ms. Kendricks and Dr. Bender down in the same room and ask them what the clips inside The Coffin were for."

"What do you think?"

"At first, I'd thought they were there to hold up drapes or something."

"You mean like pads? To protect things being hauled in the box?"

"No, not that. Like they do with a real casket. You know, decorate it inside. Make it look more fetching. More inviting."

"Why would the pilots need to do that?"

"Well, one idea I had was they were transporting stuff they were putting on display. Or transporting stuff for clients who did."

"What kind of stuff?"

He was showing some weariness at my drumbeat of

questions, but he soldiered on. "Sculptures, maybe. Or antiquities. Tribal rugs. Historic costumes. Rare musical instruments — who knows?" There was no misjudging the sarcasm in what he said next. "The violin they played on the *Titanic* sold for a cool $1.7 million at auction, remember?"

I decided to go slower. Only a few hours ago, the brain I was talking with had been in a coma. "Lots to think about."

When he didn't respond right away, I thought his awareness had gone somewhere else. But it hadn't. He was revisiting how things had happened.

"Our lateral thinking really got going after they left the thermometer in the box."

"You said, '*Our* lateral thinking'?"

"Yeah, Judson and me."

"The pilots left a thermometer?"

"Yeah. After one of their trips. I always checked inside after we put the box back in the mini-warehouse. I found it."

"How did the pilots explain the thermometer?"

"Never asked them. Like most times, they'd been in a hurry. I was nearly always the one to close up. They never mentioned the thermometer, and neither did I."

"And what did you and Judson make of it?"

"Got us thinking about the clips again."

"Now that you've mentioned the thermometer, I'm going to guess they were there to secure something cold."

"Or secure something that would keep things cold. Judson had an idea. Hand me my computer, and I'll show you."

The image he showed me was a detailed 3D schematic of how the box could be transformed into an ice chest worthy of Hercules. Or at a minimum, the Greeks' cute goddess of youth, Hebe.

Judson's drawing showed the box completely lined with Styrofoam panels. The clips were holding them in place. Add a few chunks of dry ice, and anything perishable placed in an airtight metal box like that should stay cold for a long time. Or frozen.

Interesting.

I had a couple of other questions for Pogue Stockstill. Before I asked them, I needed to tell him about what I'd seen on the security tape taken in the airport lobby last Friday afternoon.

When I did, he wasn't shocked that he'd been observed giving Kendricks and Bender their send-off. Instead, he found it ironic. At least his tone sounded ironic. Or maybe it was resignation. "In this town, no good deed evades suspicion, does it?"

If he'd been intending to stir up my curiosity, that had worked. "So that's what you were doing for Dr. Bender and Ms. Kendricks — performing a good deed?"

"I thought so. Ms. Kendricks had asked me if I'd give the pilots a couple of new keys to their office when they got back. She'd had the locks changed. In fact, she'd had a second lock added to the front door."

"She say why?"

"Said somebody had been calling the office and then hanging up without saying anything. Said she was just taking precautions."

"And how is it that you knew those two at all?"

"Well, I'd had an introductory history class with Dr. Bender. And Ms. Kendricks was around the hanger a lot. She often met the pilots when they returned from trips. I got to know her that way."

"So she gave you the new keys?"

"She did. Should be in my pants pockets. Or wherever they put what was in my pants pockets."

"You mind if I take them?"

"My pants?"

"No, the keys."

"You're the sheriff."

The two keys were in the top drawer of the bedside chest. They were separate from Stockstill's key ring. I checked with him to confirm they were the ones I was looking for. Told him I needed to step out of the room for a moment. Went out into the hallway. Extracted my cell phone from the pocket of my windbreaker. Called Angie. And said if she wanted to meet me at the pilots' office suite, I had a way to get in without knocking the door down.

She said it sounded like I'd found a key.

I confirmed that I had. Two, in fact.

She asked if I had a search warrant.

I said I didn't.

She asked if I planned to get one.

I said I'd do that if we needed one.

She pondered this for a moment. "You know what that means, don't you?"

"Not sure. As I seem to be frequently reminded these days, I'm just a lowly country sheriff."

We both knew there was only one way we could enter the pilots' office suite without a search warrant. That was if we opened the door and spotted something we thought was suspicious — like possible evidence in a murder investigation. In that case, the plain view exception to the Fourth Amendment would allow us to proceed.

Otherwise, all we could do was open the door and take a peek inside. Beyond that, one of us was going to need to visit grumpy old Judge Kincannon's office again and do the paperwork for a search warrant.

I told her I needed to show up at the pilots' office suite anyway. If we couldn't enter, I needed to seal the door with crime scene tape until I could get a warrant and put a CSI team to work.

She said she was surprised I'd not already sealed the door. So was I.

I told her I'd had a lot on my platter lately.

To my surprise, she hadn't countered with one of her catty comebacks.

I thought about it later. She must have had one of her inklings. She often did when something was afoot. Those were times when she was uncharacteristically circumspect.

I went back into young Stockstill's room. Told him I was going to keep the two keys for a day or two. Stared at him in surprise when he interrupted me. He said there was something else he needed to tell me.

I reached for the chair he'd vacated. Settled into it. And listened as he told me more about the two pilots' flight to Ağrı and back than I'd ever expected to hear, particularly from him.

CHAPTER 36

One more time, I had to admire the kid's ability to cut to the chase.

He conveyed his information with all the nonchalance of announcing that he'd decided on mayo instead of mustard for his sandwich. "Somebody told the pilots, 'Flying to Turkey to play God could be a death wish.'"

As it had been doing lately, for some reason, my mind put me back in high school Spanish class. "¿Quién, qué, dónde, cuándo, por qué, comó?"

I thought these were all worthy questions to put to young Stockstill in light of his abrupt revelation.

Who had told the pilots that?

What had they thought it meant?

When had they been told that?

Where had they been told that?

Why had they been told that?

And, *how* had they been told that?

I needed to start asking those questions.

But then my mind seemed to think better of turning itself into a male version of TV's "miss no evil" Deputy Chief Brenda Johnson.

I decided on a more succinct response. One that was pretty much out of character for me. Normally, I took care not to use profanity in my professional activities.

"No shit."

It was indicative of Stockstill's frame of mind that treated my profane outburst as a nothing burger. He ignored it.

I'd seen the condition numerous times in my interrogation room. A scorpion of knowledge was eating away at his neurons. It had to be divulged before it drove him insane. And the local sheriff, it was becoming clearer and clearer, was being viewed as the perfect receptacle to receive what he needed to impart.

That ultra-melodramatic assessment of my situation was to keep me riveted to the room's single chair. If it hadn't been, what Jude the Dude's BFF said next would have been. "You know what an inequation mark is?"

I summoned the sternest "be the adult in the room" look I could manage and gave him a nod. "I know what it says in the dictionary."

"You've never seen one?"

"A few times, yes."

"The pilots got a note signed with one."

"Got a note how?"

"Somebody stuck it in the door of their King Air."

"Did you see it?"

"Yeah, they showed it to me."

"What did it say?"

"Like I said, something along the lines of 'people who fly to Turkey to play God have a death wish.'"

"And it was signed?"

"Only with the mark. The inequation mark."

This time, I didn't say it. Only thought it. No, shit.

I searched my memory. I didn't think I'd mentioned the bloody inequation mark smeared on the hangar wall to young Stockstill.

My detectives and the medical examiner's technicians had all agreed less was more in this instance. The fewer people who knew about the gruesome piece of artwork on the hangar wall, the better. That way, if someone referenced it in any of our hearings or any public forum, they'd be invited to one of our interrogation rooms to explain how they'd known about it.

That approach wasn't going to be necessary here. Stockstill had mentioned inequation marks in a completely different context. For some reason, an old radio show I'd listened to occasionally as a kid popped into my mind. It was *Paul Harvey's The Rest of the Story*. I felt my lower lip give my upper lip a pay-attention-to-this nudge. The rest of Pogue Stockstill's story about inequation marks was incoming.

CHAPTER 37

The storyteller had again found a comfortable position on his pillows and propped himself upright.

I asked if there was anything I could get him. Acknowledged his polite decline. Kept my hands folded in my lap. And waited.

And waited.

And waited.

My guess was young Stockstill was not only assessing how to proceed but whether he wanted to proceed at all. That thought was reinforced when he asked me to get up and give a message to my deputy standing watch in the hallway. No admittances until further notice. Then he wanted me to shut the door. He didn't want anyone but me hearing what he was about to say.

This was when I realized the delay in our conversation hadn't been caused by any indecision on his part about whether to proceed.

Instead, he'd been revisiting in his mind how it had all started. "I don't think the pilots expected me to know anything about the note. The only reason they'd showed it to me was because I was around the hangar and the plane so much. They just seemed to want to share it with someone. And I can understand why they'd feel that."

The tone of his voice surprised me. That and his choice of words. Stockstill seemed to be setting me up to expect he'd understood something about the note that the pilots hadn't. "So you knew something about the note?"

He gave me a hurried head shake. "Not the note so much . . . I knew something about the mark."

I had a feeling I was about to learn what. Those light gray eyes were drilling into me like laser beams. "I get the *JPost*, you know. By mail."

I didn't want to discourage him, so I dropped my chin in a quick nod. He knew it was an empty gesture, so he elaborated. "*The Jerusalem Post*. The newspaper."

That helped a little. I wanted to reinforce my comments, hoping he'd continue. "So what's going on in Israel that interests you?"

"Not so much. I mean, not to that extent. But, you know, my uncle is a reporter for the *Post*. He sends it to me. In a bundle. A week's worth at a time."

Was a nod needed here? I decided it was. And an encouraging question. But I was clueless about where this was going. So a simple "um-hum" was going to have to suffice.

It didn't.

The pause in the conversation was overly long, and I sought to start the talk again. "So you'd seen something in the Jerusalem newspaper that intrigued you?"

He seemed grateful for a reminder of where he'd been headed. "Yes, I remembered a photo of a work of graffiti. It had been spray-painted on a shuttered shop door in downtown Jerusalem. Almost covered the entire door. Big sucker. Simple, but huge. Don't really know why the object caught my eye — only that it had been a bit offbeat. Out of sync, really. If you know anything about how things operate in Israel."

"Let me guess . . . you saw a photo of the inequation mark."

"It was more than the photo."

"Let's stay with the photo for a moment. When was it taken?"

"About two months ago."

"And why was there a photo of it in *The Jerusalem Post*?"

"Like I say, it was more than just a photo. My uncle had written a feature story about it too."

"Why had he been so interested in it?"

"Well, the gist of the story was how intrigued veteran observers of Israel-Palestinian relations were by the mark."

"What intrigued them about it?"

"For one thing, how much it reminded them of a swastika."

"Like the Nazis' swastika?"

"Yes, he said it was simple and vivid like that one. And like the swastika, it was being misappropriated. Stolen from the field of mathematics. Remember, the swastika was originally created by religious people to stand for prosperity and good luck."

"All this was in your uncle's article?"

"Yes, but I was curious. I wanted to know more. So I emailed him."

"And asked him . . . what?"

"What he thinks is going on."

"And he replied?"

"Yes."

This was when young Stockstill made me privy to information that counterintelligence agents of four or five countries would likely have killed for.

He said his uncle had sworn him to secrecy. Then shared information he hadn't dared to put into his newspaper article.

"The savviest Israeli insiders my uncle could find were telling him a rogue element was operating outside normal channels in the Mossad, Israel's notorious and often deadly foreign intelligence service. The breakaway Mossad group's way of identifying themselves was with an inequation mark, and anyone receiving personal communications of any kind signed with the mark should consider themselves in grave danger."

Young Stockstill's riveting account was still ricocheting around my mind when I checked with Angie to see if she was still available to examine the pilots' office suite.

She said she'd meet me there.

CHAPTER 38

I inserted young Stockstill's keys in the door locks one at a time. Gave each a quarter turn. And both heard and felt the bolts slide back.

The pull-down shade on the door glass had been drawn to its full length. This meant our first glimpse inside the dead pilots' office suite didn't come until I pushed the door open, allowing a dim shaft of light to advance into the total darkness, but it wasn't revealing a lot. Nothing we immediately recognized other than another door. That door, leading to another room, was open but simply revealed more darkness.

That all changed when I found the overhead light switch to the left of the door, flicked it on, and took a step inside.

It's fair to say that my working eye was not adept at going from complete darkness to an explosion of colors and images. The experience stopped me in my tracks. This sent the FBI special agent who was one step behind me into action. Angie grabbed my other arm, pulled me aside, and pushed her own way into the room. But she took only a step or two herself before her body stiffened. Her first words echoed my own disbelief. "*Excuse me?*"

My comeback wasn't brilliant but fit the occasion. "Excuse somebody, that's for sure."

One more glance and we both realized there was no longer any need to be concerned about violating the Fourth Amendment.

The issue now confronting us was much more tactical. Did Angie call in the federal investigative calvary? Or did her lowly Texas sheriff pal trust that his CSI team could get the job done?

When Angie and I later relived our first impressions of the office suite, it turned out we'd fixated on different things. But we'd both come to a similar conclusion.

We were staring at the nerve center or command post or planning headquarters — help yourself to a descriptive label — of something far more imaginative and consequential than two ex-military charter service pilots could have thought up by themselves. And very possibly, something more dangerous than even government gumshoes sniffing around Abbot County for WMDs would have had any reason to expect.

Angie's eyes had been drawn to the maps. An entire wall of them, held in place with yellow push pens. At least, the ones we could see. Oddly enough, although they covered the far wall from ceiling to floor, not all the map surfaces were immediately visible. Two objects prevented this.

About two-thirds of the way down the room on that wall, there was an office desk. It had a chair pushed into its chair well and two items resting on its desktop. One of those appeared to be a sizable monthly planning calendar. The other was a black landline phone answering machine.

The other impediment to having a clear view of what was on the wall was a lumpy, faded, vintage-styled chair. It was part of a set. A few more steps into the room, and we realized that a matching three-cushion sofa — same color, same lumpiness — backed up to the opposite wall.

On the map wall side, both the desk and the chair sat a bit farther from the wall than you'd call normal. This way, if you looked from the right angles, you could peer down behind them and get at least a glimpse of the maps whose view they were blocking.

One or two of these were obviously *National Geographic* travel maps. But most were aviation maps. Maps covered with blues for water and yellows for land, interlaced with a myriad of black, blue, and purple circles, boxes, lines, and symbols. These were aeronautical charts, used to assist pilots in planning their flights. And, when the time came, complete them safely.

I soon realized most of the maps showed regions in the Middle East. I noticed two with Turkey portrayed on them. Israel on another. Syria on yet another. The eastern United States, Canada, and Greenland were depicted on others. And several showed nothing but the waters of the Atlantic Ocean.

But my one working eye didn't stay focused on the maps for long. It quickly moved on to the wall diagonal to the one that held the maps. The wall off to my left. The wall at the end of the room.

It too was covered from floor to ceiling. But by nothing that required a push pin to hold it up.

CHAPTER 39

This entire wall was a whiteboard. The only thing on it was words. Along with a few symbols.

There was a streamer or screamer or headline — whatever you wanted to call it — near the top, put there with a red felt-tip marker.

It contained two lines, both precisely centered, as if someone had calculated or blocked out their length in advance. Either that, or the writer possessed a seasoned artist's eye for handling space.

The first line of neat red letters read Code New Beginnings. Underneath that, again perfectly centered, was a second line in red marker, only this time, the letters were smaller. They read *A Step-by-Step Schema*.

And a schema it was. Of some kind.

The contents of the wall below those two headlines were dense. Detailed. Mesmerizing. Every time you tried to remove your eyes from the entries on the wall, you found them stuck to something new.

Nevertheless, my one eye tried to drink it all in. Sort it out. Assign some kind of meaning to it all.

As I did so, something else began to happen. I found myself feeling noble and self-righteous for having made the effort.

Possessive. Like I'd been entrusted with something special and wanted to protect it. I'd had a similar feeling in the past few hours. I didn't need long to figure it out. I'd felt the same way when I found Fresca at the fire station.

I began to read what else was on the wall. The most visible other feature was the repeated usage of the word *code*. Each time, it was part of a name — a code name. Each time, the code name was written in red. And each time, the code name was followed by two lines of description.

Both these additional lines were composed of smaller letters than the code names. And they were not in red. The first line was always created with a black-ink felt-tip marker. And the line or lines that followed were in purple ink.

Code Slush was the first code name. The black line that came after it was a complete sentence. "The snow and ice offer a unique chance for an amazing outcome."

The purple line beneath all that was a mishmash. Part description. Part gibberish. Part — what else? Amateur poet under the influence? "Duplicate museum experience in the Alps / borrow dune buggy from hyperplumber / ip so, facto, hush hush, rush rush, sports fans!"

The next entry introduced itself as Code Be. Again in red. The line that followed was again in black letters, and it was a complete sentence. An intelligent one. Again. "Extreme secrecy is crucial for the final flight leg and for local transport."

Next came the purple-lettered commentary. And more ridiculous jargon. "Need sure-fire popsicle carrier / pay pipers at critical borders / arrive Flagler nighttime for deep cover!"

Code Chindi was next. With another seemingly intelligent, straightforward sentence in black letters. "The scientist knows he will need to start the process somewhere a long way from Flagler."

Once again, the purple letters made little sense. "Mexican folks, make nice egg / but Mariachis make hot potato if omelet left on their grill / best bring Eve and wee one home to the garden.'"

Code Klizzie was explained with another black-letter sentence. "Remember patience pays off — and 'pride goeth before a fall.'"

The purple-prose creator didn't appear to agree. "Nuh, uh. No, no, no! / speed is doubly important / can Nobel Peace Prize (!!!) be far behind, oh, wonderful imaginators?"

There were four more code names: Code Cha, Code Lin, Code A-Chin, and Code Klesh. Each with two captions, one in black and one in purple. The first caption composed with parlor-proper manners. The other couched in near or total nonsensical verbiage seemingly offering instructions. Or kooky reasons to celebrate. Or observations that could have been straight out of *Kukla, Fran, and Ollie*. Or, in most cases, all three.

Angie was the faster reader. She didn't comment until I turned and mouthed a single word at her. "Duh?"

I lip-read her silent reply. "Insanity."

For some reason, we were both whispering. We both focused our attention on the wall with the writing again. This time, I read more slowly. And had almost reached the bottom when I had my first inkling of recognition. It didn't help much.

But I snaked my smartphone out of my pocket, engaged the right icons, and entered a couple of words on the keyboard. Faster than you could say, "Geronimo," I was running my eye down the list I'd called up from the internet.

"Navajo."

Angie reached for my arm and swung me toward her. I could see her concern that she might be the only normal person in the room. "What are you looking at?"

I moved the iPhone so we both could see the display. "The Navajo Windtalker's Dictionary."

"Navajo Indian?"

"Yes, Navajo Indian."

"Where did you get that idea from?"

"I was reading about their wartime code-breaking exploits last night on the web."

"And that has to do with our wall how?"

"Don't know that. But the code names — they're all Navajo words. Or letters too. The Navajo assign an image, like an animal or a plant or a mineral, to each letter of their alphabet."

She looked at the wall again and started reading them off. "Slush, Be, Chindi, Kleezie, Cha, Lin, A-Chin, Klesh, Gah. They do sound Indigenous. Meaning what?"

"Well, there's two ways I can answer that. The first is, I know, and the second is, I don't know."

I explained the reason I knew anything at all. I'd read on the web about how the windtalkers had converted the alphabet and key military terms into a Navajo dictionary that had left our wartime enemies befuddled. And why not? Slush, for example, was one of three Navajo words for the letter "b." When translated literally, it meant bear. "Be" was "d," for deer. Chindi was also used for "d," but it meant devil. Kleezie was "g," for goat. And so forth.

"What I don't know is what their use here is intended to mean. Or if it's intended to mean anything. It could be somebody's idea of a joke. Or—"

Angie had her own smartphone out and was taking pictures. One after the other. "Or it could be that we really are dealing with a dangerous person or persons. I'm going to get some of the bureau's language specialists involved pronto. They should have some ideas."

I had no objection to that.

But as I continued to scan the contents of the wall, I had a growing conviction. The person or persons who had let their imagination loose on that wall hadn't been kidding around. They were serious about creating a new beginning of some kind.

Another sense I had was that the whole scheme he or she had in mind was up there in plain view, step by step, just as had been alleged, even though the method and the phraseology were outlandish, and at times, spooky.

That second conclusion had led to another.

Angie and I could stay here for the rest of the week staring and fretting at that wall, and it might not say any more to us than I'd just articulated. We needed to keep turning over the rocks and connecting the dots in real-time Abbot County, not the land of make-believe. Creating our own scheme, in other words.

Step by step.

But before we left the pilots' office suite, I wanted to do one more thing. See what was in the other room.

This time, Angie turned on the overhead light and led the way as we walked into a space that looked more like an office, though not a very active one. The walls in this room were bare.

Not so much as an outdated calendar.

The end of the room closest to the door had a well-scarred industrial metal desk shoved against the wall but no chair in the foot well or anywhere else. The desk had three drawers on one side, two drawers on the other, and the standard shallow drawer over the foot well.

One at a time, Angie tried to open the drawers, but oddly, all the drawers had individual locks. And all those locks were engaged.

Seeing if there was anything in the drawers was going to require either a set of lock picks or a crowbar. Which one it would be, I'd leave up to my CSI crew, but before they started forcing drawers open, I wanted to get a search warrant. And would.

In the middle of the room sat a black, four-drawer vertical filing cabinet. It too was chipped and scarred. We knew the drawers were empty the moment we tugged on each one. They all swayed and rattled, suggesting there was nothing inside to provide them with any ballast.

Along the far wall sat a card table with two folding chairs jammed under it. Two more chairs remained folded. They were leaning against the wall close by.

The room also contained a four-shelf metal rack. It was at the far end of the wall that contained the door into the room. The rack held little. Only some old aviation magazines and a well-thumbed copy of the 2008 *FAA Aviation Instructor's Handbook*.

This time, I sealed the door to the office suite with crime scene tape. Then pulled out my walkie-talkie to instruct our CSI technicians to get a search warrant. As soon as they got it, I wanted them to give the suite a thorough going-over. In particular, I wanted to know what, if anything, was in the locked desk drawers.

All this seemed to be fine with Angie. She was already on her iPhone summoning her other mole to the Flagler Country Club. We both wanted to know what No. 2 could tell us about Thesaurus of the Gene Corporation, the genetics research company out on the Brownwood Highway.

CHAPTER 40

The maître d' at the country club greeted Angie with a hand-shake that involved both his hands.

His name badge said he was Alain. His accent didn't come close to sounding Celtic — or French — to me. It did sound cultivated, but that could have been a country club thing resulting from a lot of practice.

He acknowledged me with a curt nod and asked my colleague if she wanted a table in the big room or a room of her own. She said a room of her own. And told him she'd have another guest arriving shortly.

He stopped at the door of a room at the far end of the hallway, gave us a half-bow, invited us to enter, followed us inside, and disappeared into a small side room. But only for a moment.

When he emerged, he was pushing a serving cart. With one hand. The other hand was balancing — for the moment — a long, collapsible folding screen.

He lifted the divider off the cart. Opened its four hinged panels. Then set it in place so that it shielded the table farthest from the door.

This is when I understood. The screen would keep the occupants of that table from the prying eyes of anyone who might try to take a peek from the hallway or enter the room unbidden.

Alain did all this without a word. Then he half-bowed again. Gave Angie a knowing smile. Sent a perfunctory salute in my direction, and exited, closing the door firmly behind him.

I was amused. "Does Alain have any idea what you do behind his screen?"

Angie opened her mouth to reply but before she could get a word out, Alain was back.

This time, he was being trailed by a woman in early middle age. There was no way her plus-size figure could ever be draped to disguise one glaring fact. The diameter of her linebacker shoulders defined her width all the way to her ankles.

Her taste in clothes didn't help matters any. Today, she had selected a flared-sleeved, scoop-necked white dress with alternating rows of magenta circles and crosses. It ended about six inches above her knees and did nothing to create the illusion of a waist.

I assumed this was Angie's Mole No. 2.

Two adult males completed the entourage. One had a stern look on his face and seemed to be accompanying the lady. He looked like he was on the clock. Without thinking about it, I assumed he was a lawyer.

And the other one? He looked like he was on something too. My first thought was lysergic acid diethylamide. Then I corrected myself. *Wrong drug, wrong decade, wrong century, in fact, dude.* And this guy didn't need a drug assist. He was high on himself.

His face was projecting the same kind of look that Dr. Bender and Nina Kendricks had been radiating at the airport as they headed out the door that led to the boarding area. He was confident to the point of arrogance.

I got the feeling he'd walked into the room expecting to dominate the conversation. Part of it was the way he was dressed.

166

Black turtleneck sweater? I don't think I'd seen one in Flagler more than once or twice. One of those was in a downtown department store window. I'd thought then that the window designer had been aiming for a look somewhere between Clint Eastwood and John Wayne. But what he'd ended up with was a skinny mannequin looking like a cross between Richard Gere and Ringo Starr.

This gentleman didn't fit either of those descriptions. But as he turned around to close the door, he probably had no idea how weird he looked. His tan stockman's duster coat had shoulder pads that looked like a woman's shawl. In the back, the coat was unbuttoned all the way to his waist, and his faded jeans were bunched on top of his unlaced Chukka boots like ruffles.

His outfit wasn't the only idiosyncrasy in his appearance, but it took me a moment to figure out what the other one was. It was the jarring contrast between his black turtleneck and his flaming, shoulder-length locks and the rest of his Four Alarm facial hair, pencil-length beard included. Put him and my deputy chief, Chuck Del Emma, in the same room, and every fire bell in the building would erupt.

Angie and I never learned the lawyer's name. He announced he was there to inform the local sheriff and the resident FBI special agent that his client would not respond to any questions about crimes allegedly committed or anything else unless we had a warrant. He and Mole No. 2 were gone in less than a minute.

But the other man had left no doubt regarding his plans to hang around a while. He pulled a chair out from the table and draped the preposterous stockman's cape he was wearing over the back of it. As a consequence, the chair almost completely disappeared.

Then he pulled out another chair, turned it 180 degrees so that it faced us dead-on and lowered himself onto it, knees akimbo. His arms were crossed and parked where he'd brought them to rest — on the top stave of the chair back.

He stared a moment at me, then at Angie, then back at me. "I'm Dr. Jon Plymouth Dandurall. I understand you'd like to know more about Thesaurus of the Gene Corporation. Perhaps I can help with that. I founded it."

I had no intention of letting this be where we started the conversation. I gestured toward the door. "The little scene we just witnessed — you have anything to do with that?"

He edged backward a bit in his chair and grabbed its middle support slat with both fists. "Guilty to that. He's my corporate lawyer. He thinks law enforcement is playing a bit too rough with my employee."

"You know she could have been taken into custody on the spot."

"A chance we took — true."

"Took a chance because you think she'll get off?"

"I'd hope the judge would be fair. But no, we took a chance because I'm hoping both of you can think like a CPAP machine."

After nearly seventeen years of questioning lawbreakers, witnesses and possible persons of interest, I didn't think anything that popped out of any of their mouths could take me by total surprise. But then, if memory was correct, none of them had ever mentioned a CPAP machine.

I didn't believe I'd had one involved in a crime, much less the double murder. I couldn't even remember the last time I'd seen one at a crime scene.

What made its mention more startling now was that I happened to be a user of one of these devices. Night after night, it kept my airway clear, saving my vulnerable throat and oral cavity from a fate that would otherwise be tortuous. If you had an apnea problem, a CPAP machine was a marvel — a miracle, really. But the mention of one in this particular context seemed to me to be a total non sequitur. That irked me.

This time, I did the chair gymnastics. Pushed myself back from the table. Maneuvered my coat away from my duty belt. Disengaged my handcuffs and tossed them in the middle of the table. They landed with an ominous clunk. "Angie, I think Dr. Dandurall and I may have to continue our conversation at the sheriff's department."

That brought him to his feet. The fingers of one hand were extended, and he was tapping them with the extended fingers of the other hand with great energy. He was signaling for a time out.

"No, no! I meant I hope you can do what a CPAP machine does. It keeps things open and functioning. On track. Operating. Flowing. I'm hoping you'll keep an open mind while I explain how the two dead pilots got in over their heads."

CHAPTER 41

All I'd really counted on knowing by the end of this conversation was what Thesaurus of the Gene Corporation was all about and what went on out there in its one-story Brownwood Highway research lab.

I already knew that the company had quite a reputation. "World-renowned" was the way Clyde Hazelton had once described it.

Of course, the loquacious editor of the *Tribune-Standard* would exult about anything he felt made Flagler seem bigger than life or one of God's gifts to creation. The fact that the Thesaurus of the Gene Corporation had certain achievements that Clyde felt elevated it into the clouds had been repeatedly spelled out in the paper. Clyde being Clyde, it had often been done in an overblown, sometimes schmaltzy, fashion.

At the moment, I wasn't remembering a lot of specifics, but as Angie and I stared at the apparition in the black turtleneck sitting across from us, my mind surfaced a few highlights.

The company wasn't that old — only three or four years. It claimed to be more than a high-technology company. "Cutting-edge high science" was the way its press releases liked to brag about it. The company's spokespersons never missed a chance to point out how rare it was having an outfit like theirs in a place like Flagler. Their argument was that breakthrough ideas like the ones that had come out of their lab didn't have a habit of taking root in places like Flagler. Nor in Dallas or Houston, for that matter. At least, not often.

Ideas with this kind of originality required brilliant minds produced by, and often still working next door to, places like MIT, Harvard, Stanford, UC-Berkeley, or the University of Cambridge.

But as Clyde Hazelton liked to remind his readers, here in all their resplendent scientific glory were Dr. Dandurall and his colleagues. In Flagler. Doing their brain-stretching research, extraordinary laboratory feats, and good deeds. And sitting here at this moment, close enough to touch, was the guiding light of all this. Wanting to tell us about the whole nine yards.

I gave Angie a questioning look. After all, this was supposed to have been her meeting. With her mole.

Did she want this to continue?

I saw her tummy give a minuscule heave. She'd just suppressed a laugh. "Does the mommy bear get a vote on which cub gets the first suckle?"

The multiple meanings in her obscure response sailed over the head of our uninvited guest like a barrage of one-way boomerangs. "Say what?"

I realized it was time to play tennis — and for some reason, Angie was wanting me to fire off the first lob. "Well, it's not the pilots we're really interested in."

Our visitor looked like a child who'd just been told there was no Santa Claus. Even so, his natural arrogance made him determined not to show any confusion.

He began to toss off possible ways to explain our lack of interest like he was feeding a duck one corn kernel at a time. "So, you've already found the killers?"

I was leaning forward with my elbows on the table with my hands clasped, staring at him. I raised, then lowered, both thumbs. Gave him a thumbs down. *Sorry, Dr. Dandurall, no cigar.*

"You've been pulled off the case by higher-ups?"

I flicked my thumbs again.

"You've planted another mole in my shop?"

I looked at Angie and rolled my eyes before giving my thumbs another flick.

"You've found something highly incriminating in the pilots' plane?"

Thumb flick.

"You've had a breakthrough searching the pilots' office suite?"

Thumb flick.

"The whole thing was a botched holdup?"

Thumb flick.

"One of the pilot's ex-wives took revenge for something and didn't want a witness?"

Thumb flick.

"Your deputies wanted you out from underfoot and did this to get you away from the office?"

Thumb flick.

"The pilots were involved with Russian spies, and you turned all this over to the CIA?"

This time, I unclasped my hands and gave him the twisted-wrists gesture for "maybe, maybe not."

He reciprocated with a back-and-forth "maybe I'm getting close" head gesture. "You've got a witness to the killings?"

This gave me pause.

I wondered if he knew about Pogue Stockstill. But I recovered in a hurry, not wanting him to realize he'd gotten too close for comfort.

Thumb flick.

"You're working with a clairvoyant who told you not to muddy the water?"

Thumb flick.

"You've hired a Hollywood scriptwriter as a CSI consultant?"

Thumb flick.

"You've had too many bad dreams about all this?"

Thumb flick.

"You promised the mayor not to mention the murders?"

Thumb flick.

But that was enough. The limits to his capacity to engage in this kind of nonsense were nowhere in sight.

"Dr. Dandurall, you're an interesting fellow. And this has been fun. But we need to talk about why the pilots had been flying contraband for you all over God's creation."

CHAPTER 42

"So DeeDee was right."

This time, the question came from me. "DeeDee?"

"Daphne . . . Daphne Margaret Maples. That was her with my attorney. She's my office manager. We call her DeeDee."

"And what was DeeDee right about?"

"She said the FBI lady had gotten the wrong impression about Thesaurus of the Gene Corporation from somewhere."

I converted one hand into a cocked pistol and aimed it at Angie. "Well, that's the FBI lady sitting right there. Why don't you give her the right impression?"

This time, he squirmed in his chair like a kid being reprimanded for eating too much candy. "I didn't mean to leave that impression."

This time, it was Angie who bored in on him. "Leaving good impressions is obviously not one of your strong suits, Dr. Dandurall."

The fey confidence of the auburn-haired dandy who'd waltzed into the room a few minutes ago was now nowhere in view. Genuine humility could be close behind.

Dr. Dandurall ran one hand through his copious hair, turned sideways in his chair, and looked more defeated than

Napoleon at Waterloo. "What would you like to know about our little research company?"

Angie had the con, and unless I thought of something, I wasn't going to interrupt. She was scratching the palm of one hand with the nail of the index finger of the other one. Back and forth, at a snail's pace. I knew she often did that when she was thinking.

When she was ready, she'd use all the fingers of the scratching hand to give the hand being scratched a symbolic wipe-off and tell us what was on her mind. I'd no more than thought about it than here it came. "What is it, exactly, that your company does?"

Dandurall cleared his throat. "Well, we do . . . ah . . . designer babies."

Angie shifted her head down and stared at the doctor as if she were wearing bifocals and needed to correct for distance. "I do enjoy interviews that get straight to the point. Really? Designer babies?"

Dandurall answered by bobbing his head once.

I knew Angie was only getting started. "And you do that how?"

"Well, we've learned how to do things with male DNA."

Her response was dripping with sarcasm. "Okay, let me guess — you've created a new Tinkertoy design and named it Daddy's Natural Assets. And, naturally, called it DNA for short."

Dandurall appeared to have misread the sarcasm. "Not a half-bad analogy."

Angie smiled. "Look, this FBI lady barely passed high school biology. Mind getting to the point."

"Sure. We've found a way to keep male sperm from committing suicide."

"And doing that helps you design babies?"

"It does. Before, you couldn't use all the father's DNA in fertilizing the egg. Some of it would self-destruct the moment it got in the egg. Now, we can use it."

"This sounds like it's all under-the-microscope stuff."

"Yes, but there are practical consequences."

"Such as?"

"We can sometimes take DNA from the strangest places and use it to — like I say — design a baby."

"A 'for example,' please. Take DNA from where?"

"Well, bones and teeth, mainly. Sometimes, very old bones and teeth." He followed with a broad smile as if he'd said something funny. Or clever.

Angie and I learned more in five minutes about the mitochondrial nitty-gritty, as Dandurall called it at one point, than we ever wanted to know. But there were other issues of interest to me in all this.

I dipped my head slightly and put a question to Dandurall. "Why did such cutting-edge stuff end up being done here?"

"Don't forget — I went to undergraduate school here. And grew up on a ranch near Munday. That's about ninety miles north of here."

"I know where Munday is. And then you went off to big boys' school?"

"I went to Cambridge — in England."

"I know where Cambridge is too. And I'm going to bet I know what you studied."

"Be my guest."

"The classics."

Once again, he seemed to be reassessing his interrogator or nemesis or gamesmanship opponent or however he was viewing me. That, at least, is how I interpreted the new sharpness in his gaze. "You're right. At least, I did study the classics at first. How'd you know that?"

"Oh, you just have the look."

"The look?"

"Yeah, you know what they say about the classics. The study of dead white men by live white men."

That brought another chuckle from him. But he didn't try to one-up my riposte. "I studied the classics for a year. Then I switched back to my undergraduate major and got a PhD in biology. But you really want to know why I based our company here?"

I'd been a smart-ass one too many times already today. I let a couple of expectant eye blinks be my answer.

"The pilots."

"How did you know about the pilots?"

"I'd spotted their office when I came back to attend a Hills-U alumni thing. Saw it in the airport lobby."

"Why did the pilots interest you?"

"As you put it, I knew we were going to have a lot of contraband" — he used two fingers on each hand to form quotation marks around the word — "to be transported."

"Like suicide-resistant sperm? Not to mention a new infant and his mother."

"Maybe."

"And Flagler wouldn't be all that long a flight from Guadalajara."

He wasn't expecting such geographical specificity. Or expecting to be asked to incriminate himself so clearly. But he didn't try to change the subject. "You know why we did the procedure in Guadalajara, don't you?"

"Sure. Because it's illegal in the States."

"It is. And that's a shame. A lot of infertile couples could be helped by it."

"But that isn't the whole story, is it?"

"Pardon me?"

"Well, correct me if I'm wrong, but we've just touched the tip of the iceberg."

"Iceberg about what?"

"About—"

The reason for my sudden pause was the flood of adrenaline entering my bloodstream. For the first time in long minutes, I remembered there was a third person in the room. And from the look on her face, she was not wanting me to go where I'd been intending to go. So I didn't.

I shut the conversation down by implying this was enough for one day, told him not to leave town without telling me, and had a sudden desire to do something that brought some joy and light into my life.

Like introduce Angie to the newest occupant of my house.

CHAPTER 43

At the country club, we hadn't ordered anything to eat. This meant the food smells wafting from the facility's kitchen had gradually become a slow torture.

The moment Dr. Dandurall scurried from the room, I told Angie I had someone I wanted to introduce to her and asked her to meet me at my house. I told her I was going to stop and pick up burgers.

Once I was in my patrol cruiser, I called Helen and asked her if she could drop Fresca off at my place on her way home. I checked to see if she wanted a burger too. She said thanks but no. She already had supper plans. But she and Fresca were on their way.

When I reached my house, Angie was already parked where my sidewalk meets the curb. I motioned for her to speed up her dismount. I wanted to get her inside before we dealt with introductions. And smells.

But, as usual, she had her own ideas about how things should proceed.

As she greeted me on the porch, she reached for the bag of hamburgers, opened it wide enough to eyeball the contents, took a sniff, and said, "Yummy!" She began manipulating the burgers in the sack so she could do a count and drew in a sharp breath. "Six! So, we're having a bunch of guests you didn't tell me about?"

"I did tell you I had somebody for you to meet."

"You did. I take it they're already inside."

"Well, no. But they'll be here shortly."

"More than one person, it would appear."

"No, you shouldn't think that."

"Then the only other thing I can think of is that Jude the Dude Mayes is home from Harvard, and he's been invited to join us for burgers."

I smiled at her. "They don't call you a good detective for nothing. But no, the double-meat-cheeseburger-eating king of Abbot County won't be dining with us. At least not the two-legged one."

She let her face drop in feigned disappointment. "Well, the suspense is killing me. Not to mention, the odors."

As I ushered Angie through my front door, I saw Helen pull into the driveway.

The dog was staring at me through the raised door window in the back seat. His ears were rigid enough to be fly traps — that is to say, on high alert. I couldn't see that tail, but I knew it was busier than a windshield wiper in a Texas thunderstorm. And all this was before he got a whiff of what I had in the sack.

I called Angie back to the door and handed her the burgers. I asked her to stick them in the oven and signaled Helen not to go to the bother of getting out of the car. I'd extract my gargantuan mixed-blood mongrel from her back seat myself.

With both the smell of the burgers and Angie's unfamiliar scent for him to process, I gripped his leash tighter than usual. Walked him to the front door. Gave it a gentle push with my leg to allow him a clear view of what was inside. And invited him to go first.

He took one look at Angie and gave the leash a strong tug. He insisted on closing the distance between us and her in record time. He parked on his haunches without any order to sit from me, extended his paw, and waited for her to shake it. She did.

Then she announced it was time for burgers. Said we'd be doing it picnic-style. "Here in the living room."

This was why we consumed our evening meal seated on my living room rug. With three plates. Two normal-sized ones, each holding one burger with all the toppings and trimmings. Those were for Angie and me. And one steak-sized platter holding four burgers with only meat and cheese. Angie had quartered each of them and arranged the pieces in two rows with two layers each.

When we were finished, Fresca had a drink and went for his usual toilet break. Then we all retired to my sofa.

"I take it that space belongs to him." Angie was glancing over at my massive dog. He was in his usual position on the short end of my two-piece sectional.

As was also customary, his head was burrowed into one of my plush throw cushions. Only one of his eyes had a clear view out of the pillow, but it was not missing anything going on in the room.

That was also customary.

Maybe I'd been thinking about doing this for a while and hadn't realized it. The thought may have become even more acute after I read an article online about the order Carnivora, family Canidae, tribe Canini, subspecies domestic dog, subcategory home-body pets that shed on your carpet and settee and poop on your grass.

My buddy-to-be was a distant descendant of wolves. His far-ancient ancestors had been smart enough to domesticate themselves, thank you. All they'd had to do was enjoy our food scraps for a while, and they realized where their bread was buttered best. When our own far-ancient ancestors had understood what good predator alarms — and buddies! — they made, the love affair was on. Now that my new buddy was firmly ensconced on my couch, I knew I'd become one of the pack.

I was rubbing Angie's bare feet. Both were in my lap. It was a courtesy I often extended to the special agent assigned to the FBI's fifteen-county West Texas region. It often led to other intimacies that I enjoyed even more. "Don't really know. But you'd better not try to sit on that end of my sofa. Not unless you want a hundred pounds of non-American-Kennel-Club-registered dog flesh in your lap.

"I prefer a shih tzu in my lap, thank you."

"I would have settled for a pure breed pug. But I couldn't find a homeless man who had one."

Angie was still watching Fresca. "How long will it take him to sail off in a wooden shoe?"

I didn't answer right away because of her choice of words. I hadn't heard anyone talk of sailing off in a wooden shoe since my grandmother had died. And that had happened when I was ten years old.

My Gran had liked to read "Wynken, Blynken, and Nod" to my younger sister and me at bedtime. "It usually takes him a minute or two after he's licked his chops for the final time. But let's see if a little out-of-date children's poetry will speed the process."

To Angie's consternation — and mine — I recited the closing stanza of the famous children's poem.

Wynken and Blynken are two little eyes,
And Nod is a little head,
And the wooden shoe that sailed the skies
Is a wee one's trundle-bed.
So shut your eyes while Mother sings
Of wonderful sights that be,
And you shall see the beautiful things

As you rock in the misty sea,
Where the old shoe rocked the fishermen three:
Wynken,
Blynken,
And Nod.

When we looked over at Fresca again, the eye was shut. The snores came soon after. My observation wasn't needed, but I offered it anyway. "My dog likes old-fashioned poetry."

Angie moved one foot up to nuzzle the side of my jaw. "So does the future mother of your children."

We couldn't do this intimacy thing much longer. I needed to talk about other topics. But the question was out of mouth before I could stop it. "How many are we going to have?"

"How many what?"

"Children. How many?"

She pulled her foot back, sat up on the sofa, slipped both legs under her, and turned to face me. "How about three?"

"Why three?"

"Well, we've already got their names."

"Really?"

"Sure. We'll name them after the fishermen. Wynkyn McWhorter, Blynken McWhorter, and Nod McWhorter."

"Even if they are girls?"

"Well, if they're girls, we'll name them Wynkynia McWhorter, Blynkenette McWhorter, and Nodella McWhorter."

She giggled.

I loved to hear her do that. But enough was enough. I needed her to get serious. I needed to get serious.

I had a double murder to solve.

She hadn't mentioned it yet, but I knew Angie was still feeling pressures herself. She needed to assure powers-that-be ranging all the way from Flagler City Hall to 934 Pennsylvania Avenue NW, and very possibly down the street to that other

Pennsylvania Avenue address, that dangerous things were not being shipped into Abbot County. Or being shipped out. "You have any idea where Dr. Bender and Nina Kendricks have gone?"

We moved from naming unborn children into possibly naming national secrets in less time than it would take to wink, blink, or nod.

"I did get some information from the CIA's counterintelligence office."

This surprised me. "They've got people watching Bender and Kendricks?"

She pinched her lower lip before answering. Then sat up straighter on the sofa. "They did have. But they lost track of them."

"Mind telling me where?"

"Jerusalem."

"The Jerusalem!"

"Yes, that one. But then that's not quite accurate either. Agents saw them get on the shuttle bus from Ben Gurion Airport in Tel Aviv to Jerusalem, but they didn't see them get off."

"The agents didn't get on the shuttle bus with them?"

"Didn't have time. Bender and Kendricks seemed to realize they were being watched. Hopped on the shuttle with their luggage at the very last moment."

"But somebody had snoops watching to see if they got off in Jerusalem?"

"They did. They were expecting them to get off at Central Bus Station, but they didn't get that far. The driver said they'd asked him to stop and let them off as soon as he reached Jerusalem City limits. He normally didn't do that, but I got the idea that bakshish was involved. He said they had somebody waiting for them, but he couldn't offer any description."

"So where could they go from Jerusalem City?"

"About anywhere. Amman, Baghdad, Riyadh, Tehran, Kabul — lots of other places if they wanted to ride a camel."

"So your intel people don't know where they went after that?"

"They don't."

"What about Pogue Stockstill's metal box — the intel people have any interest in that?"

"Lots of interest. They're getting a warrant to pick it up. They want to see if they can find any traces of what's been in it."

"And Stockstill? They interested in talking to him?"

"That too. A couple of the bureau's top counterintelligence people will be here tomorrow."

"So the bureau's still seeing this as some kind of foreign spy thing?"

"Maybe."

That said, she stretched back out on my couch, dragged another of my plush pillows behind her head, put her feet in my lap again, and yawned. "You ask too many questions. All this work makes Jack a very dull boy. Jill a dull girl too."

She closed her eyes.

Of the three warm bodies who fell asleep on my sofa, mine was the only one that moved to a bed in the middle of the night.

I covered Angie with a sheet and left her with her dreams of Wynkynia, Blynkenette, and Nodella. Like most dogs, Fresca didn't like the idea of being covered. He'd scoot out from under anything thrown over him. Paw it for a while. Get it just right. Then lay down on top of it.

CHAPTER 44

Angie and I were seated on stools at my kitchen cabinet bar — close to finishing up our waffles and cheese-and-bacon omelets — when her phone beeped.

She read the text message and hurried into the bathroom to apply a dash of lipstick. When she returned to the kitchen, she'd strapped on her shoulder harness and gun.

She was gone so fast all I got was a kiss blown in my direction off the ends of her extended fingers. *Annie Get Your Gun* came to mind. That would make me sharpshooter Frank E. Butler, Miss Oakley's boyfriend. I knew Miss Oakley would either call or text Mr. Butler and let him know what was going on when she got a chance.

I'd already headed for the office when I decided to make a side trip. It really wasn't out of the way because the office of the medical examiner was only a couple of blocks away from the courthouse.

One of the detectives I'd assigned to the murder case could have gone instead — and one of them might already have done so. But the county's voluble, Greek-born ME was one of my favorite people. When I had a legitimate chance to visit her, I usually did. Sometimes, I dropped by without waiting to have a good reason.

These visits to what Dr. Konstantina Smyth — Doc Konnie, to her friends — called her industrial kitchen were always informative. More than that, they were invariably entertaining.

The moment I pushed open the swinging metal-clad doors to her autopsy room, I knew this was not going to be an exception.

She was belting out the lyrics to something. I couldn't tell if it was meant to be soft rock, hard rock, blues, folk, country, or soul. With Doc Konnie, everything sounded about the same.

I caught a few words. Had to do with something that was missing and she didn't know what it was or how to fix it.

She invited me into her office, moved a half-empty box of sugar-coated donuts to the other end of her sofa, and motioned for me to sit.

"John Mayer's 'Something's Missing,'" she informed me before I could ask. "A lament, neh? He's got it all — money, friends, girlfriend, people to love him. But it's not there, this something. It's gone, and he not even know what it is. But that not a problem for me. I know what I missing, dear Sheriff. A hand. Yassou, a hand I am missing."

"You are referring to the pilots, I assume."

"Neh, they are in the cooler." I'd known ever since graduate school that the Greek word for yes looked like "neh" in our alphabet. And sounded like "no" to English-speaking ears. She'd said, yes, the dead pilots were in the cooler. "But not the missing hand. One pilot, his right hand — vamoosed. Not to be. The boys say they looked up every skirt in the hanger. Did not find it."

I knew her ME technicians hadn't gone looking up any skirts at the hangar. They'd simply done their usual exhaustive survey of body parts, body fluids, and other body traces. And apparently were unable to locate one of the pilot's hands.

No one at the office had mentioned this, so I now knew none of my people had yet talked with Doc Konnie. If they had, word about this development would have almost certainly gotten to me.

Doc Konnie was notable in the Abbot County law enforcement community for four things: her acute observational skills, her love for pop and country music, her mangling of the English language, and her appetite.

I declined a donut. "So our killers had to have taken it with them?"

She wiped her fingers on a napkin. "The hand?"

"Yes, the hand."

"Neh, that I would think."

"You ever have this happen before?"

"Not even in the full blood of the moon."

I wanted the opinion of the nationally respected forensic pathologist who occupied the Abbot County medical examiner's office. Why would a killer have taken off with the severed hand of one of his or her victims. "Any ideas about what it might mean?"

She seemed to move her whole upper body when she shook her head. "So we storm the brain, eh?"

"A good idea. Let's brainstorm."

"You do your write pad, neh."

"Yes, I'll take notes."

"So you write this . . . 'Because it there.'"

"Sorry, because what's there?"

"The hand, Sheriff, dear. The hand. People who make a crime often want souvenir. Maybe hand was souvenir. So he took it. Because it there."

I wrote her idea down. "Because it was there." This wasn't exactly what I was wanting from the ME, but it was a start.

When I looked up, she was watching me patiently. "Now, your turn."

"To show it to someone. Proof of action, so to speak."

"That a good one. You ready?"

"Righto."

"To run tests."

"Tests?"

"Like us ME does. Blood tests. To prove no should be flying plane, maybe, neh."

My turn. I hadn't wanted our brainstorming to get too serious too quickly, and it looked like it wasn't going to. I decided to make things even goofier.

"To practice painting his nails."

That brought a giggle from the ME and sent her fishing for something equally zany. "Ah, let's see . . . So wife could try cannibalism recipe."

And we were off and running.

I didn't cheat. I always looked her in the eye when I delivered an idea. Only after she acknowledged it in some way did I write it down. "To impress the boss."

As she often did, she piggybacked on my idea. "Bring somebody fear."

I decided to try something in egregious bad taste. "Take to kids' show-and-tell at school."

Doc Konnie didn't have children, but she knew bad taste when she heard it. "Etch! You to marry that pretty FBI agent, neh? She need to know about your back side." She meant my *dark* side. But she had one too. "Scare wife when she open refrigerator."

I suggested maybe the killers sold jewelry. They planned to embalm the hand and put it in a case to help display their rings.

She said maybe they were soldiers who wanted to show their troops how dangerous war could be.

I suggested one of the killers might never have liked his hand, so he was going to attach the new one.

She suggested maybe one of the killers had a hidden gentle streak and wanted to give the hand a nice burial.

And that's where we left it.

I thanked her for helping the local sheriff storm the brain and said we needed to go to lunch some day soon.

I had already reached the lobby of her office when I had an idea. Maybe we shouldn't mention the missing hand to anyone quite yet. This way, someone might let a reference to it slip. Then we'd have a suspect.

I walked back into Doc Konnie's autopsy room, and she agreed to leave any mention of pilot No. 1's missing hand out of her report for now. She gave me a hug and walked me to the door.

As I headed down the hallway to the parking lot door, I realized she had begun to warble another C&W song. At least, I assumed it was a C&W song.

I extended a hand to her, suggesting she could always count on that hand to be there, that any time she needed a friend, she could count on the hand to lift her up again. Or words to that effect.

When I got back to the office, I checked on Google to see if there was such a song as "Put Your Hand in Mine." There it was. Recorded by C&W singer Tracey Byrd in the late nineties.

Reading about it gave me an idea about the dead pilot's missing hand. What if it was going to be thrust into the face of someone who didn't know it was coming?

Or maybe it already had been.

The missing hand might have stayed on my mind longer if not for what I noticed as I approached the door to our department office suite.

I had another unannounced visitor.

CHAPTER 45

This one didn't appear to be a law officer. At least, he wasn't wearing a uniform or, as best I could tell, carrying a gun. I wasn't sure what he had on his mind, but from the serious look on his face, I was about to find out.

When he saw me, he shot to his feet and extended his hand. Said his name was Christoph Ebner. Suggested I call him Chris. And asked if I could spare a little time.

I gave him the sheriff's standard lightning-swift eyeball-once-over and told him I'd need a minute.

He looked older than my recent visitor from Guadalajara. And, unlike the Mexican police chief, he was clean-shaven, but he was still into the hirsute look.

His dark brown hair had receded enough to leave his forehead as exposed as the end of a watermelon. But his hair tumbled away from the crown of his head everywhere else and plunged to his shoulders, where it started to curl upward. It came around almost to his chin on both sides.

His mouth was a bit on the small side. It was locked in a smile that I guessed remained no matter what his mood. Because he didn't seem to be in a smiling mood at this moment.

Fresca was watching all this. He was stretched out in his bed on the far side of Helen's desk. He hadn't taken his eyes off our visitor.

Helen edged her chair closer to the end of her desk. I lowered my head so she could whisper in my ear. "He says he needs to talk to you about a missing box."

I straightened. Stood immobile for a moment, allowed the upper part of my body to do a half-turn, looked at him again, and wondered if my first appraisal of him had been too swift. Too casual. Too careless.

Was this stranger another bit player in Bender's and Kendricks's never-ending potboiler of a drama? Or was he something else? Like a danger of some kind?

Helen was watching me closely. One nod from me, and I knew she'd push the panic button under her desk, bringing every deputy in our ready room flying through the door again, guns drawn. I shook my head and thought for an instant about what I could do to lower the tension. I decided to ask my visitor if he'd like a cup of coffee. When he said he would, I waved him toward my office as Helen headed for the kitchen.

I invited him to sit at my anemic little conference table. Before joining him, I reached in a drawer of my desk and extracted a folder containing reproductions of the photographs Special Agent Knoke had shown me. I selected the one showing the box being loaded into the pilots' plane and gave it a gentle shove toward my visitor. "Can I assume this is the box you're concerned about?"

He picked up the photo. Lowered his head slightly. Gave it a long glance. Raised his eyes to stare at me without any accompanying movement of his head or any change of the expression on his face. Looked back at the photo again. Then glanced at me with what I read as a look of resignation. Perhaps, even defeat. "Perhaps we should start again."

He took his wallet out of one of his back pants pockets and removed a business card. It identified him as Christoph Ebner, PhD, Mummy Preservation Expert, Western Austria Museum of Anthropology, Innsbruck, Austria.

"The box in the photograph interests me. But I'm more interested in the box I built to preserve a mummy. The box was shipped to Flagler, then went missing. The people at the Austrian consulate in Houston said I should contact the sheriff. Which is you, I believe."

I pointed to the box in the photo. "Is your box bigger than this?"

"You shouldn't think of my box being like this."

"So how should I think of it?"

"Like a large refrigerator laying on its side — only one you can see into from all the sides. And from the top."

"So it's a display case."

"Well, more than a display case. It's actually an elaborate preservation unit that keeps a mummy's body frozen at a precise temperature and humidity."

"That sounds expensive."

"It is."

"Where was your case shipped to in Flagler originally?"

"To 7 Days: The Experience, the museum and amusement park."

"Your mummy too?"

"No, I didn't ship my mummy. It's too valuable. I shipped an extra preservation and display unit like the one I built for Tito, the Ancient One — the mummy at our museum in Austria. I built an extra display unit as a backup."

At this juncture in our conversation, the ah-hahs began to arrive. The biggest one was realizing the box in my photo had a much more complicated history than I'd had any reason to suspect. And now there was another box, if you wanted to call it that, in the picture.

My visitor said Tito, the Ancient One, had been found in an ice cave near the edge of a glacier in the Alps in western Austria. He was believed to be the oldest mummy ever found in reasonable enough condition for scientists to study it in detail. And they'd been doing that at his museum and institute ever since.

I knew it was time for another visit to 7 Days: The Experience. This time, I'd insist Roberts let me see behind the drapes in the Day 5 wing. I had little doubt about what I was going to see there.

But I was wrong.

CHAPTER 46

On my previous visit to 7 Days: The Experience, I hadn't been able to see what was inside the Day 5 wing at all because of the ceiling-high, wall-to-wall drapes.

And if the drapes, hanging from an elaborate pipe scaffolding, hadn't been obstacle enough, Roberts had two armed guards pacing back and forth in front of them.

This time, his receptionist said Roberts was out of town. It didn't matter. This time, I had a warrant, which I gave to her. But this time, the guards in front of the Day 5 wing were gone. Not the coarse, white canvas drapes, though. They were still there.

I stood watching them for a moment. Occasionally, a ripple would start across them only to die out as quickly as it had arrived. Other times, the drapes would catch a breeze — like sails on a ship — and billow outward slightly before collapsing back on themselves.

Between two of the curtains, I found a split that my chief deputy and I could ease through. We went in single file and knew in an instant why the drapes were so huge.

They were intended to keep curious, prying eyes from seeing something even larger.

A full-sized replica of Noah's Ark.

Del Emma whistled. "We've just stumbled into God's toy workshop."

I liked his analogy. "Can't be Santa's. Saint Nick would never get that thing down a chimney."

"He'd have problems long before he got to that point."

"Too big a task for his and his elves' skills?"

"Probably that too. But he'd never get his elves to build it without forming a union."

The object was clearly eye candy created for its shock value. And it worked. Even though the space was huge, the vessel still looked monstrous.

The cabin structure running about two-thirds of the length of the upper ship made it look even larger, a bit like an elongated Chinese pagoda.

Both the bow and stern of the ship were stunning examples of carpentry. The planks at each end of the craft curved ever so slightly upward as they approached two Bunyanesque cutwaters, one at the prow and one at the rear. Overall, the effect was an extraordinary symmetry.

The gangplank connected with the deck about mid-ship. Walking along it in orderly fashion, behaving harmoniously as all God's creations should, were pairs of every living thing you could imagine — and some I wouldn't have.

I could identify goats, sheep, cattle, pigs, lions, eagles, ravens — species the Bible frequently mentions. Giraffes, elephants, gorillas, hippos, kangaroos, cats, and dogs, which the Bible doesn't. Plus exotic creatures that could only have been a figment of some Hollywood special effects studio's wildest dreams. The garish fiberglass zoo of creatures zigzagging up the incline left no room for anyone to walk aboard.

The huge, jaunty marquee-type sign suspended above the ship was unnecessary but apt. *Mother Ship of the World's First Zookeeper.* If nothing else, you could credit Craft Roberts with turning over every imaginable, exploitable stone. The display was going to be irresistible to museum visitors, even the Biblical skeptics.

My deputy chief walked over to the boat and ran his fingers along its gleaming surface. "This thing's as carefully lacquered as a violin."

I touched the splendid finish myself. "God said to build it of gopher wood. But I think this is pine."

"What's gopher wood?"

"Bible commentators have never been exactly sure. Could even have been pine."

This was when my deputy chief spoke up. "It's all so over-the-top. Why is Roberts so uptight about anyone seeing his Noah's Ark replica?"

I kicked that around for a moment. "Maybe there's more to see."

We'd noticed that Day 5 wasn't confined simply to one large open space. Both sides of the expansive chamber had doors spaced like meeting rooms opening off in a conference hotel's central lobby.

All of them needed to be checked.

We decided to start on the left-hand side of the chamber because those doors were closest.

At the first one, I twisted the nob and pushed the door open. Del Emma and I found ourselves staring into near-total darkness. I found a light switch, flicked it on, and we both blinked hard from the sudden glare.

The room was empty.

Not a chair.

Or even a wastebasket.

We tried all the doors on the left-hand side. None was locked. And all the rooms were empty. Nothing in them at all. Only blackness — and total silence.

Same thing on the right side.

After a long while, we approached the final door and heard a muffled thud. It sounded as if something heavy had been dropped a small distance. Instead of making a sharp clanking noise when it hit the concrete floor, it had made a dull clunk. Its landing had to have been cushioned.

We both froze in place and listened hard. Hearing nothing more, we drew our weapons, and I eased the door open.

CHAPTER 47

The first thing to grab our attention was the large, brightly lit display case. It hogged the middle of the room.

At almost the same instant, we noticed something else. A woman was kneeling about halfway down the side of the glass case. She'd taken a ball-peen hammer out of her purse, then apparently dropped it. It had landed on her purse, then slipped off onto the floor. That had to have been what made the noise Del Emma and I had heard.

It was Dr. Adele Lovejoy, the dean of the Hills-U Bible Department. She had her hands pressed together, and the tips of her fingers were touching her chin.

I holstered my weapon. My mind made a judgment so quickly I didn't have time to remind it to be ecumenical.

Very Catholic-looking pose.

For certain, not a pose I'd ever have expected from the very Protestant dean of the Bible Department at one of Flagler's very evangelical-minded Bible colleges. Those places didn't have a Catholic bone in their body. And we Protestants tended to pray sitting up. Or standing.

Then I realized she wasn't praying. She was reciting.

And I recognized the passage.

It was the second of the seven so-called Penitential Psalms. King David's Psalm 32. This was a favorite of almost every Old Testament professor I'd ever taken a class from. And my homiletics professors had often recommended it as a sermon text.

Del Emma and I hadn't arrived in time to hear the first seven stanzas. So we were hearing the rejoicing part. The grateful psalmist was exulting at having a Lord who offers mercy to those who find righteousness and trust in him.

The dean was speaking in the dulcet tones of someone who had come to terms with herself and her malfeasances. Like someone at peace. At least, that was the initial feeling I got as I listened to her.

To the end, her voice, if subdued, remained serene and certain. And, inerrant to the text.

> I will instruct you and show you the way you should walk,
> give you counsel with my eye upon you.
>
> Do not be like a horse or mule, without understanding;
> with bit and bridle their temper is curbed,
> else they will not come to you.
>
> Many are the sorrows of the wicked one,
> but mercy surrounds the one who trusts in the Lord.
>
> Be glad in the Lord and rejoice, you righteous;
> exult, all you upright of heart.

I ran a quick eye over the case.

Just as Dr. Ebner had described, the sides and top of the hefty-looking affair were made almost entirely of glass. That afforded the onlooker an unobstructed view of nearly everything inside. That, of course, was the point.

I could see four slender metal poles, two on each side. They extended from the case's top to its bottom. Each one had a series of flexible extensions clamped on it. At the tip of each of these extensions was a shiny metal instrument.

I assumed these to be sensors. Maybe to measure the temperature inside. Or humidity levels. Or gaseous conditions. Or all three.

I didn't know.

But it was clear that the creator or creators of this unusual apparatus had intended it to be protective of something greatly valued.

That prized object had to be the one lying in full view on a shiny steel, roller-equipped table sitting inside the device.

I'd seen conveyances like this one many times in the Abbot County medical examiner's autopsy room. And, if not there, pushed against a wall in Flagler General Hospital's ED. Nearly always, unless they were sitting empty, they were occupied by a lifeless body, covered by a sheet.

A corpse.

This one wasn't.

The figure occupying this one was not covered by anything. It was lying there in its birthday suit, scrunched over on its side.

The dean glanced at me, waiting to see my reaction. "They're saying it's Noah's."

She took my silence for what it was — an indication of how confused I was. So she offered more information. "The mummy. They're saying it came off Mount Ararat in Turkey. They're saying it's Noah's mummy."

I was still struggling. "Who's saying it's Noah's mummy?"

"All of them. Dr. Bender, Nina Kendricks, Dr. Dandurall. Craft Roberts. The dead pilots said so too. The whole ugly, avaricious, thoughtless lot of them. They're all evil to the core. And they're all going to burn in hell for trying to steal Flagler's soul."

I let her outburst reverberate in my ears. And thought more about it.

The sentences were coherent. That's to say, the grammar was correct. Polished, in fact. And there was a logical flow to her ideas. But considered in total, the only way to describe it was lunacy.

It made absolutely no sense at all.

As the silence in the room grew, she turned to face me. For the first time since stepping into the room, I was able to get a good look at her eyes. And the thought was all over me in a flash.

The dean was verging on madness. She'd been agitated the last time I saw her — but I'd thought it had been a rational response to events in Flagler.

I'd wanted to ask her if she knew anything about the deaths of the two pilots. Or where Dr. Bender and Nina Kendricks had gone — or why. What did she know about this mummy? Where had it really come from? What was it doing in Flagler? And who was responsible for it being here?

Maybe, I'd still get to do all that. But all I could think about was getting the dean to Flagler General Hospital. She needed to be admitted to the psychiatric unit.

Once I got that hammered, I wanted a further word with Dr. Christoph Ebner about preserving mummies.

Especially this one.

CHAPTER 48

One of my deputies found Ebner at the South Breeze Motel. I phoned to ask if he'd eaten. He hadn't. So I suggested I pick him up and we go to dinner at one of my favorite restaurants.

Carmichaels Steak House was also one of Flagler's nicer restaurants. I took people there when I wanted to impress them. Or wanted something from them. Or both. By the time Ebner and I finished our salads, I'd almost forgotten my professional motives for arranging the meal. He was smart. Congenial. Seemed to be open and candid. Interesting beyond his value to my investigation. I genuinely liked the guy.

Prior to this trip, he said his knowledge of Texas had come mostly from watching the movie *The Outlaw Josey Wales*. That, and reruns of *Dallas* with his mother-in-law.

I told him I'd never managed to get into the swing of *Dallas*. I'd met too many characters in real life like J.R. and Sue Allen Ewing to find their TV exploits entertaining. But I said that Clint Eastwood's movie was one of my favorites too.

Eventually, we got around to the subject of mummies. I asked whether he thought someone had found Noah's mummy.

He smiled. "Well, there are rumors."

I didn't want him to take this too lightly, so I didn't return the smile. "But you don't think Noah has been inside either of the boxes that have created such a ruckus in Flagler?"

"You want me to be honest?"

"I'd love to put you under oath on the question."

"Well, if you did, my answer would still be the same."

"And that would be . . ."

"Truth be told, I don't know what has been in those boxes, even the one I built."

"So can we go back to my original question — do you think anyone has found Noah's mummy."

There was the smile again. "Not really. But if he's lying up there alone on Mount Ararat, I hope somebody finds him soon."

I thought coming at the subject from a different angle might give me an idea of where to go next. "So you doubt there ever was a Noah?"

"Well, it's what scientists do, you know."

"Doubt?"

"Always."

"So you've researched Noah's mummy?"

"Not his mummy. But I'm okay with the idea that there was probably a Noah."

"You can probably get into Sunday School with that."

"No Sunday School classes in Austria. It was catechism classes or nothing. In my case, nothing. My parents were atheists."

"You're one too?"

"More like agnostic. Too curious to be an atheist."

"So where do you get your information about religion?"

"The internet . . . mostly Wikipedia."

He said he'd found the subject of Noah and the Ark more interesting than he'd anticipated. And noted that Genesis wasn't the only ancient account of the great ship builder's exploits. In fact, in his opinion, the Genesis account didn't even rank as one of the most interesting ones.

I remembered some of the other accounts from my Old Testament classes but was fuzzy on the details. I welcomed Ebner's freshening of the story. "There's something called the *Midrash*. It says Noah was late one day feeding the lions on the Ark and one of them bit him in the leg and severely injured him."

I was familiar with the *Midrash*. Another of those traditional Jewish Biblical commentaries. But I hadn't opened one of its volumes since graduate school, and I couldn't remember ever consulting it about Noah.

I went straight to the obvious question. "You've closely examined the leg of the mummy we saw in the case, of course."

"There's no need to examine it closely."

"You can tell if there is a leg injury through the glass?"

"You'd be able to see it plain as day, even if you didn't know to look for it. This mummy doesn't have one. And if it had been Noah's mummy, there'd have been even more to see."

"More injuries?"

"More distinguishing characteristics."

He told me about *The Book of Enoch* — another ancient Jewish commentary. Tradition said it had been written by one of Noah's great-grandfathers. I knew that, but what I didn't remember ever hearing was what Ebner told me next. He said *The Book of Enoch* seemed to claim that Noah was an albino.

I did a double take. "Say that again?"

Ebner was getting more relaxed at recounting his tale. "I remember the exact quote. 'White as snow, and red as a rose; the hair of whose head was white like wool, and long, and whose eyes were beautiful.'"

He added that if Noah's mummy was ever found, confirming his albinism wouldn't be difficult. "If you can't tell with a quick glance, I think you can test the mummy's DNA. In fact, it would surprise me if this hasn't already been done on the mummy in the case."

I asked him why he thought this.

He said he suspected this mummy and its preservation case hadn't been at Craft Roberts's museum for very long after its arrival. "I think Roberts found some folks who wanted to test the mummy's DNA. And he loaned it to them — for a substantial sum, of course. And decided not to pay me until he knew where the mummy was going to end up."

After that, my new friend, Dr. Chris Ebner, mummy preserver par excellence, and I ordered dessert. He had another cuppa joe. I had another iced tea. Then I asked if he'd like to watch the latest Clint Eastwood movie on my TV's streaming service before I took him back to his motel.

He said he would. But we never got around to turning on the TV at my house, much less watching the movie. We soon realized we hadn't come close to exhausting everything there was to be said about a certain museum and amusement park owner and a certain mummy.

CHAPTER 49

The longer we talked, the more I realized Craft Roberts had loomed far brighter on Ebner's radar than he had on mine.

I also realized the talented museum official from Austria was more than a mummy preserver. He was also an accomplished mummy detective.

For one thing, he'd sniffed out what Roberts had actually been planning all along with his Noah props. "He's been planning an exhibit called The Sea Captain Who Saved God from Himself."

It took an extra half-second to get my head around that. "Oh, that's cheeky."

Ebner acknowledged as much. "But right on point. The 'saving God from himself' part, I mean."

"So you and Roberts talked about all this at length?"

"Well, on complicated projects, I like to know what the client is thinking."

"And what did you decide?"

"I remember the exact moment I realized how much thought he'd put into his Noah exhibit. He said we were all fortunate that Noah knew how to use a hammer and saw and that his loyalty to his God had been so strong. Otherwise, the whole human experiment would have gone down the drain when the Almighty got hacked off. Literally."

That was about as good a summation of the Bible's Noah account as I could remember hearing.

But this was neither the time nor place for Bible stories. At the moment, I had the undivided attention of a world-class expert on mummies. And he'd learned more about a mummy in our midst in his first day in Flagler than I was going to learn in a week of probing.

He wasn't revealing his sources — at least not yet. But he began to tell me some of what he'd been told.

Ebner said its modern history could be traced to the melting of the glacial fields on Mount Ararat.

According to experts, in the past forty years, the glaciers had shrunken almost thirty percent because of global warming.

This had exposed parts of the mountain that had been covered in snow and ice for thousands of years. One of those areas was the upper Parrot Glacier.

This glacier was well above 15,000 feet high on Masis's — Ararat's — north side.

"They found the mummy lodged under a rock outcropping encased in a kind of large ice cube."

"Who found it?"

"Couple of mountaineers. People climb Masis year-round, you know. It's almost like an amusement park for the Crampons Crowd."

"And the mummy had been there for more than four thousand years?"

"That's what they've concluded. The outcropping had kept it out of the clutches of the glaciers. Otherwise, over the centuries, it would have been chewed to bits. And the cold — the top of Masis is snow-covered year-round — kept it frozen."

That explanation cleared up some of my confusion but

more took its place. "You're telling me they found the mummy last fall and didn't move it all winter?"

He confirmed this. "They kept the location a secret."

"But why wait until September to bring the mummy out? Why didn't they do it in early summer?"

"It took that long for Roberts's agents to handle the bribes."

"Bribes for whom?"

"Officials in the region. They had to get them to agree to a price for allowing the mummy to be helicoptered off the mountain. And then to agree to allow your dead pilots to fly to Ağrı and load it. Then fly it out of the country to Flagler."

"Why didn't Roberts's people rent their own helicopter?"

"Only the Turkish military is allowed to fly helicopters on Mount Ararat. And there is the problem of the PKK — the Kurdistan Workers' Party. They infest the mountain in many locations above 6,500 feet. And they're dangerous."

The disconnect I'd felt before still hadn't gone away. "Look, I know Roberts. Pretty well. He's a good promoter. But he's not capable of putting the nuts and bolts of something like this together by himself."

The look on Ebner's face told me he wasn't going to disagree.

Then he affirmed the hunch that had sent a lightning bolt through me a few hours earlier. He said a whole bunch of people in Flagler had been involved in bringing the mummy here. The ringleader, he said, was the college religion professor, Dr. Bender. He'd been the one to realize almost immediately the publicity value in claiming it was Noah's mummy, even if there was little to no evidence to prove this was so.

"At first, Armenia had loomed big in his plans. He'd planned to piggyback on the idea of how important Noah has always been to its citizens. The way he explained it to me, Noah is an important reason why the Armenians see their country as a kind of Christian Tibet. In fact, they see themselves as Noah's descendants."

He kept going with his story. He said the Armenians had officially adopted Christianity as their religion in 301 AD, but their hand had been in the game before that.

Two of Jesus's apostles, Thaddeus and Bartholomew, were said to have been evangelizing in Armenia in the mid-first-century. Both, in fact, were believed — at least by Armenian traditionalists — to have been martyred and buried in the country.

I kept my reaction to this information to myself. But it was along the lines of, *Yikes! And I'm the one with the divinity degree from Yale.*

He wasn't finished. "You know why their national flag is red, green, and blue, don't you?"

I assumed he was still talking about the Armenians, so I instructed my face to continue to look captivated.

His face certainly looked that way. "Those are the colors Noah saw after he landed the Ark. And the view of Mount Ararat from the Armenian capital, Yerevan — it's spectacular. But they can't go there. The Turks won't let them. So Dr. Bender offered to arrange for the mummy to be extracted and given to the Armenians so they could display it in their national museum. If, of course, they paid him to do that."

"But it didn't happen?"

"No."

"Because?"

"Because Dr. Bender, Dr. Dandurall, Ms. Kendricks, and Mr. Roberts connived with the pilots to keep the mummy for themselves. The archaeologists they hired to bring the mummy off the mountain packed it with dry ice in a metal box at the airport in *Ağrı*. The Armenians thought it was going to be flown to Tbilisi in Georgia, then to Yerevan. Instead, Roberts and his friends had the pilots fly it to Istanbul, pack it in more dry ice, and fly it on to Flagler."

"Where did Roberts and crowd find you?"

"I'm not hard to find. All you need to do is search for a mummy preserver on Google."

"So Roberts asked to buy one of your preservation and display units for his museum."

"Yes. And that wasn't a problem. I'd built the extra one as a backup for the Ancient One, so I had one available."

"I'm assuming he hired an airfreight company to fly it here — it's too big for the *Orville 'n Wilbur* pilots to have handled."

"Yes, that's what he did."

"And you came over to the States too to make sure it worked right."

"I did. Stayed about two weeks. It worked fine."

"Then what did you do."

"I went home."

"And now you're back in Flagler because Roberts didn't pay your bill?"

"That's right — he didn't."

"Did he say why?"

"He said he didn't need a real mummy anymore. Or a pricey case to keep it in. Said he was hiring a 3D technology special effects team in Hollywood to create a replica of Noah's mummy. Said it would look better than the real mummy. And he wouldn't have to worry about keeping the replica at a constant twenty-one degrees Fahrenheit and ninety-nine point four percent humidity rate."

"But then he changed his mind, at least momentarily. I'm guessing that was because he found some folks who would pay to rent the mummy for a while."

"Yes. As we say in Austria, that's the way the avalanche crumbled."

"What a sweetheart our Mr. Roberts is."

"Isn't he? Makes you want to turn him into a mummy himself."

Clearly, my new friend had a good grasp on a lot of the why's and wherefore's of a world-traveled mummy. But I wasn't sensing he'd come close to suspecting how the full story fit together. And why it had led to two people central to so much of it — the two pilots — being brutally murdered.

I didn't really hold his ignorance against him. I didn't know anyone who had worked out that puzzle. I hadn't. Angie hadn't. Dr. Bender and Nina Kendricks might have, but they'd disappeared down the rabbit hole and I couldn't ask them. Not until they returned. *If* they returned.

The pilots might have had the best understanding of all, but I couldn't ask them either. For certain, they weren't going to return.

I took Dr. Ebner back to his motel and told him to be sure he called me before he left for Austria so we could have dinner again. I reminded myself on the drive back to my house, tomorrow was going to be another demanding day.

Before leaving to pick up Dr. Ebner at his motel earlier, I'd had a brief phone chat with the head of my CSI team. He said they'd forced open the desk drawers in the pilots' office suite. In two of them, all they'd found was a bunch of old catalogs, magazines and the like. But the other drawer had contained a collection of notebooks.

Everything they'd found had gone straight into three standard file boxes. These would be waiting on my office floor when I got to work tomorrow. My plan was to scan all of them, one notebook at a time.

That was still the plan right up to the moment I walked into my office suite.

CHAPTER 50

Another visitor was seated in Helen's office. Obviously, waiting to talk to me. This hadn't quite reached the point of being a predictable routine yet. But it was verging on the monotonous.

Our guest stood.

This allowed me to make my first assessment about him. He was a little short of six feet tall. Well-built. "Stocky" would be an acceptable adjective.

My second assessment had to do with what he wore around his neck. I'd never seen anything like it before. It was a necklace supporting a kind of metal cross, a heavy one, from the looks of it.

There was nothing Catholic about it. Too florid in its design. Too ornamental. But clearly, it was meant by its wearer to be taken seriously. He no doubt did. If I got a chance, I'd ask him about it.

My third assessment stemmed from the individual's overall appearance. He was a walking advertisement for a barber-shop specializing in exotic looks for men. He had a coal-black, matte-textured haircut and an expansive horseshoe mustache to match. He had a soul patch beneath his bottom lip and, beneath that, an exquisitely trimmed, boxed beard in two thicknesses.

He saw my eyes roaming his face. "My family is from Armenia."

He extended his hand and told me his name was Special Agent Ara Efendiyan.

Helen handed me his business card. It said he was with the FBI's Directorate of Foreign Intelligence Section in D.C.

I gave an exaggerated tug on an imaginary beard. He understood the question. "The bureau indulges us when we need to blend into exotic places and peoples."

"And the charm thing?"

"It's a khachkar pendant. K-h-a-c-h-k-a-r. An elaborate cross, obviously. People from Armenia have been carving and casting and craving them since the ninth century. It's like wearing a Star of David or a Hamsa if you're Jewish."

I waved toward my office. Motioned for him to take one of the chairs around my wobbly conference table. And lost no time asking a question that had been rolling around my mouth for days, like a slow-dissolving jelly bean. "Where, exactly, is Armenia?"

He extracted the ringed pocket notebook that seemed to be ubiquitous with FBI agents — Angie had one too — and tore out a page. Placed it on the tabletop between us. And began to draw upside down.

His first figure looked like the outline of a great shark if you were viewing it from the side. "The Mediterranean Sea."

Then came a ragged oval that abutted the top of the shark's tail and extended a goodly distance to my right, continuing well past the shark. "Turkey."

He said if you go east for nearly a thousand miles from the west coast of Turkey, you'll come to a thin little sliver of a country that's shaped surprisingly like a miniature Italy.

He drew such a shape on his makeshift map. "It's an isolated, rugged, volcanic little country. High mountains. Forbidding plains. And countless social and economic problems in between. That's the sovereign Republic of Armenia."

I wanted to appear amenable to Armenia, so I said I was assuming he'd been there.

He confirmed this with another history lesson. "I'm a third-generation Armenian-American. My great-grandfather escaped from the 'Medz Yeghern' — the 'Great Crime,' the genocide — from Adana, in Turkey, in 1915 and came to America. Seven million of the world's eleven million people with Armenian ethnicity live elsewhere, you know. I made my first visit back to the old country when I was eighteen."

I covered his drawing with my right hand and spread my fingers. "That's all fascinating. But I'd like to talk to you about a mummy."

This didn't seem to come as a surprise to him. "That's one of the reasons I'm here."

CHAPTER 51

O nce I removed my hand, he closed the cover of his note-book. But he didn't do what I thought he'd do next.

He didn't put it back in his pocket.

He pushed it a little closer to me and left it laying between us like a congealed fried egg, one long-since grown cold.

I thought he might be trying to intimidate me. But when he didn't pay any more attention to the little tablet, I didn't either. "Our sources have turned up the most remarkable story."

Looking away quickly, I repressed a chuckle. I also kept a snippy retort to myself. *Remarkable is the only kind of story we seem to do in Abbot County these days, Special Agent Efendiyan.*

He pushed himself away from the table far enough that he could crook one leg and rest it on the other leg's knee. "You probably know the details better than I do, but you've been dealing with a group here in Flagler we call terroristic in D.C. The ringleaders all have Armenian names, similar in composition to mine."

He reached for his notebook again, said he'd write them down for me. When he tore out the page and handed it to me, I looked at what he'd written: *Garbis Migirdicyan, Razmig Haroutiunyan and Hachik Torosyan.*

I'd never heard any of those names. For that matter, I wouldn't pretend to know how to pronounce any of them.

The idea that emerged was one of those left-field-originating developments. Popped out of nowhere. *Thank you, left field! Thank you, mind! And thank you, Alfred Adler!* Freud's buddy had called his therapy technique "Acting as if." Now seemed a good time to give it a try.

I leveled a steady look at my visitor. "Part of our Armenian problem, are they?"

The FBI special agent said he thought they were. Then he told me why.

First, he was reasonably sure he knew who had destroyed our wind farm. It hadn't been some brilliant new hacker group. But prior to this, the Armenian Cyber Warriors had limited themselves to hacking government websites in Turkey or neighboring Azerbaijan. And they'd always used DDoS — distributed denial-of-service attacks.

"A DDoS attack is where hackers use the internet to overload a target's computer systems. What happened to your wind farm seems to be something new, at least for them. You might say they've upped their game. This worm was inventive, complicated. But the dudes got incredibly lucky with the thunderstorm's arrival. There's no way they could have deliberately timed things that well."

Second, he said it was getting more and more difficult to tell who was on the Armenians' "A Team" and who wasn't.

"It used to be that the really serious, clever Armenian activists all spoke *Western* Armenian, not *Eastern* Armenian. And they didn't carry Armenian passports. They were all from the diaspora, and they had U.K. passports. Or French. Or Argentine. Sometimes, American."

The academic part of my brain was finding this backstory interesting. But the sheriff part was getting impatient. "This is important how?"

"Well, these days, if you run into these characters, you can't tell the level of resourcefulness you are dealing with by listening to how they talk. And it used to be that you could."

This was when I realized my loquacious companion wasn't going to stop until he reached his end game.

"Eastern Armenian is primarily spoken in current-day Armenia, Russia, Iran, Syria, and Lebanon. Western Armenian is softer; it often uses *k*'s instead of *g*'s, *i*'s rather than *y*'s, for example. And, frankly, it sounds more urban, civilized, intellectual. That's because we Armenians living in the west have had a lot more opportunities to improve ourselves. And how we speak Armenian is one of the places it shows up first."

Having said that, he added we law enforcement types needed to be aware — this was his third point — that there *was* an "A Team" on the loose.

"We've been tracking it for a while. It calls itself either The Brothers Haykaken or The Brothers Haigagan, depending on whether you are speaking Western or Eastern Armenian. Either way, it means The Brotherhood Pertaining to Armenians."

He went on to explain that The Brothers Haykaken — or Haigagan — appeared to have roots in the old ASALA organization. "You may not have heard of it, but ASALA stood for Armenian Secret Army for the Liberation of Armenia."

He explained the ASALA lasted for about fifteen years. Killed a bunch of people — mostly Turks — in attacks and assassinations. Petered out in the early 1990s.

"Their goal was to get Turkey to admit to the great genocide. And they wanted Armenia given back to Armenians using the boundaries President Woodrow Wilson had proposed in his Treaty of Sèvres in 1920. The treaty was never ratified, though. In fact, the whole experiment called Armenia has been hanging on by the skin of its chinny chin chin for the past 1,700 years."

I'd never had a conversation like this with an FBI special agent, not even Angie. Be interesting, I thought, to keep it going a while longer. That was the reason for my simple question. "And still is?"

The blank look on his face suggested he'd lost his train of thought.

I gave him another nudge. "Armenia — it's still taking it on the chin, is it?"

That helped him reconnect with his narrative. "Still is. The Romans, the Parthians, the Byzantines, the Mongols, the Arabs, and the Turks have all tried to extinguish the Armenians, often literally."

"You mean, they've done that recently?"

"Recently enough. The Ottoman Turks slaughtered a million and a half Armenians between 1915 and 1923. Then what little was left of historic Armenia was occupied for sixty-nine years by the Soviet Empire. This left millions of Armenians scattered to and fro around the globe in the diaspora. But three million stayed behind. In 1991, they declared independence."

He said The Brothers Haykaken represented something new. A merger of sorts. On the one hand, the youthful, restless energies in the Republic of Armenia. On the other, the growing financial capabilities of well-educated new generations of Armenians of the diaspora.

He said both groups wanted to mount a defense of all things Armenian that hadn't been seen in a long time. Perhaps not ever.

I sensed that his end game had arrived. "For some reason, Abbot County has become ground zero for The Brothers Haykaken's first big operation."

I don't know why my memory chose that moment to surface an old Chinese proverb, but there it was: "If you have two loaves of bread, sell one and buy a lily."

If not a lily, at least a mummy.

The FBI special agent seemed to think a good place to start was finding Garbis, Razmig, and Hachik.

It wasn't difficult. According to our databases, they shared the same residential address.

I asked Special Agent Efendiyan if he wanted to come along. He said he wouldn't miss it for the world.

CHAPTER 52

The location was a nondescript, two-story eightplex. It sat on one of the side streets crossed by Bison's Cut Drive on its way south through the hills.

At eleven in the morning, the neighborhood looked very much like what it was: a bedroom community to residents who worked elsewhere and a dormitory community to college students. In a word, at this time of day, it looked empty.

The apartment manager looked like he could have been a graduate student himself. He said each of his three renters wrote him a separate monthly check — and had been doing so ever since they'd moved in together at the start of the summer term. He hadn't seen Garbis, Razmig, or Hachik since last Saturday. All of them had left their apartment at about dinner time.

I sought clarification. "Left together?"

"Right."

"In the same vehicle?"

"In Garbis's beat-up old white van."

He said Garbis, Razmig, and Hachik were all graduate students in religion but not at the same university. One was studying at the University of the Hills, another at Cummings University, the third at Butler-Atkins. But they lived together.

"I admit that's kind of strange. But then, these guys are kind of strange."

I cocked my head. "How so?"

The guy's eyes were deep-set. When he squinted like he was doing now, they almost disappeared. "A lot of the time, they didn't really act like students. Didn't seem to leave the apartment much. And they were always asking questions about where to find things."

Once again, the special agent and I proved great minds think alike by voicing the same question at the same time. "What kind of things?"

The manager thought about that for a moment. "Like where to find a grocery store that sells Frito pie. I don't think they knew a lot about Flagler. About America, for that matter. Maybe you can buy Frito pie ready-made at a football game, but you ever been in a supermarket that had premade Frito pie on the shelves? Garbis Migirdicyan, Razmig Haroutiunyan, and Hachik Torosyan are three of the most unusual College Joes I've ever come across." He was already reaching for the key ring on his belt. "You wanna see their place?"

Once again, my companion and I answered in unison. "No, but thanks." We explained that we had to do something before we could pay the grad students' digs a visit. We needed to get a search warrant.

Special Agent Efendiyan said he needed to do something else. Get back to FBI headquarters in Washington. But he'd be most curious about what we found in the so-called grad students' apartment. Especially if it was a mummy.

CHAPTER 53

With Special Agent Efendiyan no longer available, I asked Del Emma and Detective Salazar to accompany me.

About eleven the next morning, Chief Deputy Del Emma knocked on the door and announced our presence. "Sheriff's department! Search warrant! Open up!"

He did that twice. Turned the key. Took a peek inside. Eased the door open wider and stepped through. Salazar and I followed, taking care not to trip on each other's heels. Our SWAT team instincts were turned to high.

The air in the apartment was still, stale, clingy — the place felt . . . what? Abandoned? My instincts said we wouldn't find anybody at home.

Chief Deputy Del Emma took the first-floor bedrooms and the main bath, which sat between the two bedrooms. Still on the first floor, I took the living room, the breakfast nook adjoining the kitchen, and the small mud room leading to the back door. Both of us were soon shouting, "Clear!" Detective Salazar needed longer since he had to climb the stairs to the second floor and search an entire floor by himself. But we heard him shout out soon enough. "Mother of all that's holy, what *is* this?"

Del Emma and I were quick to join him, and our eyes were soon taking in the same gory scene.

The wash basin in the bathroom was flecked with dark stains and, in a few places, streaked with crimson. A bloody towel had been discarded on the floor.

There was one of those all-purpose first aid kits open on the commode lid, and on the basin, a half-used roll of blood-smeared gauze had been discarded between the cold and hot water faucets.

Salazar turned to stare at me. "Didn't you tell me about a broken window in an empty apartment you visited the other day?"

I confirmed this. "Found evidence of an injury too."

"You checked with the hospital's ED?"

"I did. They didn't have any info."

"Well, I think we've found where the guy went when he left the apartment."

I concurred.

We'd know which Armenian it was as soon as we could get Garbis, Razmig, and Hachik in the same room.

I asked Matt to take possession of several items and transport them back to the office. One was the laptop computer we'd found on the kitchen table.

We'd also found the Armenians' passports. I sent those along too.

I told my deputy chief and my detective I'd lock up. I wanted to sift through the contents of the wire baskets we'd found stacked on the kitchen table.

In the bottom basket, the first item I spotted was a folded copy of the features page from the local paper of three Sundays ago. I remembered the lead story on the page because I was quoted in it.

I'd been explaining that one of the most important examples of semiotic power — the power of signs — in any community involved the symbols of law enforcement. One of my quotes summed up my thinking.

"When people see evidence of the law officer's presence, their behavior usually changes. In most cases, for the better.

They observe speed limits more closely. They're more polite to the people around them. They behave better."

That was why, I'd told the reporter, I drove my own patrol cruiser home every night and parked it in front of my house.

"I want you to know I live there. That this is my home. And that I care about the safety and well-being of the people around me."

In the copy of the article I was holding, my quote was circled in red ink that looked to be from a ballpoint pen. But the circling wasn't what bathed my brain in adrenaline. It was the note that appeared at the end of a line drawn from the circled quote to the page's margin. "We need this guy's car!"

The apartment around me was beginning to feel eerie. Alien. What was I dealing with here?

It didn't feel like stupidity. Stupidity doesn't plan. These folks showed signs of planning several moves ahead even if things didn't always go as expected. And this seemed to be getting personal. The newspaper article had been an electrifying wake-up call.

There was one thing I was going to do as soon as I got back to the office tomorrow morning. Hire a locksmith to change the locks on my outside doors. But what I spotted sitting on my conference table the next day made me forget all about locksmiths.

CHAPTER 54

The severed hand looked like a large, if misbegotten, piece of seaweed. It was floating near the bottom of a capped, wide-mouthed, liquid-filled glass jar.

Helen found the jar when she arrived for work. She said it had been jammed in a box on the hallway floor right outside our office suite's door. Obviously, someone had placed it there after we'd all left the night before.

"Someone," she added, "with a sardonic sense of humor."

I acknowledged that leaving a jar containing a severed hand behind qualified as sardonic. But she said that wasn't all.

She pointed to handwriting on the top of the box. It was an address. "Sheriff Luke McWhorter, Director of Spare Parts Department, Abbot County Sheriff's Office Lost and Found, Flagler, Texas."

The ludicrous address itself would have kept Helen from touching the box.

But then we had a rule around the office. The only unexpected items given automatic entry to our workspace were those with markings of the U.S. Postal Service or one of the parcel delivery services. Anything else had to be examined by our CSI staffers before it was brought inside.

Two investigators had hurried to our suite with a portable Kevlar-reinforced drape. They used it to encircle the box containing the jar. Then they used their mobile X-ray unit to take a look at the box's contents.

They decided the package contained no explosives. But this hadn't allayed all their concerns.

Next, they cut through the wrapping paper and the tape holding the box shut and lifted out the jar like it was a rattlesnake that had swallowed its tail. With gloved hands, they carried it to my conference table and began dusting it for fingerprints. They were still involved in the task when I'd entered the room. So far, Helen said, no prints had been found.

I noticed one other thing lying on the table. A sheet of white paper. It bore several smudges of fingerprint powder because it had also been dusted.

Helen called the sheet to my attention about the same time one of the technicians turned it right side up. He shoved it toward me so I could read what was written on it.

The sentence was in decent cursive: This is what happens when people play God.

Underneath this, as a kind of signature, was an object I recognized. It was the symbol that had been painted — in blood — on the wall of the hangar where we'd found the massacred pilots. Once again. I was looking at an equal sign with a slash through it. I'd probably have given it a great deal more thought if Angie and my fact-seeking dinner party had not proven so complicated so quickly.

CHAPTER 55

The idea was Angie's.

Alain picked and outfitted the room.

I selected the guests.

The plan was to seat everyone who might know anything useful about Noah's mummy around the same table. See what they might volunteer. See what they might let slip. Then direct questions at them. And decide if we were hearing any new evidence that would suggest the great Ark-building patriarch, Captain Noah, had made it to Abbot County. And if he had, where his remains had gotten off to. And, most important of all, who had been involved in arranging all this.

If we did our job well, we might also learn something about the murders of our two pilots and get an inkling about who else could be in danger.

Angie had wanted to bring Special Agent Efendiyan back to town and give him a seat at the table, but I demurred.

"He's too fixated on this being an Armenian thing."

"All of it?"

"The pilots murders, the mummy mystery, the Gallup emails, the threat against you, the attack on the college kid, the severed hand — the whole grab bag."

"You don't think it could be an Armenian thing?"

"Honestly, I don't."

"So what is it?"

"For the most part, I think it's an Abbot County thing."

"You really think our little prairie proletariat could cook up this kind of international incident?"

"I think the two pilots could have come close to doing it all by themselves."

But they hadn't had to. I was sensing that any number of our good West Texas folks had been more than happy to lend a hand. Too many to be seated, Agatha Christie style, around a dining table at a country club.

I insisted on having two of my people present. My chief deputy and my head forensic investigator, Douglas Hackmore. After that, I went for people I knew had first-hand knowledge of the events I was interested in. For certain, now that he'd continued to improve from the blow to his head, I wanted Pogue Stockstill there. Plus I wanted Dr. Dandurall. Ideally, Dr. Bender and Nina Kendricks would be present, but we were unlikely to track them down in time. I thought about asking Christoph Ebner, the mummy preserver, to return and join us. But the loquacious Austrian, good observer though he was, seemed to have a knack for being one step behind and one hunch too late. Besides, nearly all his knowledge was second hand. And he had a tendency to become mired in details. In addition, there was the expense of bringing him back all the way from Europe.

So how many participants did we have? For that matter, how many did we need?

Dwelling on that thought, I remembered anthropologist Robin Dunbar's research on the maximum number to invite if you wanted a successful dinner party. Well, this hadn't been the precise research question Dunbar had been interested in; actually, he'd asked how many people the human brain can relate well to in a given setting. It had been others who worked with his findings who had decided on the right number for a successful dinner party: seven plus or minus two.

From five to nine persons. Seven seemed like the right number.

The analytical "me" reminded the venturesome "me" that I wasn't planning a dinner party. For its trouble, my fact-seeking self was then informed by my daredevil self that this was exactly what I was planning. As I totted up the people I already had in mind to receive invitations, I realized I was one short.

Who was to be the seventh person?

Two people came to mind.

Either Dr. Konstantina Smyth, the medical examiner. Or Craft Roberts, the museum/amusement park entrepreneur.

Both might be problematic. Left to their own devices, either of them could easily turn my experiment into a circus. Doc Konnie, by veering off in unexpected directions. Roberts, by making it all about him.

I decided on Doc Konnie.

If things got dull, she could at least sing for us.

CHAPTER 56

Angie said the place to stage our gathering was the country club. Her call to Alain, the maître d', mobilized the process.

Alain promptly posed a question. Did I want to seat my guests around a round table or a long table? Angie put me on the phone. I asked the country club waiter what he recommended.

He asked if I wanted the conversation at my dinner party to trend more toward the formal or the chummy. I told him that, in the end, I needed these people to volunteer useful information. When he shared his conclusion, I immediately understood how out of my league I was when it came to setting up dinner parties.

His recommendation was a square table. But not a completely square table. A *nearly* square table. He said two trestle tables pushed together would do the trick. This was how I learned that a trestle table consists of two strong end pieces connected by a longitudinal cross-member and capped with a tabletop.

When Alain shoved his two trestle tables together, he had a six-foot-by-five-foot table and comfortable seating for seven. A nearly square table. Cover it with a white tablecloth, which he'd done, and you'd never know how he had cobbled it together.

But I could see how putting seven people at a nearly square table was going to leave them with little choice. Either they joined the conversation, or they were due for an awkward, boring experience.

I didn't want it to be boring, so at noon the next day, when my six guests and I were seated around Alain's nearly square table, I sought to put them at ease. "We want you to enjoy this."

Angie was determined to do her part. "What Sheriff McWhorter means is that no one will be forced to eat wearing handcuffs."

That brought a few chuckles. But it hadn't exactly relieved the tension. It could even have been considered a faux pas.

I tried a speedy rebound. "What Special Agent Steele meant to say was she will let you wear her badge if you ask nicely."

That brought some more laughs. I felt we were back on track. I thought introducing each of the people sitting at the table might be a good way to keep things moving. When I'd finished doing that, I got to the point.

"I bet you're hungry." I knew a truly stupid look was cascading across my face like an avalanche. I blinked hard to slow it down and gave Alain a wave. He and two other waiters began depositing plates bearing our salads in front of each of us.

Forty minutes or so later, we were finishing our dessert — apple crumb pie à la mode — and accepting or declining coffee.

I was encouraged.

The conversation during the meal had gotten off to a slow start, then picked up energy. As best I'd been able to gather, it had been the kind of getting-to-know-you-a-little-bit-better stuff I'd been expecting. Now, it was time to see if my bold use of Angie's FBI expense account was going to pay dividends.

I tapped my dinner knife against a glass and watched nearly everyone at the table give their mouths one last swipe with their cloth napkin.

Angie and I had talked about how to start. We'd both agreed

that inviting guesses about what this odd dinner party was about would be a good beginning. But we'd disagreed on who we thought would be the first to respond. Angie had picked Dr. Dandurall Said he was a know-it-all who'd want to control the conversation. I'd picked Dr. Pogue. For the same reason.

Time to find out.

I did the honors. "Would anyone like to take a guess as to what this is all about?"

The voice that piped up had a distinct Greek flavor to it. "A missing hand." Doc Konnie, of course. Any discussion of body parts would make her the foremost participant.

I told her one part of her answer had hit the bullseye. The part about something being missing. But it wasn't a body part we needed to discuss. It was a whole body. A mummy. And the question wasn't whether it was missing. It wasn't any longer. The question was why it had been brought to Abbot County to begin with. And what had been done with it since its arrival.

I said everyone sitting around the table had been asked to be present because I believed each of them could contribute to answering that question.

I knew the first person I called on was going to be uncomfortable but I couldn't let that stop me. I intended — and Angie had agreed — to make this an act of communal story-telling. And stories work best when they start at the beginning. My problem was that I had no idea where this story started. I decided to do some exploration.

"Pogue, you could make this easy. Just tell us what was in the box the first time you removed it from the pilots' plane."

He looked startled. Probably because I'd called on him first. But it could also have been the thought that he might have opened the box to find himself face-to-face with a 4,000-year-old mummy.

His reply suggested as much. "Oh, geez . . . I'd have had a heart attack."

I didn't want him to stop there. "Because of what the pilots had told you would be in the box?"

"I've already told you, they didn't talk about what they were hauling."

"Never?"

"Well, hardly ever."

"How about the first time?"

"Christmas presents."

"Excuse me?"

"They said they'd brought back Christmas presents."

"But you mentioned a thermometer?"

"That was another time. You asked about the first time."

"My apologies, I did."

"The first time, the box was empty."

"And all the other times, you never saw a mummy?"

"Never did."

If there was anyone at the table who was going to impeach young Stockstill about what had been in the box, it was going to be my head forensic investigator.

After I'd talked with the college student at the hospital, I'd asked Doug to apply for a search warrant. Once he had it, his instructions were to saw off the lock on the pilots' storage unit, load up the metal box, take it back to his lab, and examine it from top to bottom.

He'd done this and sent me a report.

He said he'd found nothing to suggest it had been used to haul a mummy, but he hadn't found anything to suggest it hadn't been, either.

I toyed with what I might do with this information right up to the moment I turned my head toward Professor Dandurall.

I asked if he thought the pilots could have left any prints on the box when they'd removed it from his laboratory.

CHAPTER 57

I knew I was being deceptive and that bothered me a little. Bothered the preacher part of me more than the law officer part.

And I instantly understood why. The preacher part of me reported to a higher authority than the law officer part.

The law officer part of me had an immediate "yes, but" response. No less an authority than the U.S. Supreme Court had given its blessing to a law officer's lying about finding fingerprints at a crime scene. I'd once memorized the case title of this decision for an exam in a criminal justice class: *Oregon v. Mathiason, 1977*.

Hackmore ducked his head. Glanced up at me once. Then decided he was thirsty and reached for his water glass.

Dandurall appeared stricken. He knew he was trapped in one of those "have you quit beating your wife?" quandaries. The moment I saw the look on his face, I knew my suspicions were correct. The box had made at least one trip to the laboratories of the Thesaurus of the Gene Corporation.

But the scientist wasn't giving in that easy. "That's a cheap shot, Sheriff, and you know it. You don't know if there was a Noah's mummy. And you certainly don't have any evidence of one being in any box at our laboratories."

"What would you say if I told you I had a witness?"

"I'd say you're a liar."

"What if I told you that witness was sitting here with us right now?"

"Then I'd say we had two liars in our midst."

"Well, you could say that. But you'd be off by one."

"I don't know what you mean by that."

"I mean that I actually have two witnesses sitting here who saw the box in your laboratories. So, following your logic, we have three liars in our midst."

At this point in our post-dinner developments, eyes were doing a variety of things.

Young Stockstill was feeling cleared. He was enjoying his spectator's role as he basked in his innocence. My two employees appeared to be riveted by their boss's performance in a drama I knew they'd be talking about for the rest of their careers. Doc Konnie's eyes were locked on the centerpiece on the table. Hydrangeas in a soup tureen. Some of Alain's magic. I had no idea where he'd found the flowers on such short notice.

Dandurall looked up once. He shot me a glance that said he knew the jig was up. I thought so too.

At one time or another, there had been a mummy in the box. It had been imported by the two pilots. It had spent time in Dandurall's research facility.

But was the mummy Noah's mummy? And had it gotten two people murdered?

What I had to decide now was which of my fellow diners knew things I needed to know to answer those two questions.

CHAPTER 58

The answers came before I could even ask the questions. And they came from the mouth of the last person in the room I'd have expected to hear it from. My chief deputy.

He may have been thinking out loud. "We need to talk about the elephant in the room."

Initially, Del Emma seemed to be as surprised as anyone at what he'd just said. But when he hazarded a look in my direction, I could see no sign that he was regretting his outburst.

On the contrary, he looked determined. Resolute.

The way he was handling his napkin was a sign he wasn't finished. He had twisted the napkin into a makeshift rope and knotted it around one of his fists. "Sheriff, you will remember you gave me instructions to comb the pilots' office suite for anything we'd missed. I did that. And I discovered something that was very interesting. Very revealing, you might say."

There it was again. My chief deputy's flair for the dramatic. But then, I had to give him credit. Every time I'd witnessed him put his theatrical self on the stage, he'd earned an A+ for weaving a compelling tale. He proceeded to do so again. He explained that the revelation had come from the large monthly desk pad calendar that been sitting on the pilots' desk.

The pad had covered a year's time — with one sheet for each of the months of the year. Each sheet had daily blocks of writing space for notes and reminders. The top two sheets had been clean — no writing or any other marks of any kind. Not so, the sheets underneath.

On the third sheet, the pilots had begun to jot things down. And once they had started, they'd been meticulous. And voluminous. They'd entered notes in space after space. Day after day. Month after month.

Del Emma quit twisting his napkin and laid it beside his plate. "The entries I found most fascinating began about eight or nine months ago. That was when the pilots started making trips around the country."

He said he'd found their destinations puzzling at first. "They were flying all over. Wyoming, Oregon, Colorado, Missouri, North Carolina, Virginia, Florida. Sometimes, they'd name the towns they landed at. Occasionally, the airports. And these were always quick trips."

To say the least, this information astounded me. "You hadn't told me any of this."

"I haven't seen you since I visited the pilots' office suite."

"Did the notes on the calendar sheets say what these trips were about?"

"Once in a while there'd be a hint."

"I'm going to guess they were scouting for something."

"I thought maybe real estate."

"Where'd this idea come from?"

"Notes they made. They jotted down things like 'not close enough to town' or 'too visible from the road.'"

"So they were looking for a rural property?"

My chief deputy moistened his lower lip with the upper one. "That's what I'm thinking."

My questions were nowhere near extinguished. "For themselves, or for someone else?"

238

"They never mentioned airports."

"So they probably weren't looking for a place for themselves."

"You don't get that feeling."

"Maybe we should take that calendar pad to the office and go over it again."

"I think we should. But I'm pretty sure I know what it's going to tell us."

With eight pairs of eyes boring into him, my deputy chief knew it was time to quit milking the drama. "For whatever reason, the pilots were looking for a place to house the mummy's baby and her mother. This would mean they were planning an abduction."

I eyed him closely. "And you know what that means."

He didn't hesitate. "They were abandoning their associates in their 'save the world' Code New Beginnings plot."

I saw Angie reach for her purse. Extract her little notebook. And write something. She tore out a sheet. Folded it in two. And bad manners be damned, stretched across two of the other diners' table space without apology to hand it to me.

I reached for it. Opened it. And silently read the two questions. "Who lied? Why?"

I glanced up at her and shaped a single word with my mouth, knowing she could read my lips. "Everybody."

At this point, I expected people to start excusing themselves from the table. The way napkins were being tidied and laid aside, the exodus could start at any moment.

But this was before Pogue Stockstill did what bright young minds have a habit of doing. Blowing other people's thoughts and strategies out of the water.

You could sense he was thinking out loud again. "So this means the two pilots died and I almost got killed for nothing. Nothing at all."

Eventually, I was going to need to say something because I didn't think anyone would pick up the conversation at this point. But I was wrong.

Once again, it was Doc Konnie who spoke. "So sorry you hurt, Pogue. That not a plan. We uncorked too much to bargain for."

And once again, I marveled at how events in Abbot County could turn on a dime. I pondered the information available in those few words. Some of it I'd suspected. But some of it I'd never dreamed could be possible.

There *had* been a plot. It had involved the pilots. Others in Flagler had also been involved. One of them I'd always thought was largely apolitical — the medical examiner. It had been a deadly plot. And I had no assurance that its consequences had run their course. Or, for that matter, if they ever would.

One other thing.

I was absolutely certain Noah's mummy had somehow been at the heart of it all.

CHAPTER 59

The next morning, I was sitting at my desk still pondering the events of the previous day when my personal phone chimed.

It was Angie.

After listening a moment, I fired a fusillade of questions at the woman I loved. She could only conclude that I was a) surprised b) confused c) concerned and d) perhaps feeling threatened. But I hadn't told her why yet.

Helen was hearing all this. She made it almost as far as her desk before launching into what she called the Grainger Cha Cha Cha. As I'd told her more than once, this was a patently silly piece of theatrics. The Grainger Cha Cha Cha broke out when she was dying to know what was going on but wanted to make it appear that she was paying no attention whatever. She intended the dance to minimize her presence. But it always made her the most obvious thing in the room. *Any* room.

I realized I needed a little more privacy if I was going to continue cross-examining my caller. I stepped into the hall.

"So you're not in Flagler?"

"No, sweetheart, like I said, I'm with a Crimes Against Children Task Force in Gallup."

"Gallup, as in New Mexico?"

"Yes, honey, as in New Mexico."

"When did you arrive there?"

"About thirty minutes ago. We flew to Dallas last night. Caught the last flight to Albuquerque. We all got up at the crack of dawn to drive into Gallup."

"And you couldn't tell me about this."

"Couldn't, no. Sorry."

"And what crimes are the children of Gallup being threatened with?"

"Are you in your office?"

"No, I'm standing outside in the hallway."

"Can you arrange to go somewhere more private?"

I told her I could be in my car in less than a minute. She said she would stay on the line but to say nothing else until I was inside my vehicle alone and with the windows rolled up.

Once I reached my vehicle, I did more than that. I locked my car doors, turned on the AC, and checked my phone's battery supply. If necessary, I could use my two-way radio and have my dispatcher connect me with the FBI's emergency radio network. But if Angie was already concerned about keeping our communications secret, I didn't want to have to do that. My phone's battery indicator said I was good to go for another hour. I told Angie as much.

What she said next was the strangest thing I'd ever heard over my phone — from her or anyone else.

She said someone was threatening to cut off the hands of Gallup's children.

That comment, plus what I'd observed in the jar on my conference table, made me want to flex my wrists merely to see if my hands were still attached. Instead, I flexed my tongue, and that was a mistake. I repeated what she'd told me, word for word.

"Somebody is threatening to cut off the hands of Gallup's children?"

She thought I was having trouble hearing her. Her solution

was also a common one. She thought she needed to talk louder. "*Yes!* Hands! Their hands! Sever them! Detach them! Cut them off!"

I didn't have to think about it. The issue wasn't anyone's hearing. She was verging on hysteria. What I needed to do was help her make sense of what was happening in Gallup. Be her instant-analyst-from-afar. Help her feel in control. In such circumstances, questions can be good. "Do your IT people know where the emails are coming from?"

She seemed to appreciate the chance to refocus. "They said Eastern Europe."

"Anonymous emails often come from Eastern Europe."

"I know that."

This was when I remembered the Navajo words we'd found written on the wall of the pilots' office suite. "The children being harassed — are they from the reservations, by chance?"

"No, so far they've all been children of Gallup jewelers."

"Really?"

"Yes."

"Any idea why?"

"I think it's because of where most of the jewelers are from?"

"Where's that?"

"Some little village on the West Bank, in Palestine."

I heard myself whistle. "*Palestine?*"

Angie confirmed that I'd heard her right. "Weird, isn't it?"

I had an idea. "Maybe their parents' competitive instincts have gone too far."

"I was considering that until about thirty minutes ago."

"What happened then?"

"The parents all got another email."

"What did this one say?"

This time, she didn't bother to try to hide her frustration at my inability to offer any miraculous insights about what was happening in Gallup. I hadn't done so because I'd not had any. All I was feeling was surprise. And there seemed to be a new one each time she opened her mouth.

I was wondering what the sharp-eyed, sharp-witted FBI special agent — the one I loved more than life itself — would throw at me next.

"Criminy, Luke! The email said people in Gallup needed to ask Sheriff McWhorter what happens when people play God."

I didn't have to think about it. Now wasn't the time to tell her about the hand floating in the jar. She didn't need more uncertainty and confusion dumped on her. In those categories, she was already in the emotional red zone.

I might be soon myself. Because what I needed to do now was start examining the other thing I'd noticed when I walked into my office.

The file boxes from the pilots' office suite.

CHAPTER 60

The boxes were jammed against the wall. Two of them were labeled *Files*. The other one said *Notebooks*.

Their lids were crisscrossed by strips of red sealing tape. Every few inches on the tape, the word *EVIDENCE* appeared in large black letters.

In a way, Angie deserved to be here when we went through the boxes. After all, she'd been the first one to try to open the desk drawers. But Angie was going to be tied up in Gallup for at least another day. I couldn't wait for her.

Stepping into Helen's office, I asked her to do two things. First, see if there was an empty room in the court-house where a bunch of files and notebooks and God only knew what else could be spread out. Then see if Detective Rashada Moody could spare me a couple of hours. If she was available, I had a rush assignment for her.

Helen walked out into the hallway and started toward the west stairs. I knew where she was going — to the part of the courthouse on the second floor we insiders called Old Bailey. It was where our courtrooms were located.

Of course!

All our judges were at the annual state bar association convention this week. Their courtrooms would be empty.

My office manager returned in less than two minutes to tell me old Judge Kincannon's courtroom looked like a good choice. Then she resumed talking on her phone to the person she'd just put on hold. A few moments later, tilting her phone away from her mouth, she said Detective Moody would be joining me there in five.

I picked up one of the boxes, took two steps into the hall with it, and realized I needed Helen to follow me. I couldn't leave the boxes unattended in the courtroom, and I had two more trips to make.

Helen instructed me to put the box I was carrying down on the hall floor and pointed up the stairs. I knew when I was being ordered out of sight.

I was seated at Judge Kincannon's long table for opposing counsel when three of my deputies entered the room, each one lugging a box. I asked them to deposit the boxes on the table.

Detective Moody arrived as the last of the box-deliverers exited. She let her black faux-leather-grained satchel drop from a higher distance than was necessary. It landed in an empty chair with the intended thud. For some reason, it was my day for being made an example of. "That office manager of yours is a Simon Legree."

I kept my next thought to myself. *The fiery creature who just chewed you out, partner, happens to be one of your employees.*

I suggested to Detective Moody that we break the seals, remove the lids, and give the contents a cursory look while they were still in the boxes. "All I got from CSI was there were two drawers filled with files and such. And another drawer pretty much jammed with composition notebooks. You know — the kind you use in high school English class."

I knew the moment I said that to expect another dyspeptic remark from Rashada. It was swift in arriving. "I finally quit attending my high school English classes. My verbs never conjugated."

I didn't reply.

She removed her dark jacket and draped it over the back of the closest chair. I was no expert on women's fashions, or on colors for that matter, but if anyone had asked, I'd have described the jacket as being a navy-blue blazer.

Now that she'd taken it off, her ruffled blouse was in full view, and it was eye-catching. The blouse was an all-consuming white, buttoned all the way to her neck.

Its most visible feature was two wide seams of white ruffles. On each side, these plunged off her shoulders and met close to where I was guessing her belly button resided. Another billowy explosion of ruffles encircled the bottom of the blouse, giving the appearance of a short skirt. Her flawless, slightly tapered jeans completed her ensemble. Her boss had to admit she seemed to have an eye for fashion and did so. Silently.

She arranged the first box so that it was square to the edges of the tabletop and turned to look at me. "Your box or mine?"

I almost said, "Ladies first," but caught myself. "You're closest."

She ripped the sealing tape from her box. Began rifling through its contents. And didn't speak again for several minutes. When she did, her tone was dismissive. "Men's stuff."

I'd found the same thing in my box. Military magazines. Catalogs for camouflage clothing. Catalogs for guns. Catalogs for survival gear. A few issues of a journal on Asian conflicts and Al-Qaeda. Publications by something called the Strategic Studies Institute at the National War College. Aviation magazines, most of them having something to do with helicopters. Nothing of interest, as best I could tell, to our murder investigation. At least, nothing on its face.

We both pulled a chair over to the third box. This was the one labeled Notebooks.

I broke the seals on the box, removed the lid, reached inside, and began extracting notebooks. I placed them in a single stack between us.

The covers were not all the same color — so far, I was seeing purple, black, and green — but all the sturdy covers had the same swirling, marbled image dominating its design. They looked exactly like the "comp books" with the taped-looking spine I'd often used for notetaking in high school and college.

My deputy took the notebook on top, and I took the next one.

We began to read.

CHAPTER 61

To me, it was sort of like reading a diary. A dual diary.

It didn't take but a page or two for me to understand I was reading descriptions of the two pilots' experiences. Experiences? That might not be the right word. Adventures?

This didn't seem to always be in the strike zone, either.

Observations, meditations, contemplations, ruminations, speculations? As I reflected on what I was reading, all these words flitted through my mind. But none was a consistent fit. Sometimes, they worked, sometimes, they didn't.

But one thing was coming through as clear as the proverbial clanging bell. The two pilots had not been ordinary joes. Not in Afghanistan. Not in the Marines. Not as helicopter pilots. Not as charter pilots. Not as keepers of a journal. Not as whatever else was going on, and — there was that bell going off in my head again — something clearly was going on.

And strictly speaking, it was two journals being kept, howbeit in a single notebook.

The two people doing the jotting were coordinating their entries. By date, by topic, by intent, and by a desire that the circumstances being written about be understood. But after that, the arrangement of the entries was close to being enigmatic.

For example, it was not always the same person who wrote under a date first. And occasionally, one person's handwriting was the only handwriting under a particular date.

Most times, one of the journal keepers wrote first under a date, then, on a facing page, the other added a comment. Or an amplification. Or a disagreement. Or a disparagement.

There didn't seem to be any reluctance to be blunt. Even nasty. That is to say, there didn't seem to be many holds being barred. And yet, a high degree of compatibility had clearly been felt by the two.

The notebook I'd picked up had a green cover. The date on the first page that contained writing was April 19, 2015.

The first handwriting under that date was that of the person I soon came to think of as The Commander. He used bold but controlled letters. Placed them almost as upright as the edge of the page but not quite. There was a slight slant to the right. Consistently.

After a moment, I found the word I was looking for. This individual's handwriting seemed dignified.

But that's not to say there were no departures from the norm. For example, he'd inserted hyphens between the three words in New York City. And he was into grouping. Words were often broken into syllables. "Mis construction." "Bro ken." "Ad ded." Or the letters in a single syllable might be separated by spaces. Like "m e a nings." Or "clari f i e d."

For the entries I'd read so far, he'd always used a ball-point pen with black ink. And he tended to think in complete sentences.

Not so, the other writer. I found his calligraphy fascinating. The letters had the look and feel of cursive. But almost no letters actually touched. And to this individual, controlled slants were a lost art. Letters leaned every which way. Not wildly. Just without conveying much interest in appearance or consistency. Like the *l* in like inclined slightly to the left. Right next door, the accompanying *i* sloped slightly to the right.

I called this person The Roamer. Already, I had spotted two different ink colors for this individual. Blue and purple.

But as I began to turn the pages, I realized I was ignoring the handwriting differences. Not because the two styles of the writing were so different, although that was reason enough to make me want to keep turning the pages. My compulsion to hurry, and yet not miss a single available insight or observation, was because I began to understand what these notebooks might be capable of doing.

Which was?—

In a very real sense, resurrecting my dead pilots.

Meaning what?—

Bringing them back to testify about events leading up to their own demise.

Done how?—

By dropping clue after clue after clue in their own words.

Or it might not turn out to be that at all.

I was resisting a growing urge to ask Detective Moody what she was finding in her notebook. I hadn't done so because I was a bit afraid. Fearful, first, that the contents of the notebooks she was reading might not be transporting her on the kind of revelatory express train I was riding. But also, that she might be growing weary of all this time spent looking at them.

My notebook had opened with these sentences, written by The Commander:

We took the day off to bar-hop in downtown New-York-City. (Manhattan to the cognoscenti!) It wasn't wasted time. We had a fascinating conversation with two ex-Israeli military guys in a new place in Lower Manhattan called Old Bubbly's Bar.

Then, the ink color and handwriting style changed, along with the language style and the points being emphasized. The commentary on the encounter at Old Bubbly's Bar was now taking place on the facing page. The Roamer was in the house!

His first entry was a correction. *Fascinating — not! 2 Jewish typicals. 'Been there, done that' mouth-offs. Or 'do this, don't do that (if you want to know what's good for you!)' showoffs. Yadda yadda yadda! Yetch!*

The Commander had a rejoinder. It sounded indulgent. He was apparently accustomed to his buddy's spouting off. *Lad, if the Pope ever served you communion, the first thing you'd tell him was his wine was flat. Besides, these guys gave us good advice on handling officials in Turkey.*

Over on his page, The Roamer's response was in all-caps. *AS IF THEY'D KNOW A MUMMY FROM A MOMMY! MUCH LESS, HOW TO SMUGGLE ONE!*

That particular exchange went on for another page-and-a-half. The Commander always wrote on a left-hand page, The Roamer on the facing right-hand page, starting at the same depth on his page that The Commander had left off at on the facing page.

The pages in these notebooks were sturdy enough that you could write on either side — that's to say, front and back. But since The Commander always wrote on a left-hand page, this meant that the first page containing any writing in one of the notebooks was always the back of the first page. Page two, you might say. Page one would be blank. Always.

Figuring all this out had left me standing almost motionless for several minutes, flipping pages back and forth in a single notebook.

Then I felt I'd seen enough in old Judge Kincannon's courtroom.

Seeing what was in the notebooks — or more accurately, how what was in the notebooks had been recorded — had triggered a curiosity. A question was growing in my mind, and the answer was in the pilots' office suite.

In addition, the pilots' entry for April 19, 2015, brief though it was, had done something else. It had ignited a suspicion. If my gut feeling proved to be true, it was going to take my detectives' and my investigation of the pilots' murders down a very different road than the one I'd been envisioning.

CHAPTER 62

Detective Moody wasn't spending a lot of time in any one notebook. But she had a steady routine. She'd pick one up from the stack. Open the cover. Use the thumb of her right hand to apply enough thumb pressure to the first page to make it bend. Then, slipping her other thumb under the bow in the page, flip the page over so she could glance what was on the other side.

After an instant, she'd sweep her eyes along the two table-tops, walk to a certain location at one table or the other, and deposit the notebook, squaring it with any others nearby.

Then, it was back to the stack to take another notebook.

She did that until she brought her routine to an abrupt halt. She was standing at the gap between the two tables. Her next move was to reach for the table farthest from where I was standing and give it a tug. It didn't move. Too heavy. This was when she waved for me to come help her.

I knew what she wanted to do. Join the two tables so they provided one long, uninterrupted work surface. And that had my approval. I'd been about to suggest this myself. It was obvious she was arranging the notebooks by date.

This had to mean she shared the same suspicions I had.

If we were lucky, these notebooks were going to provide us with the history of a macabre crime — the pilots' appalling murders. And, with a little luck, more than these crimes' history. We might have eyewitness accounts to years of events leading up to these crimes. Not in the words of the killers, but in the words of their victims.

And we had more than simply the victims' words. We had an unusual window into how two gifted imaginations had interacted with each other.

I was already suspecting we were going to end up crediting these gifted imaginations with something else. The pilots had somehow managed to involve my isolated, countrified West Texas county in a deadly international kerfuffle. One that was fraught with colliding ambitions, a thirst for vengeance, and numerous opportunities for betrayal. And ending this conflagration, or so it was my hunch, was going to be like extinguishing a gasoline fire.

I could discuss all this with Rashada later. Right now, I needed to make sure she wasn't seeing something I was missing. "The notebooks go back a spell, don't they?"

She seemed absent and didn't look up right away.

Not until she had reached the location she had in mind for the notebook she was holding. Even then, I earned only a quick glance. Then she pointed to the notebook at the far end of the second table. "That's the earliest I've found. It starts with October 3, 2011."

"What's the first entry about?"

"Going home."

"Where were they?"

"Afghanistan."

"How did they sound?"

"Weary."

"What was on their minds?"

"Getting out of Dodge. Getting back to family, friends. Finding themselves girlfriends. I don't know what else. You really need to read these notebooks for yourself, you know?"

"I know. And I have been reading some of them. But tell me something . . ."

I'd have thought my directness would have caused her to turn toward me. But she hadn't done that. She continued to face the table.

The remaining stack of notebooks was within reach, but her hands had dropped to her side. Her head was downcast. I could see enough of her face to realize that her eyes were too. Something was going on, and I didn't have a clue. Maybe it would surface.

For the moment, I decided to stay focused on . . . well, the moment. She had a first-rate mind. A first-rate investigator's mind. I wanted it to help us resolve Abbot County's current crime conundrum. "Tell me what you think we're going to find when we've read through all these notebooks?"

She still didn't turn in my direction. She put the notebook she'd just picked up back on the stack. Used both her hands to feel the notebook's edges, first on the sides and then at the top and bottom. Made a tiny adjustment to make sure it was sitting perfectly square with the notebooks beneath it. Then went still. And stayed still for a length of time that was, to me, beginning to feel awkward.

Then she answered. "I think we're going to find . . . " She stopped and started over. "I think you're going to find that these two pilots were a lot more than they seemed. A lot more than merely two local businessmen running a charter service."

The distress in her voice was so palpable I let the matter drop. In fact, I changed my mind about what I wanted to see happen with the notebooks here in old Judge Kincannon's courtroom. I'd been thinking we'd get them arranged in chronological order. Then, at minimum, each take a peek in all of them, keeping our eyes peeled for clues to anything that might have produced a detrimental outcome for Abbot County. And, if we started finding things, talk about them.

Now, I decided that getting the notebooks in chronological order would be enough for one day.

I suggested as much, and Detective Moody and I continued our routine of opening a notebook. Checking to see what the date of the first entry was. Then placing the notebook where it belonged in the growing arrangement on our tabletop workspace.

Getting to the bottom of the stack required another half hour. When the last one was checked and placed, I turned to face my deputy. "Thank goodness, that's that."

At the time, she was a couple of steps away. Then, no steps away. She reached for me. Drew me forward until our bodies touched. Then our lips.

I was too stunned to speak.

When she finally took a step back, she looked up at me. Smiled her beautiful pageant-girl smile. Reached for me again. Tightened her clutch, laid her head on my shoulder and held me close for a moment. And only then backed completely away. "I've wanted to do that for a long time. Now, I've done it. There's a letter of resignation on your desk. I'm going home to East Texas to run for sheriff."

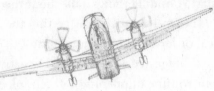

CHAPTER 63

After Detective Moody's dramatic departure, I decided I had to bite the bullet. Read — or at the very least, skim — all the notebooks myself. The task wasn't something that could be delegated.

Besides, the physical and mental activity might help restore order to my hormones more rapidly.

I'd watched Rashada exit the courtroom. She'd grabbed her jacket and purse without a backwards look.

She might visit our offices one more time to pick up her personal gear, but I had a feeling she'd already done that. My suspicion was that she was gone from my life — irrevocably.

If so, it had been a spectacular exit. Especially in the presence of a forty-two-year-old bachelor who had gone all the way to Yale for better life credentials but still hadn't got very far from home.

I packed up the notebooks. Then, I picked up my phone and conveyed a request to Helen. Asked her to summon a couple of deputies. I needed two of them to lug the "men's stuff" boxes to our evidence storage room.

Getting the box with the notebooks to my patrol car was something I thought I could manage myself. And I did manage it by dividing the trip into four stages.

Stage one involved getting the box from the courtroom to the courthouse exit nearest my reserved parking space. Stage two involved holding the door open with my foot, squeezing through with the box and lugging it from the exit to my vehicle. Stage three involved pushing the button on my car key that opened my truck door and balancing the box on the leading edge of the vehicle's trunk well. Stage four involved half-heaving and half-shoving the box over into the trunk.

That still left me with Fresca to deal with.

I could have left him for Helen to drop off at the house later. But heading home and leaving her to continue looking after my behemoth of a mutt at the office seemed an imposition too far. But I knew, dog logistics being what they are, this was going to delay my notebook reading.

Getting him to my vehicle involved only one stage — keeping him from tugging me off my feet as he charged ahead on his leash.

Once we reached the house, I knew it would again be a one-stage operation. At least, until he'd done his number in the backyard.

At the house, I put a couple of dental sticks in his bowl for him to chew on, then returned to my vehicle and repeated the stages I'd used to load the box of notebooks, only in reverse order. I lugged the box into the dining room, sat it momentarily on the tabletop, pulled a second chair closer to the one I planned to sit in, moved the box to it, occupied the first chair, and started to read, beginning with the first notebook.

CHAPTER 64

Just as Rashada had said, it opened with a date.

October 3, 2011.

I quickly sensed what she'd said she sensed in the authors: boredom, homesickness, a desire by the pilots to get on with their lives and find real meaning in them.

On their interminable tour in Afghanistan, keeping the notebooks had apparently been a way for them to deal with some of the feelings of remoteness and ennui.

The discussion about Code New Beginnings began in the second notebook.

In their jottings, both of the individuals referred in passing to their strategy-making studies at the National War College in Washington, D.C. They appeared to have come around to the idea that they could make a real difference, not only in Afghanistan but in the entire Middle East. But they were going to need a strategy. Thus, the gradual development of their schema — the one they eventually ended up outlining on their office suite wall. Their basic idea seemed to be that they could make the whole thing happen with one good and mighty deed. What it was, I wasn't sure. I hoped to figure that out in my reading of the later notebooks.

While at the war college, they'd also both sat through the college's course on the history of code breaking.

As Marines, they'd taken special pride in learning that Navajo "codetalkers" had served valiantly in all six Marine divisions in the Pacific during World War II.

No doubt, this had been where the pilots had learned the Navajo words — or letters from their alphabet — they'd used as names for their code stages. This could have been done on a whim. Or there might have been actual method in their madness. I didn't know. This was something I was still hoping the notebooks would explain.

It was all idealistic. Naive, frankly. Almost juvenile. In so many ways.

Or was it?

CHAPTER 65

A s the pile of notebooks at my elbow grew higher, I found
myself drifting more and more off into my own thoughts.

My own world.

I was nearly forty-two years old and only now showing
a few signs of a real sense of direction. I'd had the extremely
good fortune of having a beautiful, talented woman come
into my orbit. I'd wooed her — and won her. And could look
forward to living my life with her.

Apparently.

I hoped so.

If Angie ever got wind of what had happened in old Judge
Kincannon's courthouse earlier today, she might start second-
guessing her decision to be tied to me.

Isolating myself in that room with another beautiful,
talented woman — especially one who apparently had eyes for
me — might have been unwise.

Much more dangerous, I now understood, than I would
have ever supposed, had I thought much about it in advance.

But had I thought about it in advance?

I could still feel Rashada's supple lips pressed tight against
mine. Pressed tight, and lingering. At the same time, her fingers

had been planted in the small of my back, drawing me forward into her embrace and clearly in no hurry to release me.

I was going to wonder until my dying breath whether I'd set the whole encounter up out of a reluctance to move my life forward.

There were more than a few signs I was dragging my feet in that department.

The issue of what I was going to do with my career in the long-term still hadn't been resolved. Was I going to stay in law enforcement? If not, I might have wasted nearly two decades of my life.

And if I stayed in law enforcement, the question was . . . stay where?

In Abbot County?

I could only run for sheriff so many times even if I won reelection again.

Stay somewhere else in Texas?

I could probably get an administrative job with a state agency in Austin. Or possibly a command position with the Texas Rangers or maybe hook up with some investigative agency operating out of Dallas or Houston.

But where did those kinds of outcomes leave me — leave *us* — if and when the FBI transferred Angie somewhere else? Trapped in one of those clumsy, dangerous long-distance relationships?

I could still hear Angie's instant rejection ringing in my ears. "Not for me, Luke-a-roo, baby! When I hear your voice, I prefer to have a body attached to it or at least one close by."

But staying in law enforcement meant consigning that expensive divinity degree from Yale to, at best, only occasional use. If, that is, I ever made use of it in a career sense at all.

So far, that twenty-minute stint in the pulpit the other day had been the first time I'd used those skills since leaving divinity school. I had to admit the experience had caused a bit of a stir in my chest. I could still move people's emotions. Cause them to reflect on what Saint Paul had called the substance of things not seen, the evidence of things to be hoped for. I'd seen that in their eyes as they'd filed past me at the church-house door after my sermon.

And either way — whether I decided to keep wearing the star or make a career change and wear the cloth — there was still the issue of becoming a father. Or not.

Did I want children?

Time wasn't going to be on my side a lot longer. Most women wanted children. Angie did. If I didn't, sometime soon I was going to find myself in one hell of a predicament.

But then, sitting there with the pilots' notebooks stacked all around me, I realized I was already confronting a predicament.

In my case, it was a bit early. Most men didn't experience mid-life crises until they were between their late-forties or fifties. But already, I was feeling a profound sense of uncertainty. I waited for my subconscious to supply a word. It eventually did. A profound sense of . . .

. . . *incompleteness.*

"Say what!"

This was when I realized I'd spoken aloud for the first time since I'd sat down at my dining table and started looking at the notebooks.

I silently repeated the word to myself.

Incompleteness.

At that point, I stood up. Reached for the box with the notebooks. Swung it around so that extracting the last notebook from its "end of the parade" location was a snap. Ignored the quickening in my breathing and a new palpable thump in my chest. And introduced a pronounced departure from the routine Detective Moody and I had used from the beginning in our examination of the notebooks.

I didn't cradle the notebook in the crib that the fingers of both hands naturally make when you are holding something to be read. Instead, I shifted the notebook to where it was resting completely on the extended fingers of my right hand.

This didn't mean the left thumb and fingers had no role. They had an important role. They could be in control of the entire notebook, if that's what I wanted. But it wasn't. The only pages I was interested in were at the back, so this was where I put those fingers to work.

As my left thumb allowed a few pages at the rear of the notebook to flip past, my right thumb was allowing me to scan these pages one or two at a time.

In short order, I reached the page where the pilots had begun their final entry in this notebook, the page that included the date for that entry.

And this was when my suspicions — my expectations, by this point — were confirmed. The final entry of the final notebook in our box marked Notebooks was not so final after all.

It was fourteen months old.

This meant our library of notebooks, intriguing as it was, wouldn't be providing us with the most recent clues to the pilots' activities. Not unless we found additional notebooks. That was assuming, of course, that additional notebooks existed. I had no idea if they did. And if they did, I had no idea where to look for them.

Our understanding of the pilots' deaths was, therefore, suffering from a severe case of incompleteness.

That word again.

I thought about all this over an early sandwich. Then through an evening of mindless TV viewing due to an attention-deficit problem.

I kept seeing this image in my awareness.

One of a wall filled with red, black and purple words, plus a symbol or two. A particular wall in a particular two-room office suite that was located not that far from the scene of a particularly grisly double murder.

The first time I'd viewed what was on the wall, I hadn't understood very much about what had been written there. Only that a lot of it looked like it could have been lifted straight from Lewis Carroll's nutty poem, "Jabberwocky." All mimsy were the borogoves. That's what some of the stuff streaming across the wall looked and sounded like — pure mimsy from the borogoves.

Now, I wanted to look at it again. I knew I still wasn't going to understand everything, but I had a feeling about it.

Several feelings, in fact.

I was pretty sure I knew which parts of Code New Beginnings had been written by The Commander. And which parts by The Roamer. But I sensed that more was to come from the two deceased pilots.

I was feeling that if we gave them rapt attention and showed a little respect and appreciation for their cleverness, they would join us. Sit there with me and another person or two. And engage in earnest dialogue about what had led up to the unspeakable events in the hanger.

I knew the idea was weird — too weird ever to explain to anyone but Angie. But the sensation had a cinch on my certainties that was too powerful to ignore.

I even felt those lumpy, faded, vintage-styled pieces of furniture had been placed in the pilots' office suite for this express purpose. To help us get to the bottom of this. Find the culprits. And understand their involvement.

When this happened, I knew who I wanted to be sitting in the chair: me.

But since Angie wasn't available, I had to think about who I wanted to be sitting on the sofa facing me.

When I figured it out, I sent Helen a text asking her to see if they could join me first thing tomorrow.

CHAPTER 66

D r. Jon Dandurall and my chief deputy were standing near the door to the slain pilots' office suite. I heard the opinionated scientist before I saw him.

He was up close in my chief deputy's face, waving both his hands in the air. As he shouted, he looked like he was hacking away at some invisible menace.

I suspected it had nothing to do with the untimely deaths of the former occupants of the offices we were about to visit. More likely, Del Emma had expressed an opinion about something — anything. And "Doctor D" had immediately erupted in argumentative opposition, merely for the sake of arguing.

Dandurall hadn't worn his turtleneck. He was wearing a button-down collared dress shirt and a halfway chic tie beneath his sports jacket.

I adjusted my approach to the pair so they'd be less likely to see me until I was ready. After all, this was an airport. There was nothing inappropriate about aligning yourself better with the runway before landing. When I was ready, I issued a demand. "Gentlemen, quickly now. Give me an eleven-letter word for something you can make a man from."

Their answers came in near-perfect unison. "Gingerbread!" They'd gone from total involvement with each other to total involvement with the unexpected new party without missing a breath or a beat.

I feigned disbelief that I was witnessing such a scene in an airport. "I do believe you've both arrived with just the right attitude."

All three of us turned to face the door. The jaunty mood dissipated the instant we stepped into the pilots' offices. And it should have.

We all understood the events that had brought us together were too tragic and macabre — and too needful of explanation — to waste any more time carrying on like schoolboys.

I parked my laptop on the end of the desk closest to the chair. Stared at my computer for a moment. And decided not to raise the screen right away. The room would have enough distractions without my trying to take notes or look up things on the internet at the same time.

My guests seated themselves on the sofa. I settled into the chair. Then, eyeing the pair opposite me, let the rarity of the occasion sink in.

All that red hair.

Out of curiosity, I'd once checked Wikipedia to see how common red hair was in America.

Its nabobs had opined that America had more people with high levels of a reddish pigment called pheomelanin in their physical makeup than anywhere else in the world.

No one had a firm count. It could be as few as six million people and as many as twenty million. In terms of a percentage of our population, we were nowhere near being the auburn-haired capital of the world. Scotland took that honor — with fourteen percent. Ireland was next with ten percent. And here I was in the room with two flaming examples of the phenomenon with me.

But I hadn't finagled this meeting because of these two individuals' flagrantly noticeable pigmentation. I was running short of people to help me sort through the challenges detailed on that wall.

I didn't know when Angie would be available. Rashada was probably gone forever. Dr. Bender and Nina Kendricks had disappeared. I had other deputies, but none I wanted to take away from their regular duties and drag into all this. So this pair was it — and I'd invited them there because I thought they'd do.

Both had seemed intrigued by the wall scribbles from the moment they'd waked through the door. I wasn't surprised by that. But I was by what Dandurall did next.

Barely an instant after he sat down on the sofa, looked up at the wall, and began to read, he leaped back to his feet. Charged to the wall. And began to ram a finger at the entry for Code Chindi like he was accusing it of something.

Turned out he was.

Not the entry, as such. But the people who'd made the entry. "Holy Mother! *These guys played me like a fiddle!*"

My one good eye and both my chief deputy's hurried to read what was provoking him so.

It appeared to be what the pilot I'd nicknamed The Commander had written with his usual dignified efficiency. "The scientist knows he will need to start the process somewhere other than Flagler."

But it wasn't the black-lettered part of the Code Chindi entry that seemed to be agitating the good doctor the most. It was The Roamer's purple-lettered part. "Mexican folks, make nice egg / but Mariachis make hot potato if omelet left on their grill / best bring Eve and wee one home to the garden."

Dandurall was shouting. "How many people have seen this?"

I felt I owed him an answer. "Just the two of you. Plus the local FBI special agent."

Now I had a question that needed to be answered. "Why does it matter?"

I didn't get a reply.

He was too absorbed in reading the other material on the wall. Entry by entry. Code by code. Reading and pointing. Using both hands at times to make connections. Then taking his arms away and backtracking and rereading.

He took a couple of steps away from the wall so he could take in more of it and started talking. Not talking, exactly. More like cogitating out loud.

He was talking himself through Code New Beginnings step by step. Through the schema. Like he was seeking to figure out where the scenario of events outlined on the wall might lead.

I knew the feeling.

I'd been trying to do that from the moment Angie and I had first entered the pilots' office suite.

I realized I was literally leaning slightly in the wall's direction, not wanting to miss a single word he uttered. Not that he noticed. The wall had him mesmerized.

Until it didn't.

CHAPTER 67

It all happened with an abruptness that startled me.

Dandurall backed up almost to the center of the room. Put his hands on his hips. Spent several more seconds staring at the wall. Then announced his conclusion. "I don't think everything they knew is up here. The codes aren't finished."

He approached the wall again. Reached high on it with his left hand, and rested that index finger once again on Code Chindi. Then made an arc with his body and his arms so expansive I feared he'd pull his shoulder joints out of their sockets.

This allowed him to start tapping the last entry with the index finger of his right hand while he continued to tap Code Chindi with his left index finger. He was now stretched from Code Chindi to Code Gah. "No, they didn't. They didn't finish."

More muttering followed. More calculating. More analysis. Then an announcement. "Well, the bastards!"

I didn't think he could maintain that posture much longer. I was right. About then, his back shouted uncle. He retreated from the wall. And put his hands on his hips. "Not bad at all. Damn clever, in fact."

I'd been observing Dandurall as closely as he'd been observing the wall. And doing my own calculating. I needed to be careful how I re-entered his awareness. I needed him to view me as something other than a superior to him. I didn't even want him to see me as an equal. More as an earnest, good-intentioned subordinate, seeking help with the hard stuff.

The way to do that?

I decided to position myself as Dr. Watson to his Sherlock. Not permanently. But for as long as it took to get him to share what else he knew about the pilots' deaths. Otherwise, it was going to be too easy for me to end up as Professor Moriarty. If not viewed like an enemy by him, at least like a rival, and this would make him hold back.

Perhaps the right question would do the trick. That idea gave birth to another. *Might a trick question be the right one? One way to find out.*

"Are the pilots' deaths a murder/suicide?"

Doctor D had been in the midst of a return to the sofa. At hearing my question, he stiffened. "Surely, sir, you jest."

Okay, that worked. He'd realized I was still in the room. Maybe I could build on that awareness. "It might explain a bunch of things, don't you think?"

His posture was still unmoving. "Name one."

"Why the pilots' notebooks for the last fourteen months are missing."

"Name another."

"Why this looks less and less like some kind of — quote, unquote — happy new beginning."

"Keep going."

"Why the pilots seemed to be involved in one mysterious act after another."

"Any more?"

"Well, let's try one closer to home. Why you've been trying so hard to convince folks that the pilots were in over their heads."

From the look on his face, I thought I'd hooked his instincts for self-preservation with that one.

This could have been the moment he returned to the couch after all, joined my long-suffering deputy chief, and told both of us what Code New Beginnings was really all about. Explained why a 4,000-year-old mummy had been brought to Flagler, only to be shuffled back and forth between our town's drama-makers like an unwanted birthday gift. Maybe spill the beans about what he was actually doing with the laboratory anti-suicidal-sperm techniques he was so proud of. And share his thinking on whether the killer or killers would strike again and, if so, where. And at whom.

But it wasn't.

He looked toward the door. Turned back toward the wall. Reversed himself with another half-turn of his body. Swallowed hard several times. Launched glances at several objects in the room, none of which came close to being in my direction. Then he charged to the door, shoved it open, and fled.

I glanced at Del Emma but didn't rush to put brackets around what had just happened. The events of the past few minutes would establish their sense of closure on their own time. When they did, my chief deputy and I could initiate the conversation we were going to need to have.

My rash suggestion about a murder/suicide — that just popped out of my mouth, but I wanted to think about it some more. In fact, I was thinking about it a lot.

Why?

Because it made about as much sense as any other death scenario I could suggest at the moment.

There was one problem, of course. The question of the peripatetic hand. How had it gone missing and then, a day or two ago, managed to put in a reappearance?

But this didn't rule out a murder/suicide. It simply required that at least one other person be at the crime scene besides the killer or killers.

That might not be a problem, either. We had an eyewitness who could put not one but two other people there. We'd been assuming these two were the killers. At least, I'd been assuming that but they might only have been eyewitnesses themselves.

Of course, if that were true, they'd taken their role with extreme seriousness. All that blood spatter on their buddy suits. They'd gotten up close and dirty.

I gave my chief deputy an opening. "You ever run into things like this in South Florida?"

His laugh seemed to originate more from sympathy than amusement. "Oh, all the time. I just never paid them much attention."

That got him the puzzled look he was fishing for.

This time, his chuckle was more relaxed. "The perpetrators always spoke Spanish."

"So you don't?"

"Well, a few words. Like 'Buenas noches.' And 'Hola, me llamo Chuck.'"

I suspected he knew a lot more than that. I revisited my languages classes of long ago and pulled some Spanish words out of my memory. "¿Qué hacemos a continuación?"

What do we do next?

But before either of us could say anything more, the door swung open. Nina Kendricks walked through it, followed by Dr. Bender. Kendricks was clutching a couple of loops of the crime scene tape.

Her first words scrambled my thoughts.

"Where are the pilots?"

CHAPTER 68

I couldn't get my eye to quit staring. At their clothes.

The pair was almost certainly wearing the same outfits Angie and I had seen them wearing in the video. A video made days ago. The video in which they'd had an intense conversation with Pogue Stockstill and then disappeared out the airport lobby door leading to the boarding apron, presumably to catch a plane.

Kendricks removed any doubt about the clothes with what she said next. "Don't touch us. We've been on airplanes most of the last forty-eight hours. Can't remember the last time I showered."

Her eyes gave the room a quick sweep. When they came to rest, it wasn't on anything in the front room. They were fixated on the desk in the back office. She could see it plainly through the door. She was still staring at it when she tipped us to her real concern. "The notebooks — are they missing?"

I caught my chief deputy's attention and pointed to the chair. He moved over to it.

Next, I invited the pair to seat themselves on the couch.

In a few seconds, I was back with one of the chairs from the second office. I unfolded it and took my own seat.

I sought to reassure Ms. Kendricks. "The notebooks are safe in my office. At least, most of them. They weren't all in the drawer, were they, folks?"

The pilots' office manager dropped her head, and I couldn't see her eyes. But Bender's eyes were darting all over the place. He looked like he was trying to work all this out.

It wasn't hard to guess most of the questions he was wrestling with. What were two of the county's senior law enforcement officials doing in the pilots' office suite? How had we gotten in without doing at least some visible damage? How had we managed to open the desk drawer without doing more of the same? How did we know there were notebooks missing? And the crime scene tape — why had it been there to begin with?

I saw him blink. Twice. This time, looking right at me. "Something's happened to the pilots, hasn't it?"

This moment shouldn't have felt inopportune. I'd been expecting it. But I still felt sandbagged by it. And, in an instant, I understood why. I'd been busy myself pondering things that didn't add up.

Why had this pair worn the same clothes for days? What was the reason for their exhaustive travel schedule? Why hadn't they gone home when they got off the plane instead of arriving together at the woman's place of work? How did Dr. Bender justify being on such an intense safari or whatever it was with Ms. Kendricks to start with? He was married, wasn't he?

My neck may have literally snapped back. Not sure. But I realized with a jarring abruptness there was something else I hadn't dealt with yet.

Their question.

"Yes, the pilots . . . I'm sorry to say they're dead."

CHAPTER 69

You've heard people talk about things getting deathly quiet. My simple pronouncement seemed to have brought about that kind of silence in the room. And stillness.

I couldn't detect any movement. Certainly, not on my part. I don't believe I'd so much as blinked since the last time I'd heard my voice.

It was no surprise to me that Bender's face had remained unchanged. He seemed the stoic type.

Nina Kendricks wasn't emoting much, either. She wasn't turning to Bender for support or condolence and wasn't offering him any. Hadn't so much as reached out to touch his arm. That seemed to put one of my questions to bed. *So much for them being an item.*

So what were they? Somebody's operational team? Ideological sympathizers? Cooperating adversaries? Teacher and student? Mentor and acolyte? Next door neighbors? Brother and sister?

Kendricks tossed the crime scene tape on the sofa between them. "Crap!" And sent her first look at Bender. The glance hadn't seemed to be one of recrimination. More one of resignation — and regret. Her words reinforced that. "All that hurrying wasn't enough. We're too late!"

Bender was staring at the landline phone on the desk. I'd had it on my mind too. "If you thought these guys were in jeopardy, why didn't you call them?"

This time, Bender was the one who replied. "Couldn't be sure who would answer. Even before we left for Jerusalem, we knew we were all probably dealing with deep shadow types."

I glanced at both the people sitting on the couch. Wanted to see if either had noticed how my eyebrows shot up.

It wasn't so much that Jerusalem was in the picture again. It was the reference to "deep shadow types."

I'd never used the term. I'd never heard anyone else around the Abbot County Sheriff's Department use it. I wasn't even sure I knew what it meant.

I intended to ask but wanted my questions to draw a coherent story from this daredevil pair.

That was why I didn't address my first question specifically to either one. Until it needed to be something else, it could be considered a "to whom it may concern"-type inquiry. I decided to start with The Holy City anyway. "So your destination on this trip was Jerusalem?"

Bender stayed in the lead. "Not really. Our final destination was Deir Dibwan. That's in the central West Bank, east of Ramallah."

The uselessness of that explanation irked me. *Why didn't he just tell me it was on the dark side of the moon?* But I didn't want to come across as any more of a geographical ignoramus than I was. "So, a suburb of Jerusalem."

"Not really."

"Okay, I get it. You're bored and we're going to play Twenty Questions."

That brought a fleeting smile from both of them. But it also brought out the professor in the professor. "No, not at all. Thanks to near-constant warfare for 4,000 years, partitioning by the United Nations and spaghetti-like borders, and road networks, that part of the world can be confusing."

"So a town *not far* from Jerusalem."

Bender got the point, not that it helped much. "To be specific, thirty-nine point kilometers. Takes about an hour and twenty minutes to drive it — if you observe the speed limit. And the road is so hilly and curvy, it's hard not to. Just take Begin Boulevard and Route 50 north out of the Holy City."

I wanted to keep him amused. "Then go left at the first traffic signal, correct?"

This time, he didn't so much as crack a grin. I realized he was trying to picture a traffic signal along the route.

Seriously?

I assured him I was joking. This was why I assumed the joke was being turned on me when he volunteered a new detail about his and Nina Kendricks's recent travels. "But we didn't go to Deir Dibwan first. We went to Gallup."

That had to be Gallup, New Mexico, again. A curious remark that I had no idea what to do with. I didn't do anything with it.

He shifted on the sofa so he could gesture at the wall with all the scribblings. "Maybe Code New Beginnings can help us get to the bottom of the rest of it."

CHAPTER 70

Del Emma noticed it first.

I became aware of what was happening when I noticed Del Emma.

He'd fished his hanky out of his back pants pocket and was offering it to Ms. Kendricks. Tears were streaming down both sides of her face.

She reached for the handkerchief and used it to pat her cheeks down. Meticulously.

Next, she blotted around both eyes. After that, she took her time unfurling the square of fabric to its full size. Then raised it to her nose. And blew. Hard.

I let matters ride for what I hoped was a decent interval and asked point blank. "You had a close relationship with the pilots?"

She blew her nose again on my chief deputy's handkerchief. Whispered a wordless "thank you" to him. Refolded the cloth to its original shape and tucked it in her bag with almost ritualistic care. Looked at him again. "I'll launder this for you."

Del Emma did what a gentleman is supposed to do — waved it off as being of little consequence.

Her body shuddered.

I knew it was involuntary. The body sometimes does that when the brain speed-processes something complicated or confusing.

"Relationship? No, nothing like you're thinking. Nothing romantic. I learned a long time ago not to get involved that way with people I work for. Or work with."

I kept watching her. That explanation was leaving too much unexplained. If I waited, there was going to be more.

When it came, my brain served up another familiar sensation. The one where part of it chose to look on from a distance while the rest of it sorted things out.

It had new information to work with. That was because Ms. Kendricks had seemed to sum up everything she knew about the deaths of the two pilots in a few meaty words.

"Ever hear that Dostoevsky quote? About how power is given only to those who dare to stoop and take it? That's what the pilots and the rest of us . . . me, Zack Alonso, Dr. Dandurall, some people you've never met and never will . . . had planned to do, you know. Dare to step into history and give a little bit of it a new power and a new beginning."

The Dostoevsky quote — yes, I'd heard it. Professor Lovejoy had used it only a few days ago to describe Dr. Bender. I was startled to realize I'd never known Bender's full name. Now that I'd heard it, I was startled all over. *Zack Alonso* Bender, was it? Who'd have guessed?

And Dr. Dandurall? He'd been in this room only a few minutes ago.

People I'd never met and never would? Some of them from Gallup, apparently. And a wide place in the road north of Jerusalem called Deir Dibwan.

All involved in some mad plot that had ended Sunday morning in the twin propeller blades of a much-traveled private aircraft in one of Flagler's airport hangars. In a bloody, mysterious tragedy that had killed two people. Hacked them up like hamburger.

It was a plot certain to have been hatched in this office suite. The two individuals sitting there had obviously been involved in the hatching. And that wall down there at the end of the room seemed to have been where the recording secretaries — the two pilots themselves, if you could believe it — had posted their notes as the grand scheme had been thought up and worked through.

If only they could be here to supply the final details. Or, at minimum, their notebooks for the past fourteen months. How had the Scottish poet said it? The best laid schemes o' mice an' men / Gang aft agley.

I glanced at my deputy. He occasionally glanced at me but most of the time, he was eying the other two in the room. He obviously had a ton of questions for one, or both, but he was having trouble deciding who to question first and what question to start with. "I want to talk to you both, but we'll wait on that. Why don't you vamose for now?"

He said he was going to his patrol vehicle for more crime scene tape.

His exit from the room seemed to be a signal for Bender and Kendricks to rise to their feet. But before they exited, they seemed to feel they needed to explain where they were going.

Kendricks said she needed a powder room. She followed this thought with another one. After all their traveling, what she really needed to do was go home, shower, and crawl into bed. Bender piggybacked on the idea. He needed to get home too. Said his wife was going to be wondering why he wasn't home already.

They looked at each other as if wondering if there was anything else they needed to share with each other. Apparently, they decided not. Both were up and out of the room without another word and were gone in a few heartbeats, their luggage trailing behind them like devoted puppies.

For the first time since Del Emma and I had turned the locks on the office suite, I was alone with my thoughts. And my own bladder. I needed a powder room myself.

Availing myself of that most fortunate of male capabilities — the ability to urinate standing up — allowed my mind to zero in on something else. Something Dr. Dandurall had said.

He'd been studying the Code New Beginnings entries on the wall when he'd erupted at one of them.

The last one.

Code Gah.

After first reading it, he'd literally charged the wall. Began hammering at it. And shouted that they — meaning the pilots, I'd assumed — were bastards. But he'd apparently meant that to be a backwards compliment. After looking at the wall a little longer, he'd added that they'd been "damn clever."

For some reason, about the time he said that, the idea had occurred to me that the pilots' deaths might have been a murder/suicide. I'd suggested it to my companions, and the room had erupted again. This was why our conversation had never returned to Code Gah.

Now, it was time for me to take a closer look at it. At what The Commander and The Roamer had named after Navajo language's letter *r*. Like their other code names, it could also be translated literally. To Navajos, among other things, it meant rabbit.

Hurrying back to the pilots' office suite, I perched myself on the end of the sofa. And commenced staring at the wall.

At the final entry, most of all.

At Code Gah.

The Commander's summation was efficient and proper like all his others, although a little more poetic than most of the ones he'd written. "Expect the head's logic to bow to the heart's rainbow."

The Roamer's entry was similar to all his other entries. There was the usual juvenile nuttiness. But I also sensed serious instructions were being transmitted. "Theme song is Video con Dios, my love! / Noah sailed on a barque, not an ark / be sure to lip-read the horses' mouths."

I walked over to my laptop. Flipped the screen back. Lit it up. Then spent several more long moments gazing up at the wall again at what The Roamer had written under Code Gah.

That gave me several ideas.

I instructed my computer to go to the imaging service, VideU, and searched for "Noah's Bargue." I watched as it identified fifty-five results in the folder.

Jackpot. It was them. Looking at the dates on the videos, I realized the pilots hadn't left many blind spots in their activities in the past fourteen months. Or at least, not many blind stretches. If we didn't find satisfactory explanations for what had happened in the hangar last Sunday morning, and even if we did, I was destined to spend several hours watching videos soon.

I clicked on the first one — the one headed "Origins of Code New Beginnings."

The horizontal thumbnail image at the left of the headline showed the two pilots crunched close together in front of their King Air. One of them had been holding the phone out at arm's length so they could take an "us-ie."

Opening the file, I watched as Quitaque Haynes explained that this was probably a hair-brained scheme. But he and his buddy thought they might have hit on a way to keep people like them from having to go to places they had no interest in going. And, truth be known, any business being in. Like Afghanistan.

CHAPTER 71

That first video had been posted fourteen months ago. So, one mystery cleared. We hadn't found the final fourteen months of the notebooks because they'd never existed.

The pilots had turned to making videos. According to VideU, fifty-five of them.

I did the math in my head. More or less, one a week. A quick scroll-through of files in the Noah's Barque folder confirmed this.

It was clear that Ike Breezer had been the man behind the camera for most of the videos. If I'd been directing the videos, that's where I'd have stationed him anyway. For appearance's sake.

Kway Haynes had been by far the more photogenic of the two. I didn't want to say that he'd had a natural beefcake look. But that was the reality.

Something about the solid set of his squarish shoulders established the pattern. Moving upward, Mother Nature's architect had stayed with the plan. Squarish chin, manly mouth, airbrushed nose, Hollywood-ready eyes and brows, all topped off by designer-styled sandy brown hair. If he'd had a bad angle, it wasn't showing up in the videos.

On the other hand, Breezer's face was off-kilter no matter where you focused. In the few videos where he appeared, one of his dark eyes always seemed puffier than the other. He was balding, but not equally on both sides. His thin lips didn't enjoy a compatible symmetry with his nose, which lacked symmetry itself. It bent slightly to the left.

And . . . And *I needed to quit this!*

Both these poor dudes were dead. Chopped up like slabs of meat. I needed to find a video that gave me some clue as to why it had happened.

I scrolled to the last one. Noted the date of the posting — "6 days ago." Read the headline. And, as seemed to be happening more and more these days, I heard myself announce my reaction, hoping all the while no one else was listening. "Don't fuck with me!"

Unless this was a terrible joke by a very nimble and inventive internet troll, I was about to learn how the pilots had spent some of the final moments of their lives.

At least, the headline fed that expectation. "Arriving with Mr. Code New Beginnings and His Mom-to-Be!"

The accompanying image showed a very pregnant woman framed in the doorway of the pilots' King Air. Ike Breezer had just helped her through the door. Kway Haynes was on one side of the stairs, reaching up to steady her. The video continued with the woman descending the stairs and being escorted by Haynes to a waiting golf cart.

CHAPTER 72

Staring at the video of the pregnant woman descending from the pilots' plane, I realized something that left me frozen in my chair.

I'd made a wrong assumption.

When my chief deputy had told me about the notations on the pilots' desktop calendar, I'd assumed our killer — or killers — at the hangar last Sunday morning hadn't been from Flagler. I'd pictured them as having arrived from somewhere else. To invade our peace and quiet as deadly interlopers. Probably from another distant continent.

And I'd assumed they'd been drawn to Abbot County by the pilots' naiveté and greed. By Haynes's and Breezer's horrendous misjudgment in accepting as cargo a controversial mummy taken off the icy slopes of Mount Ararat and then hauling it in the wrong direction. It was supposed to have traveled east and they'd transported it west. All the way to Flagler. And allowed it to be passed around like a department store mannequin.

My mental scenario also assumed that the killers, having accomplished their mission, were long gone. By now, no doubt, they'd already slept a night or two in their own beds. Most likely, back in Tel Aviv or Jerusalem or Amman or Riyadh.

But that was then, and this was now.

I now understood I might be 180 degrees off-base about the origins — and intentions — of our killers.

There might have been no need to import a pair of killers. Thanks to the finger pointing — deliberate or not — by the pilots themselves, I'd had a consciousness-arresting thought. The idea had been triggered by the extraordinary array of wall renderings, calendar notations, and computer videos available in the pilots' office suite. The killer might have already been here. *And I might have just finished having lunch with him. Or her. Or them.*

Another thought had tripped over the heels of that one. If I'd not lunched with the killer or killers, I'd dined surrounded by people every bit as vulnerable to being killed as the pilots. Killed by the same interloping parties. And killed for the same presumed sins. For having plotted against the plans of the surreptitious group that had spawned them. Against the momentum of history. And, against the assumed will of God.

What should I do next?

Put them all under surveillance? Or, if they were victims and not perpetrators, under house protection?

I really didn't have enough deputies to do that for very long.

Besides, this was an opinionated, independent-spirited bunch.

Doc Konnie might indulge a deputy stationed in her autopsy room during the day, but she was going to squawk at having one follow her home at night. Young Stockstill had just been cooped up in a hospital bed for days. Restricting his movements again and assigning him a Glock-wearing babysitter wasn't going to sit well. And there was the pair of Kendricks and Bender. One was highly intense and drama-prone and the other was hopelessly inquisitive and adventurous. I'd have better luck trying to keep tabs 24/7 on a visitation of horny kangaroos.

Besides, around-the-clock observation of that many people was going to attract notice. Sooner or later, Clyde Hazelton would get wind of it. Once the *Tribune-Standard* put out the word, the whole town would know. Including, if they picked up a newspaper in the airport or their hotel, the killers. That is, if they were still here. Or if they were to return.

I thought it a much better plan to establish a twenty-four-hour guard over the most likely target of all. The pregnant mother. Once the baby was delivered, the protection could be extended to her newborn. They'd need security indefinitely, but not from me. In the longer term, I'd turn the problem over to my fiancée and the Feds.

First, I had to find the mother-to-be.

The hospital hadn't admitted anyone resembling the woman in the pilots' video. Our local emergency ambulance service had no record of having transported anyone meeting her description. I had Helen spend a couple of hours calling all our local obstetricians, but that didn't get us anywhere. I called Flagler's homeless shelter and a couple of churches with programs for single mothers, even though I realized what shots in the dark these were. None of these outreaches generated a lead.

I couldn't remember when I'd felt my idea quiver so empty. For a moment, I felt a tinge of despair. Then I remembered that quote about despair being anger with no place to go. There was one more place I could go. Or rather, at least one more individual I could seek out. My mind bequeathed a new name for him. "Mister Airport."

Pogue Stockstill, the college student.

No one had seemed to know more about the pilots' movements than he had. Where would he think the pilots had sequestered their pregnant passenger?

I found him in his dorm room at the University of The Hills. Allowed him a quick joke about how I should take out adoption papers for him. Gave him a terse explanation for my visit. And watched him respond with a finger snap. "Of course, their late-nighter!"

I professed ignorance of what that was. He was already headed for the door. "Come on — I'll show you."

The drive took about twenty minutes. If we had started from the airport, it would have taken less than four. On our drive, Stockstill explained that the pilots' over-nighter was a two-bedroom kitchenette apartment "a hop, skip, and jump" away from the airport. He said it was where the pilots often stayed when they had an early morning flight or a ridiculously late night arrival.

We knocked on the door, and it produced an instant response. A scream for help.

The door was unlocked. When young Stockstill and I entered, one glance told us what was needed. An ambulance. A hugely pregnant woman was sprawled in the room's only armchair. She was clutching a bloody towel between her legs. She moaned, then screamed again. "My baby is coming! We need a hospital!"

We did, indeed.

I summoned the paramedics. Saw the patient off to Flagler General. Loaded up young Stockstill and transported him back to the university. Then radioed my dispatcher and told him to assign three deputies to the hospital ED and a newly arrived mother-in-waiting. And then to assign deputies to find Dr. Dandurall, Doc Konnie, Dr. Bender, and Nina Kendricks and provide them with protection.

I'd dropped Stockstill off in front of his dorm when I got a status report. The hospital ED and the pregnant mother, Dandurall and the medical examiner were covered. No problem locating the latter two. Both had returned to work after our luncheon.

But Bender and Kendricks were nowhere to be found.

They needed to be.

And, at the moment, I was our department's expert on the pair. No one knew more about their favorite haunts, personal vicissitudes, preferential quirks, and the games they played when they didn't want to be found or found out. I needed to get back to the office and direct the search.

This was why my chief deputy and I didn't arrive at Flagler General Hospital until mid-afternoon.

I wasn't certain how long we'd be able to remain there. The professor and the pilots' office manager remained at large. The hunt had to be continued.

CHAPTER 73

Del Emma and I parked in the sheriff department's assigned reserve space and hurried through the emergency room doors.

The receptionist was eager to assist us. Her eyes dropped to the badge penned on my shirt. From there, her eyes moved to my face. Del Emma was treated to the same routine. His badge was scrutinized. His face too.

This seemed to reassure her.

And emboldened her to do what good receptionists do when they aren't getting the information they need. Ask another question. "Is this person a man or a woman?"

"A very pregnant woman brought in by ambulance," I told her.

The hospital employee was now in serious interaction with her computer keyboard and screen. The data was flowing. "We have a woman in our delivery room now. If you'd like to have a seat in the waiting room with the other expectant fathers, I'll have someone step out and update you."

An instant later, all three of us understood that this delay wouldn't be necessary. Whatever had been happening in the delivery room was now spilling into the hallway.

Two individuals clad head to toe in blue buddy suits, black ski masks, and respirator cups provided the first indication that not everything was kosher. The pair burst through a pair of swinging doors in the hallway a dozen or so steps from where we were standing. The sound of the doors slamming back against the wall had quit echoing in the hallways, but I could still hear it ringing in my ears.

Each of these persons took a couple of steps. Then, on their heels, two more people charged into the hallway.

Both were holding pistols.

Each of them took aim at one of the fleeing persons and fired their weapon. Each target crumpled to the floor and lay there unmoving. Instinctively, I knew they were dead.

The gunmen froze in their tracks. Glanced in both directions. Then started running full tilt toward the emergency room exit. That's to say, straight at Del Emma and me.

They noticed us waiting with our guns drawn. This was when they applied the brakes so forcefully they began to skid on the waxed floor.

When they recovered, they aimed their own weapons at Del Emma and me. And sent two thunderous crashes careening through the hospital hallways.

I thought both bullets pierced the glass exit doors behind us, but I was too busy to check. I was about to return fire when both figures disappeared into one of the hospital's wings. But not, as their luck would have it, into one of its patient wings.

Those wings have emergency fire doors at the end. Push the doors' panic bars open and you could exit the building.

The wing that had swallowed the shooters was a storage wing. The fire door for that wing was chained shut.

I was aware of all this because the fire department had been involved in a long running dispute with the hospital over the practice.

Chaining up an exit door was not only potentially deadly in case of a fire. It was also illegal. I also knew you needed one of the maintenance department's keys to be able to get into any of the storage rooms. Security for what was stored there was the whole idea behind the chained fire door. So I thought the pair with the murderous trigger fingers were trapped.

I also thought they would surely surrender, and both my deputy chief and I shouted warnings calling on them to do so.

But they didn't.

CHAPTER 74

Del Emma was crouched behind the receptionist's desk, talking into his mobile radio. Anyone observing all this might reasonably have expected him to be whispering. But this wasn't the case. He was shouting at the top of his lungs.

He ordered our dispatcher to start a Code Red response toward the hospital. But warned him to keep deputies out of the building until he learned more from us. Our SWAT team was to take up positions in the parking lot and await further orders.

I heard our dispatcher ask if he should relay any instructions to the hospital.

My chief deputy told him the watchword of the hour was duck. Take cover. Lock your doors. Keep your head down. And, by all means, the hospital's security people should stay the hell away from the emergency room entrance. The sheriff's office would handle things there. I had a vagrant thought as I listened to this. Deputy Chief Del Emma wasn't teaching Sunday School at the moment.

While my deputy chief was communicating with headquarters, I was watching the two people menacing us.

Stationed on the wall opposite the shooters' hideaway, there was one of those wide-angle convex mirrors that eliminate blind spots at corners.

Every move the pair made was as plain as day.

I watched as they tried to open one door after another and realized for the first time how they were dressed. They were decked out in blue medical workwear including scrub caps, and they had stethoscopes draped around their necks.

At this point, space in my mind for logical thinking was at a premium. But dawn can't resist the rising sun forever.

When the implications of what I was seeing in the corner mirror soaked in, my knees almost buckled. Or they would have, had I not already been squatting. The two persons visible in the mirror had been in the baby delivery room posing as obstetricians. The fear flooding over me was for the mother-to-be, the unborn infant, and the hospital's real baby delivery staffers, all of whom were still there. *We needed to get into that room!*

I was about tap Del Emma on the shoulder and signal it was time to advance. That was when the reasons for my concern charged out of the dead-end hospital wing.

They were coming to us.

At top speed.

I don't know whose bullets hit who. All I knew was that my colleague seemed to be emptying his gun firing at the two charging gunmen at the same time I was emptying mine.

And today's advantage goes to the good guys!

Just another of my instinctive feelings. I was pretty sure both our accosters were dead before they hit the floor.

The adrenaline was attacking my nervous system in such ravenous quantities that I'd quit trying to think like a rational human being. This isn't to say I'd turned into a maniac. I felt exceptionally calm. "Preternaturally so" I believe Merriam-Webster's purists might have said it. But I was operating on automatic. I'd turned into a machine.

Later, I'd come to decide this was because of my training. And feel grateful for it. But for now, it only felt like I was doing what was necessary, then moving on to the next. And doing it again. Determined to keep doing it as long as was necessary.

Preternaturally so.

I reached for my mobile radio to request paramedics, then remembered where I was. Surely, we were about to be flooded with paramedics.

And doctors, nurses, security personnel, crash cart pushers, gurney wheelers, floor managers, accounting office people, janitorial staff, cafeteria workers, radiology techs, ultrasound techs, medical lab techs, therapists, pharmacists, and dietitians. And Pink Ladies.

Yes, lots of Pink Ladies!

Let the hospital good times roll!

I approached the two shooters. Sidestepped the pooling blood. Reached for their carotid arteries and checked for signs of a heartbeat.

I could feel none.

Next, I rolled the first of the ski-mask-wearers over, ripped the surgical mask aside and took a firm grasp on the balaclava. Jerked it straight over the person's head and . . . and . . . and again sensed that my universe was falling apart.

Well, not falling part. But reordering itself at a speed approaching the velocity of light. Faster, if nothing else, than I could keep up with it. Even preternaturally so.

This dead person was someone I recognized.

It was no longer a mystery where Nina Kendricks was. She was lying inches away from where the toes of my boots ended. From the rigid look on her face, I knew checking her carotid artery wasn't necessary. She was dead.

But I'm a sheriff, so I did what sheriffs are supposed to do. I checked it anyway. She was still dead.

There was one other person whose non-working carotid artery should be checked, but I'd leave that to someone else. I knew the answer. Dr. Zack Alonso Bender was dead too.

I didn't get to my feet. Not immediately.

I assumed the sitting position my personal trainer had been trying to teach me. You cross your legs at the ankles, then you put one hand flat on the floor and lean on it. Next, you bring the opposite leg up and place that foot flat on the floor. This leaves your other leg in a squat position. I planned to remain in that position until the activity around me forced me to move. Or until it became so uncomfortable I couldn't do it anymore.

Sitting in this position seemed to be helpful as I began backtracking from these events to other events.

I now knew who had killed the two pilots. It had not been the Middle Eastern terrorists that the FBI's counterterriorist experts and their counterparts from half the rest of the world had been so worried about. It apparently could have been. But the would-be assassins must have gotten to the hangar scant moments too late. By that time, the deed had been done. And the real killers were gone.

So, committed guerrillas that they were, they'd done the next best thing. They'd cut off one of the dead pilot's hands. Then retired to their temporary Flagler living quarters and contemplated what mischief they could pursue with their item of bounty. This was apparently when they'd read about the pilots' deaths in the local newspaper. This had brought the local sheriff to mind. They'd put the severed hand in a jar and managed to have it delivered to him.

But Nina Kendricks and Dr. Bender weren't finished.

When they arrived back from wherever they'd been over-seas, they sniffed out where the pilots and Dr. Danderall had stashed the Palestinian woman they'd recruited in Gallup to bear the mummy's child. Checked on her regularly. And when they'd realized she was gone, donned their camouflaging garb and headed for the hospital.

At long last, they'd thought the linchpin to their audacious plot was about to arrive in the world. And the major warring parties of the Middle East would have something magnificent to share. A baby! Half Israeli, half Palestinian. *A mummy's baby with roots reaching all the way back to Noah, if there had been a Noah.*

The two foreign-born assassins shadowing the pair were right behind. It was an extraordinary lesson in how the universe works that both parties had showed up in the delivery room at almost the exact same time.

And the fact that my deputy chief and I had been right on their heels was almost beyond the pale.

I intended to tell my trainer to forget her crossed legs sitting exercise. It was too much to ask of a forty-plus-year-old Yale Divinity School graduate's hip joints and knee sockets.

I was still contemplating how to break the news to her when I heard the unmistakable cries of a new infant.

Then more cries.

I pushed to my feet. Approached the delivery room. Took a couple of steps into the brilliantly lit space. Swept my eyes over the swirl of people doing busy things in it. Saw one nurse tucking a knit cap down on the head of a tiny figure obviously not long arrived in this world. And observed several other medical types were involved in intense activity between the mother's raised, draped legs.

This confirmed my suspicions based on what I'd been hearing. The mummy had contributed to the birth of twins.

A few minutes later, gazing at the newborns through the viewing window of the nursery, I strained to absorb the rest of the story.

The mummy had contributed to the birth of identical twins.

A few days later, Angie and I watched from the hospital sidewalk as the U.S. Marshals Service loaded the mother and her babies into a vehicle. Destination: the marshals' Witness Protection Program. WITSEC.

I never asked Angie exactly where they had been taken.
Didn't want to know.
Not then. Not now. Not ever.

SOME MONTHS LATER

Flagler had a new restaurant — one that had my hearty endorsement. And it wasn't only because of my love for Mexican food. I also considered the owner of Guadalajara's Mexican Food a personal friend.

Guadalupe Reyes said she'd opened her new restaurant to keep up with the Garcias. The joke was that there weren't any Garcias who owned restaurants in Flagler, Mexican or otherwise. But if we'd had any, they'd have to hustle to stay ahead of Mama Reyes.

She'd urged her contractors to finish her new restaurant building in record time. Then she'd imbued its interior with all kinds of imaginative touches.

The special-order toilets, for example. They'd come from the Talavera ceramic artisans in the heart of Mexico. When you walked in on the fixtures unawares for the first time, you hard-braked. This was because of the riot of pinks, oranges, reds, purples, yellows, greens, and blues on the lavishly decorated toilet bowls and on the good mama's hand-painted potty seats.

Rather than the nonexistent Garcias and their restaurant, the real reason Mama Reyes had opened a new business was because of Flagler's nervous energy.

A wave of it had swept over Abbot County a few weeks following our horrendous spell of mayhem and murder.

You'd expect that the person in charge of finding enough deputies to direct all the traffic would have been among the first to notice. It was impossible for me not to.

For one thing, there were all the truck-mounted cranes and flat-bed, machinery-loaded trailers harrumphing day and night around the county's highways and roads.

Rather than the economic disaster we'd all feared, the wind farm's destruction had ushered in an economic boom. A sizable army of skilled workers had dismantled and hauled away the destroyed equipment. Another sizable contingent had arrived to install new and improved electricity-generating machinery worth hundreds of millions of dollars.

It was obvious that Abbot County's place as a world leader in wind power was being restored.

I was asked to conduct a brief graveside service for the two pilots. In my remarks, I'd suggested only God knows what our season and our time are meant to be. And precisely how our actions and intents fit into the larger order.

I closed, as I liked to do at most funerals I conducted, by reciting the entire text of theologian Reinheld Neibuhr's famous prayer:

God grant me the serenity
To accept the things I cannot change;
Courage to change the things I can;
And wisdom to know the difference.

Living one day at a time;
Enjoying one moment at a time;
Accepting hardships as the pathway to peace;
Taking, as He did, this sinful world
As it is, not as I would have it;

Trusting that He will make all things right
If I surrender to His Will;
So that I may be reasonably happy in this life
And supremely happy with Him
Forever and ever in the next.
Amen.

As for the Armenian grad students, I never met any of them. So I never got a chance to ask Garbis Migirdicyan about any weird intentions involving my car. Or, for that matter, to ask him about anything else, including our Abbot County mummy saga.

As the story was recounted to me, a jet chartered by the Armenian Embassy had arrived in Flagler the morning after a break-in at Nina Kendricks's apartment. By mid-afternoon, Garbis, Razmig and Hachik were apparently tucked safely behind the embassy's walls in the nation's capital. Not long after that, they were gone from the country entirely.

I'd taken a few items from their apartment as evidence. But all the trio had wanted returned were three cowboy rain slickers that Angie and I had found in one of their closets. Apparently, the Armenians thought the coats would impress their girlfriends back home.

FBI Special Agent Ara Efendiyan had his own best-guess scenario about the trio. He thought the Armenians had come to Flagler to go to college without knowing each other. They'd made each others' acquaintance through The Brothers Haykaken, then made higher-ups at the anarchist outfit aware of ways to do real damage in Flagler. Like destroy the wind farm.

Whatever the complete story was, the Armenians would not be missed in Flagler.

To my deep regret, Dean Adele Lovejoy's mental illness was severe and enduring. In retrospect, it had been in plain sight the day I'd visited her office. But her skill at inventing nonexistent realities had been so effective, I'd been snookered like so many others.

Her uncharacteristic behaviors should have been tip-offs. And her elaborate stories about Professor Bender. The notes she'd claimed he'd given her. Her description of the professor's travels to eastern Turkey. Her story about the travel book about Mount Ararat. None of this had turned out to be true.

As for Dr. Bender and Nina Kendricks, we never learned where they had been prior to their abrupt, disheveled appearance in the pilots' office suite that day.

We did use airlines and customs records to confirm they'd made at least one trip to Deir Dibwan, the little Palestinian village. But this had taken place sometime — some months, actually — before the video Angie and I had viewed. The one that showed them walking from the ticket lounge out onto the boarding apron at the Flagler airport.

On that occasion, we concluded they'd never boarded a flight at all. Had merely gone through the pretense of walking through the boarding doors, then sneaked around the outside of the building back to the parking lot. My guess was they had looked so bedraggled that afternoon because they'd been doing something strenuous outside. But what, I never had any idea.

As for the mother of the newborn twins, she was said to be in her thirties, single, childless, bespectacled, short, a fast walker. She had a community college degree in history and geography from a two-year school in Gallup. Her most distinguished physical feature were her dark eyes. They were always moving, always trying to take in everything. Once she heard gossip about the mission involving a baby, she volunteered to take on the difficult assignment of being artificially impregnated and bearing a child who might leave its imprint on Middle Eastern history. She ended up with two.

At 7 Days: The Experience, Craft Roberts missed his May target date for unveiling the new Noah and the Ark exhibit, but it was open and packing them in by early July.

I learned more from Clyde Hazelton, the managing editor of the *Tribune-Standard*. He was the first one to tell me about what Roberts was planning contemporaneous with the unveiling of his mummy exhibit. He was staging Joseph Horovitz's cantata, "Captain Noah and His Floating Zoo."

I asked Hazelton if he thought the mummy was Noah's. He said Roberts had spent a bunch of money having the mummy examined and tested. Said his experts had done carbon-14 dating on contents found in the mummy's stomach and had pegged its age at about 4,000 years old. That made it ancient enough to be Noah's mummy.

But he said evidence didn't much matter in this case. Either you believed there was an actual person named Noah or you didn't.

If you did, then you didn't question whether God could have ordered the guy to build a big boat. Fill it with a small zoo. Keep it afloat in a great flood. Dock it on a high mountain called Ararat. Then instruct Noah, at the ripe old age of 950, to climb 15,000 feet high and lay himself down to die close to where his boat originally landed. And now, more than forty centuries later, arrange for the old gentleman to show up again to prove to doubters that his stories were true.

I told Hazelton he ought to put all that in a feature article. He said he was planning to.

The mummy was impounded by order of a Federal District Court judge in the District of Columbia. Still housed in Chris Ebner's preservation case, it had been flown to Virginia and put on temporary display at the American Museum of Forensic Anthropology. In all likelihood, its ultimate destination was going to be decided at the United Nations. Turkey, Armenia, Israel, Palestine, and the State of Texas were all embroiled in a monumentally complex legal debate over who had first dibs on its ownership.

The inequation mark showed up one more time, in the most unexpected place.

On the saddlebag of one of two shiny, close-to-brand-new Yamaha motorcycles we found parked right outside the Emergency Department's entrance the day of the ED showdown.

The handwritten note said if the owners of the Yamahas didn't manage to see the light of a new day, the motorcycles were to be considered the personal property of the local sheriff. They were a gift. A payback for his skills — these were the writer's exact words — "for handling people who liked to play God."

The only signature was the equal sign with a slash through it.

EPILOGUE

Somewhere along the way, concentric circles of chaos quit surging across our little West Texas pond.

I had waxed eloquent about all this one day in late spring as Angie and I took a drive down U.S. Highway 283. We'd talked about riding the Yamahas but had decided we wanted to take Fresca with us.

We didn't go all the way to Mason, so we didn't see the most spectacular views of the spring wildflowers available in the Texas Hill Country.

But the carpets of bluebonnets and Indian paintbrush were still gorgeous enough to put me in a pontifical mood. Or maybe it was the beauty of the woman I was riding with. Most likely, it was both.

In any event, while parked on a slight rise that allowed us to view the flower-dappled meadows below, I did my best to sound like a Yale Divinity School graduate and not a country sheriff.

I allowed that Flagler's skies these days were bluer, deeper, purer than before. That our community had, in reality, leaped its own River Styx, even out in vacuous emptinesses of often-bone-dry West Texas.

And this was allowing our community to fling off the inertia of indecision and ennui.

Solace, release, resolution and perhaps discernment and the beginnings of forgiveness had given Abbot County, Texas, new room to breathe. We were doing it the only way available to us: one step, one relationship, one act of consoling, repairing, rebuilding, and replacing at a time.

Angie found my outburst of purple prose hilariously funny. She doubled up a fist, reached over and jabbed me hard in the shoulder. "*Ride 'em, cowboy!*"

From the back seat, Fresca barked his approval.

ACKNOWLEDGMENTS

I'm indebted to these individuals for their assistance with the Sheriff Luke McWhorter mystery series:

Brandon Allen, MD, Assistant Medical Director, Adult Emergency Department, University of Florida Shands Hospital, Gainesville, Florida. ED procedures and terminology.

Amy L. Beam, EdD, owner of Mount Ararat Trek travel agency of Dogubayazit, Turkey, and Barbados. The realities of climbing Mount Ararat.

Jennifer Blanton and Penny Goering, Texas Search and Rescue, Austin, Texas. Care and handling of cadaver dogs.

Leo Halepli, Istanbul and Green Bank, West Virginia, the first Turkish citizen of Armenian descent ("a Bolsohay") to be offered a position in Turkey's Secretariat General for EU Affairs. Turkish geography and culture.

Heather A. Reed, Site Manager, Buffalo Gap Historic Village, McWhiney History Education Group, Buffalo Gap, Texas. History and geography of the Callahan Divide area of West Texas.

Marco Samadelli, PhD, Researcher at the Institute for Mummies and the Iceman, South Tyrol Museum of Archaeology, Bolzano, Italy. Mummy preservation and all things Italian.

My deep appreciation for their support and assistance to ECW Press of Toronto, Canada; co-publishers, Jack David and David Caron; Jen Albert, fiction editor; Chidera Ukairo and Samantha Chin, editorial coordinators; and Emily Schultz, sub-editor.

My grateful thanks to Charles Boulos and Michèle Carrier of Montreal, Quebec, Canada, for providing quality control in spades for the Sheriff Luke McWhorter books.

My life-long companion and business partner, Sherry, has spent an untold number of hours vetting every twist and turn in these works. Her sense of how the world works is uncanny and her imagination boundless. So is my love for her, and my appreciation of what her selfless spirit and zest for living bring to my work. My grateful appreciation too to daughter Kim Lynch for lending her dad her remarkable critical and descriptive skills; daughter Mendy Klein for her unflagging encouragement; son-in-law John Stytz for contributing his technological expertise; son-in-law Matthew Klein (DVM) for manuscript-vetting and advising me on animal issues; grandson Ian Stytz and granddaughter Kaitlyn Klein for their interest; and my brother, Stan Lynch, for his editing skills and astute content suggestions.

Friends, family, or fellow authors who generously answered questions and/or critiqued early drafts include Jay Brandon, Dan Coleman, Skipper Duncan, Stephanie Jaye Evans, Perry Flippin, Larry Hahn, Joe Holley, Victor L. Hunter, Gary John (EdD), Howard R. Johnson, Scott Kinnaird, Larry Lourcey, Major General Don Lynch (U.S. Marine Corps, Retired), LaRae Quy, Robert M. Randolph and Harold Straughn.

My thanks to staffers at the *Roswell* (N.M.) *Daily Record* and the International UFO Museum and Research Center in Roswell for responding to questions about the 1947 UFO incident.